Praise for *A SEAL at Heart*

"A romance with real heart, from a talented writer who has deep personal insight into what it takes—and what it means—to be a Navy SEAL."

—*New York Times* bestselling author Suzanne Brockmann

"Two wounded souls find healing through love in Elizabeth's romance. Readers will find this book an accurate reflection of what's happening in the world today and perhaps be uplifted by its message of hope."

—*Booklist*

"Elizabeth's series starter is, like the title, filled with heart and action. Vivid descriptions of military missions, and the pain that can come from them, make this a page-turner."

—*RT Book Reviews*

"The connection between Jack and Laurie is instantaneous and combustible."

—*Publishers Weekly*

"An exciting and poignant read that gives insight into the dangerous and stressful life of a SEAL even as it shows the magnitude of the sacrifices and commitment of these amazing heroes."

—*Night Owl Reviews* Reviewer Top Pick

a SEAL FOREVER

ANNE ELIZABETH

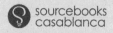

sourcebooks
casablanca

Published by Sourcebooks Casablanca, an imprint of Sourcebooks, Inc.
P.O. Box 4410, Naperville, Illinois 60567-4410
(630) 961-3900
Fax: (630) 961-2168
www.sourcebooks.com

Printed and bound in Canada.
MBP 10 9 8 7 6 5 4 3 2 1

*This book is dedicated to our outstanding Navy SEALs,
our Men and Women in Uniform, their Families,
and our Wounded Warriors.*

*Thank you for your tremendous dedication, your
sacrifice, and your service. HOOYAH!*

Chapter 1

MASTER CHIEF DECLAN SWIFTON OF SEAL TEAM FIVE rolled over the side of the Rigid-hulled Inflatable Boat and slid soundlessly into the Pacific Ocean. The RIB took off without even a comment from the operator, leaving Declan to sink farther into the drink.

The temperature cooled as he swam away from the surface. Fish skirted the edges of his thighs, small shimmers of movement against his skin. He scissor-kicked his way forward. The ocean currents caught him, dragging him in the direction they wanted to go, toward shore. He lay with his arms at his sides, frog-kicking only. Above him, he could see the afternoon sunlight glistening and frothy foam chasing away the glassy surface. Down here, things were different...calmer. Peaceful, in a way few souls would understand, and yet he knew that even he would have to surface soon.

His lungs would start to ache and burn, his gut would begin to feel as if it would cave in, and that would force him to either head topside or drink in the salt water. But there was still time. This was the water in front of Imperial Beach and the apartment he lived in. He knew it very well.

Scanning the ocean floor, he gauged it would be about thirty seconds until he reached one of the many rocky breakers out here. He'd have to pull up before then, or the force of the current would smack him against the side of it.

As his body began to complain, he used both arms and legs to draw himself upward. Breaking the surface, he opened his mouth and drew in air like a thirsty man would gulp water.

The waves bounced him like a buoy. The tide was coming in and the wind was picking up momentum. Looking at the sky, he could see that there would most likely be a storm today. Over his shoulder, he spied a wave coming his way large enough to take him to shore. It would reach him in about thirty seconds.

Dec took a long, slow breath and appreciated the sun dropping into the horizon. The colors were extraordinary; orange and gold dappled the horizon as the blazing ball of light attempted to sink before the moon lifted higher in the sky.

His hands flexed, cupping the water. It had been a hot day, and the sun's rays had heated the top of the ocean, making the surface feel like a warm bath, loosening his muscles. Three months ago, he'd been in waters so frigid, with actual ice caps—the memory still made him cold. But here, the Pacific Ocean off California's Imperial Beach, was a slice of heaven.

Some nasty-looking cumulonimbus clouds were coming in. Seeing the lightning arc way off toward the distant desert, he decided it was time to go in, and right on cue, here came a perfect wave.

Swimming at top speed, Declan pushed his way through another changing current, one that sought to drag him into faster-moving waters. He went over a higher sandbar, having no intention of going to Mexico today, and increased the reach of his stroke. With single-mindedness he worked his way into the more placid surf as he homed in on a large stretch of beach.

The SEAL felt a few sea lions swimming around him, and one nosed him in the gut and another in his back a few times, assessing whether or not he'd play. *Not this time, my friends.* He continued swimming without engaging. If he stopped to play, he'd be out there for hours.

Switching to the breaststroke, his arms protested. His platoon had switched their training this month to desert-warfare techniques, and he'd been sweating his balls off in the heat. He managed to learn a thing or two, even now, after all of his years in the Teams. But it felt good to be back in the ocean, his element. He'd live in the deep blue like a Jules Verne character if he could.

Taking in a mouthful of water, he swished it around and spat it out. *Salt water, nature's peroxide.*

Pausing to focus in on the beach for a second, he saw two sunbathers to the left, occupied in a rather heavy-looking discussion, and a handful of children all the way at the end of the sand section, packing up their sand castle gear. The area abutted some rough terrain that even the tweakers and druggies didn't venture onto.

Dec bodysurfed the rest of the way into shore. With the cool sandy bottom beneath his feet, he walked up onto the beach, leaving behind the water's warmth. The wind ruffled the tops of the waves, blowing even harder from east to west.

He exited the ocean north of the arguing couple. Jogging down the beach behind them, he headed for the last building on the wide stretch of beach. It was a rather outdated seventies-style apartment complex with balconies on the top floor and a rock wall circling the entire structure. This was a fast climb topside.

His skin prickled with gooseflesh; a breeze was kicking up, typical for February. It didn't really faze him, it was just interesting to note how fast things change. That storm should be over the apartment complex in less than ten minutes. Who knew whether or not it would stick or be blown out to sea; but this area was in for a good drenching.

Taking one more glance at the sunset, he noted the time. He needed to keep moving to stay on schedule for tonight. A certain lovely lady would be having his undivided attention later this evening.

Dec found the proximity to base was workable. He could run or bike down the Strand to work, take a swift motorcycle ride, or like today, get a lift from one of the Basic Underwater Demolition/SEAL (otherwise known as BUD/S) instructors as they were going out to torture the tadpoles, or rather, teach a class.

Closing in on his apartment, he lengthened his stride. Two apartments sharing a common balcony did not make for an ideal situation, but he liked his place and the building overall. Being able to slip into his apartment via his own glass door was a serious advantage too; it helped him avoid keys jingling in his shorts or stashing a key somewhere.

Right now, between him and the one place he needed to access was a single, solitary person: his hermit of a neighbor, Maura Maxwell. The softly pretty but buttoned-up lady had moved in and barely said a single word to him, and right now she was sitting on the far end of their shared balcony with her eyes glued to him.

—⁓—

Maura watched her neighbor climb the rock wall. She slipped back into her apartment before he could engage her in conversation.

Closing the glass door behind her, she slid the lock into place. It wasn't that she was antisocial; no, that wasn't it. She was just shy. At least, that's what she told herself when it came to her neighbor. She rubbed the scars on her arm; they tended to ache when she was nervous. She wished she could reach the ones on her back and rub those too.

Her neighbor stretched and his ab muscles moved. Such a perfect six-pack! He was an Adonis.

Besides, what would she have to say to a Navy SEAL? Especially a giant man as tall as Hercules, with the shoulders of an Olympian and abs and buns that you could bounce quarters off of. That wasn't intimidating at all.

Hugging her highly prized work journal to her chest, she pulled the vertical blinds almost closed and then took a position at the very far corner so she could watch him covertly. That was a not-so-subtle hint to herself that as much as she wanted to ignore him, he captured her attention as no other man ever had. Declan Swifton made her feel like a gawky teenager.

She sighed. Since she had moved in here six weeks ago, she had managed to barely speak with him. A grunt on the landing as a greeting didn't count. His constant parade of gorgeous, bikini-clad female companions had put her off of ever wanting to "chat," and yet, at night before she fell asleep, she fantasized about what she would say to him if he were in her bed and how his body would feel against hers.

She'd probably end up babbling mathematical

nonsense at him until he rolled his eyes in boredom. No one thought equations were sexy. She didn't need two undergraduate degrees to tell her that. But the math was for new parkour techniques, and he seemed like the type to appreciate, um, physical activities.

Speaking of which, she needed to get moving before all the daylight was gone. Placing one of her many journals on the coffee table, she marched herself to the side closet near her bathroom and pulled out her wet suit. Stripping off her clothes and folding them carefully onto a chair, she then wiggled into the black neoprene. She tried not to imagine herself being squished into a sausage casing, because that rarely made a woman feel stellar about herself. She was a gymnastics and parkour instructor, but even so, the wet suit was just about the most unflattering garment ever made.

Reaching around back, she located the zipper, pulled it upward, and then secured her hair into a ponytail before stopping at the mirror. She assessed herself, deciding she looked…good enough. Not perfect, but she wasn't giving up chocolate or lattes anytime soon. A girl needed her vices.

She was eager to have a calm evening paddle beneath the stars. Four nights ago, she'd stood on the board and enjoyed an hour of blissful relaxation. Even if it was a serious exercise and core workout, there was nothing like it in the world.

Practically running back into the living room, she grabbed her newish paddleboard and paddle—she'd bought them off Craigslist two weeks ago—and headed outside. It had only taken her a day on the glassy ocean to master the trick of centering her weight and using her muscles to help balance her. It had been the most enjoyment she'd known for a long time.

Peeking her head out of the door, she let go of the breath she hadn't realized she was holding. Luckily her neighbor wasn't outside on his half of the balcony. She could make her escape without confrontation.

She hurriedly lowered both items over the railing and climbed down after them. It was awkward, and she had to be careful not to cut her feet or rip her wet suit on the rocks.

Once she was on the ground, the sand was loose under her feet. She was grateful for her gymnastics and parkour training, because every step made her feet sink. Without her balance and ability to move with the flow, she'd be sprawled on the beach.

As she finally reached the water's edge and was on firmer ground, she didn't even pause, just barreled into the frothy surf without hesitation, laid her board on top of the water, wedged her paddle against her body, and pushed off.

Climbing onto her board, she settled onto her knees and paddled out to a hopefully more manageable part of the ocean. Fighting the current was tough going as she kept rolling off the board and having to right herself again. At this rate, there was no way she was going to be able to stand and have that calm, star-filled moment.

Taking a chance, she pushed her way onto her feet and stood amid the churning waves for a few blissful moments until she lost her balance again.

By the time she realized that she was in a tricky part of the water where the currents changed quickly, lightning cracked above and the sky opened up, releasing a deluge.

Holding on to her board for dear life, Maura chastised herself. "If you hadn't been so bullheaded, none of this would have happened. All you had to do was talk to the man, and then you wouldn't be so mad at yourself."

Water splashed into her mouth and down her throat. She choked and sputtered.

Trying to get back onto her knees, she attempted to turn toward shore, but a wave bowled her over and she lost her grasp. The paddle was spirited away by the water, but she could see her board.

Swimming for it, she reached the side and pulled herself back onto it. Panic surged through her as she searched for the shore.

With the rain and the increasing height of the waves, it was impossible to get her bearings, and she could feel hot tears streaming down her face. Laying her head on the board, she didn't know what to do, other than hold on.

If only I had looked at the sky before I started... The chastisement only made her feel worse.

As the rain pounded her skin, she promised herself, "If I survive this, from here on out, I will be bolder and smarter."

Maura and her board smashed into a buoy anchored two miles out, off of Imperial Beach. Her hands grabbed onto the edges as she tried with all her might to pull herself up and anchor herself to the bouncy yet somewhat stable marker. The good news was that she attained a foothold on the larger structure; the bad news, that her board slipped out of her grasp and bounced out of her reach, leaving her with no escape other than to swim back through the choppy and turbulent waves.

Chapter 2

WRAPPING A TOWEL AROUND HIS WAIST TO COVER HIS nakedness before he stepped outside—heaven forbid he shock his neighbor—Declan walked out onto the balcony to bring in his beer cooler before it filled with water from the incoming storm.

He'd long since lost the top and he didn't want it to overflow and flood the balcony. If his neighbor's apartment got even a drop of water from something he did, she might be the type to complain. The woman was an enigma to him. He'd been as friendly as he knew how, and still she had barely said a word to him.

As he picked up the battered cooler, something on the horizon caught his attention. He put the plastic down and walked to the railing. Was that some fool out on the water? Did that person know what he or she was in for?

He went back inside, located his binoculars, and hurried back to the railing. Zeroing in on the form, he could barely believe his eyes. It was his neighbor. Maura Maxwell. Her paddle was heading for Mexico, her board was on its way to Japan with a possible stop-off in Hawaii, and she was holding on to a buoy that wasn't meant as a flotation device.

"Crap."

Pulling off his towel, he grabbed a pair of swim trunks from the drying line by his balcony door and slid into them in record speed. He hopped the railing, landing with a roll on the sand, and ran at top speed toward the ocean.

His feet splashed into the foamy surf as he ran. Diving into the first high wave, he headed for the buoy. Adrenaline surged through his body, drowning out the grousing of his aching limbs. His arms dug into the water as he dove under a high, white-peaked wave and avoided the trap of the rolling undertow. Surfacing, he continued his quest, skirting the sand dune and finally reaching his quarry: a very waterlogged and frightened Maura Maxwell.

The big question was, would she follow his instructions or did he have to knock her out? Lightning crashed above as the storm kicked it up a notch.

Well, she'd better listen, or he wasn't going to be responsible for giving her an aching jaw.

He swam closer to her. "Maura?"

She peered at him warily. "D-D-Declan?"

She looked like a cold, wet cat, and he hoped she didn't scratch. "I'm going to reach for you. When I do, you need to let go and not fight me. Do you understand?"

She nodded her head.

He put out his arm. The woman grabbed it and pulled herself to him, wrapping her arms around his neck tightly, choking him. At this rate, she was so panicked, she was going to sink them both if she didn't listen.

Pushing her away from him, he held her at arm's length. "Don't grab me. Let me hold you. If you need to, wrap yourself around one arm, and nothing else. Got it?"

His message appeared to penetrate her brain, because she let him maneuver her into position: belly up, her back to him.

As he secured her against him, he kicked out with a sidestroke—best way to bring her in, given the circumstances. Quite frankly, though, he knew he was probably going to regret not knocking her out. The ride to shore had the potential to be rocky.

As waves pummeled them, he could feel her claws sinking into his skin. He didn't change his hold or his pace. It was slow going, but it would be successful. He'd done this particular drill at least a hundred times before.

Ouch! Did she just bite his arm? Her movements were growing frantic.

He paused, treading water. "Calm down," he ordered. She stilled against him.

With his lips next to her ear, he said, "We're almost at the sandbar. You need to relax."

He felt her nod. That was his cue to keep moving. Slow and steady, he pulled her through the strong currents and toward the shore.

As his feet slid over the sandbar, a wave lifted them high enough that he could see the beach clearly. The tide was coming in quickly.

Rain continued to fall and its steady rhythm helped wash the sea salt from his eyes. Catching sight of another large wave, one that would be big enough to bodysurf to shore, he pulled her onto his body and spun them around.

The wave lifted them and carried them toward shore. Declan landed on his feet first, picking up Maura and carrying her up onto the bank. He didn't stop there, walking across the beach and taking her up the wall in a fireman's carry…not stopping until they were both on the balcony.

The rain had slowed to a light sprinkle by then. Her eyes looked like a doe's as he gazed into them. "Are you okay?"

She clung to him, shaking, not speaking.

"You need to talk to me, or I'm going to take matters into my own hands."

Her teeth chattered, and though it looked like she was attempting to nod that all was well, he wasn't buying into it. Picking her up again, he opened her balcony door, took her inside, closed it, and walked through to where he thought her bathroom should be. It was a safe bet, since it was likely that their apartments would be mirror images of each other.

Putting the stopper in place, he flipped on the bathwater and turned to face her.

The woman was as white as a sheet. Turning her around, he unzipped her wet suit. He noticed some nasty scars on her back, but he didn't utter a word of question. He pushed the neoprene off one shoulder and then off the other. Working the suit down over her hips, he managed to snag the bottom of it with his foot and lift her up and out.

Lowering her into the tub, he didn't let go until she was safely covered in the warm water. Huh, she had scars on her arms too. Whatever she'd been through, it must have been painful. It also didn't keep him from noticing how captivating she was.

His eyes stopped traveling up and down and locked firmly to hers. That green gaze of hers drew him in, inviting him to glimpse into her soul. The openness was intoxicating.

When she licked her luscious lips, his eyes moved

down, and for a brief second, he forgot that she was his enigmatic neighbor and thought only of kissing her. A woman. Naked. In a bathtub full of warm, inviting water.

Her hand shot out, making contact with his chest. Instead of pushing him away, her fingertips traced over the muscles.

He cleared his throat. "Maura…"

She looked at him like a woman who knew exactly what she wanted from a man. Again, she touched her tongue to those pink lips, and then said, "Thank you, Declan."

His name. He didn't ever remember her saying his name under normal circumstances, and he liked the way it sounded coming from her mouth.

Leaning down, he kissed her. Tenderly. Just a taste.

Salt, and a hint of her, filled his senses as the kiss deepened. Her tongue boldly sought his as he welcomed her into his mouth. Hunger ate at him—hers and his. The kiss drew him deeper into her.

Her hands were holding his head, fingers entwined in his hair, and her openness to him was glorious. He wanted her, wanted to pillage and plunder all of that sweetness to his heart's content.

With her head cradled in his hands, he pulled back. He couldn't do it. He wouldn't take from her when she had just gone through something so horrific.

She stared at him. Her green eyes taunted him, burning away his will.

"I…" He let go of her head and drew farther away. "If you're warmed up, we need to get you out of there before the bathwater gets cold." As he stood, his gaze shifted. There she was, in all her glory. Maura Maxwell naked was nothing like he'd imagined she'd be. Her breasts were ripe—just enough to fill his mouth and hands—and her body was trim and tight, with legs that went on forever. His fingers curled into fists. He was just going to have to get a grip.

The water sloshed to the side as she sat up in the tub. She pulled the elastic from her hair, making the strands spread out like a halo. She didn't make a move to cover herself. Instead she looked up at him unashamedly. "Thank you for rescuing me."

He nodded, not trusting his vocal cords. The sounds might come out as a jumble of noises, and then he'd lose his chivalrous focus for sure and crawl into the tub with her.

There was a confidence and beauty about her that drew him. His eyes followed the tiny drops of water as they ran down the valley between her breasts. He held out a towel for her, and she stepped out of the tub and into his embrace. He dried her off briskly, then pulled another bath sheet off the rack and wrapped it around her. She leaned into him and he took her weight without a sound, wrapping his arms around her and resting his chin on the top of her wet hair.

"I didn't realize there was a storm."

"I saw the signs of it. The storm came in fast."

"It did." The chagrin in her voice was obvious.

"C'mon, let's get a blanket to wrap you in. And some warm socks. You need something to warm you up from the inside too. Whiskey? Or brandy?"

"How about a cognac?" Those green eyes were lit with a blazingly brilliant fire, and the balls of her cheeks were flushed with red. Amazing that she could be so pretty when she had just almost been killed.

Declan didn't say anything. He hustled out of the bathroom, through her living room, and out her balcony door, leaving temptation behind. She could get her own cognac. Maura was the kind of woman who could make a guy linger and never leave.

He took in a long, slow breath. His life didn't lend itself to entanglements, not of the female kind. It was easier to keep relationships at arm's length. Have fun. Satisfy needs. And then move on. Being a SEAL was unpredictable, and he'd seen too many guys seek normality with ladies, only to have it come crashing down around their ears.

Closing the glass, he exhaled. Gazing into her apartment from the other side of the divider gave him an odd feeling in the pit of his stomach, like this was something that could be good. He didn't know why. He barely knew this woman. She was the quiet lady who lived next door and barely said a word to him. Christ, what was he thinking! Move on.

Scratching his head, he gave up his mental meanderings and entered his apartment, closing his own sliding glass door, blocking her out further. Outside, the storm had calmed, moving out to sea, and a quiet lull was coming to the area in stages of silence as everything settled for the night. Soon the stars would be visible in all of their glory, and he could walk the beach, enjoying it.

A knock at the front door reminded him that he had made other plans for the evening. "Oh, shit! I forgot about Sali."

It was a convenient on-again, off-again relationship that he'd had for years. When they were both between relationships, they tended to hook up. No strings, just a mutual satisfying of needs. Right now, all he wanted was to put his adrenaline rush to some good use.

Striding across the room, he opened the door to greet Sali Jensen, a petite blond with golden skin and bright blue eyes.

───∿∿───

After Sali left the next morning, Declan lay in bed, and it was painfully clear that the woman he wanted to see again was…Maura. He had been unable to stop thinking about her all night long. His mind had played through images: holding Maura close to him as he swam, carrying her, pulling off her wet suit, and placing her into the tub of warm water. And that kiss… His body got hard thinking about it.

He rubbed his hands over his eyes. What the hell!

Declan gave up on the logic of it all and got up to face the music. Grabbing a pair of jeans as he went, he stepped into them and buttoned the top button.

At least the girl next door seemed to like sports. He'd counted two surfboards, well-used Rollerblades, and a mountain bike over there. Usually he did those things with a Teammate, but it could be more satisfying to explore those interests with a female companion.

Damn, too much pondering! He was like a wind-up doll—tons of energy and nowhere to go with it. A good hard run—by himself—might get his head back on track, he thought.

Walking over to the window, he stared out at the gorgeous day. He could see early-morning joggers out doing their thing. Why not?

Checking the clock on the wall, he saw that he had two hours before he needed to be on the Amphibious Base. So he switched his jeans for running shorts and beach runner shoes—the kind with toes—and then headed out the balcony door. Stretching his muscles, he limbered up and then descended the wall. The water had made the sand a bit firmer, and it was easier to walk as he made his way down to the edge of the lapping waves. That was the ideal spot for a swift run.

Breathing in the fresh sea air, he took off at a good pace. It wasn't long before he felt an itch at the center of his back, like someone was watching him. As he glanced over his shoulder, he saw her. Maura.

She smiled and then zipped past him. "Morning."

He revved up his speed and joined her. "Good morning. You look well."

"I am. How are you? Did you have a good night?"

His eyebrows drew in. "Ah…sure."

"Declan." She peered up at him. When she put her hand on his arm, he looked at her.

She tugged him to a halt, urging him to come sit next to her on the rocks near the pier. They'd run a long way and he had barely noticed the distance. Regardless, he allowed her to lead him.

"I'm not going to be shy. I promised myself out there, on the water. What you did last night was…miraculous! Thank you." She batted those sultry eyes at him.

He shook his head and sighed. "You were on my mind several times last night."

She grinned at him. "Can I take you to dinner tonight?"

The question piqued his mischievous streak. He'd be

willing to have a lovely lady take him out. That was worth pursuing.

"Where?" He was pleased and oddly nervous at the same time. After all, a woman who went out in a storm didn't necessarily show the best sense. Best, hell. And yet she was...in her own way...compelling.

"It's a surprise. Meet you at seven?"

"How about five? I'll be hungry."

"Perfect!" she exclaimed. "I'm going to blow your socks off."

He stood. *God, I hope she isn't being literal. Then again...*

She gave him a quick hug and ran down the beach.

Time was ticking. He had to get to the base. Turning around, he headed toward home. Whatever was in store for him with this woman, he'd have to put it out of his mind for now. Work beckoned.

Chapter 3

THE DESERT AIR WAS DRY. THEY'D FAST-ROPED INTO the training area two hours before and hiked to the mountain range. Their goal was to reach and eliminate the targets before the opposing group could stop them. Going up the difficult terrain was going to cinch the Op. The other group wouldn't expect a vertical ascent and assault.

The SEALs worked their way up a sheer cliff that even experts might consider highly challenging, and it was mostly fun. Declan preferred to push himself when he could, and the rest of his Team had the same mindset. This climb met that criterion.

At the mountain plateau, they broke into three groups of two men each. Time was not in their favor if they wanted to get the drop on the other group, so they ran like their pants were on fire to get down to their lookout spots.

They'd rotated them from the last training scenario, and no one would suspect this tactic.

Leaper was making more faces than a clown. He wasn't a woodsman. Declan wasn't necessarily one either, not that he would ever consider complaining. He could easily admit that he had always felt he was more a creature of the water than of the land, but it was all part of SEAL Team: sea, air, and land. Right now, he was carrying a sniper rifle, ammo, and pack and wearing his ghillie. He'd pulled on the overall onesie and built it on the fly as they came down the mountain.

Now was not the time to point out to Leaper that he'd just tucked poison oak under his chin. The damage was done, and his swim buddy was going to be bathing in pink stuff to ease the itch tonight.

Finally, they reached their goal. Getting down on his belly, Declan crawled forward, grateful that there were no leaves to rustle and give away his position. He got as close as he dared. His vantage point showed the opposing group clearly. They were roughhousing and taking their time setting up the targets.

Damn, those guys are way behind. They probably think we're still going around the mountains. But why the hell would anyone go around when they could go over?

He signaled Leaper, who passed back the info. Hand signals were ideal, given the way sound could carry in this area, and the enemy had the same equipment, so if they were scanning channels, using the radios could get Declan's Team blown.

As silently as possible, Declan took a few sips of water and waited for the signal to shoot. The trajectory was perfect. The windage, elevation, and air pressure had been taken into account. He'd adjusted his scope, gotten the appropriate numbers set, and his mind went over the math and angles one more time to double-check himself.

His ghillie suit, basically a camo suit layered with foliage to hide him in the terrain, currently included two large brown tarantulas. His eyes had caught the movement and he gave them a second's notice as they crawled up his arm and perched on his head. Declan didn't mind. He liked spiders.

Leaper, who was his spotter, signaled him.

The rest of his team had swept the area and confirmed

the Intel. They held their positions, and there was even a backup sniper to their left in case Declan's shots were blocked. Nothing was left to chance.

Leaper gave the "go" signal.

Declan returned the signal. He kept his eyes on target as he looked through the scope. He had the first kill in sight.

Taking in a half breath, he held it and pulled the trigger. He'd learned the technique years ago from a frogman who could shoot a wart off of a tadpole. One of the best parts of the Teams was sharing knowledge. The info they passed on to each other was not only useful, but fucking lifesaving.

They got the first target even before the other Team prepped. Those guys were going to get nailed for having their pants down.

The mic gave three clicks. Anyone listening would think it was static. For him, it meant *Go!* The next target waited.

Repeating his technique, he took out the target and scanned for more. Three shots later, he'd eliminated every threat before the other Team could take out their targets or retaliate.

A series of clicks over the mic was their wrap sound: *All clear!*

Yep! Our Team won this training game. Hooyah!

Backing slowly out of his hiding place, Declan was pleased. This meant they were wheels-up earlier than intended. The tarantulas fell from his head and scrambled away.

As the sun blazed down on him and sweat drenched his back and legs, he knew that he'd performed well. They'd done this exercise three dozen times, and they'd probably do it another three dozen until everything was reflex and every angle and contingency was explored.

He made his way back. Then he secured the sniper rifle and prepared to rope down the mountain. Leaper was itching like a madman, and Declan couldn't stop chuckling every time he looked at the guy. He felt for his frog-brother. He'd been in that position before.

The air was clean and clear, and Declan breathed deeply. Pretty special up here. His guys could have hitched a ride out with the losing Team, but that wasn't the exit strategy. For the most part, unless it was necessary to deviate, they'd stick to their plan.

A congratulatory thump on the back from Leaper made Declan smile. Tromping Team ONE always gave him a lift.

Elation slid through him. SEALs loved this job. Wherever it took them, whatever he was doing, Declan knew this was exactly where he was meant to be. As a sniper, gathering Intel or pulling the trigger, fast-roping, swimming, diving, being launched out a torpedo tube... it didn't matter. As long as he could keep being a SEAL and engaging every part of his being the best way he knew how, he'd be at peace.

At the top of the peak, he took off the suit, stripped it of foliage, and redistributed the branches quickly so there was no evidence of him there—the tarantulas had long since departed—and placed the suit in his pack. He strapped his gear back in place, made sure his rock-climbing harness was secure, hooked onto the line, and lowered himself over the side.

Pushing off the wall with his feet, he made it down in record time.

Above him, freaking Leaper did a swan dive, heading down face-first. The man had a death wish at times that made Declan's gut clench. But there was no denying Leaper's skills as he zipped to a stop beside him.

"Idiot!" Declan mumbled.

"Oh, must you call me those love names when all of our Teammates are around?" Leaper made smooching sounds with his lips.

Declan shook his head. "C'mon. I'm buying when we get back. Cold ones. At least until I have to get ready for my date."

"Oh, a date! Can I come?" Leaper lunged for him, obviously intending some kind of bear hug or embrace.

Declan stepped aside and watched Leaper hit the ground. Leaning over his friend, he asked, "How's the air down there?"

Spitting out a mouthful of dirt, Leaper said, "Yummy! So very delicious!"

Declan grabbed the back of Leaper's harness and hauled him to his feet. "Maybe we'll make a new beer flavor for you. Essence of Dirt."

Leaper pointed to the place where the terrain changed back into sand and batted his eyes. "Can we make it sand, please?"

"Mercy." Declan laughed as he and the rest of the Team double-timed it back to the extraction point. After their success, they were all eager to get back home early and receive their bravo zulu for a job well done.

⌁

Teaching gymnastics was not Maura's original dream, but it was close. Her favorite part of the whole world had been competing as an individual gymnast. When that ended for her, she'd found showing others how to reach their potential touched on some true happiness, and for now that had to be enough.

Super! read the sign on top of the building. The gym was tucked into the back of a row of restaurants. A parking lot was in front of it, and to the sides were slabs of dirt filled with litter and crushed cans. The outside was painted bright orange, and the sign on the door simply stated Froggy Squats.

Maura hummed to herself. She'd been kissed last night, and by none other than Declan. Life was getting interesting. She'd discarded that last bit of shyness as she lay in the tub naked. She felt renewed, as if she could be the bold, modern woman she'd always wished to be. It was hard to fathom how amazing it had been. That man knew how to lock lips. Yet he'd seemed to... what? Want to talk? Want more?

The kiss was the culmination of everything she'd personally ever wanted to say to him—all put into one physical action, and he had done it. Reached down and kissed her. And she had been naked. The desire had been evident in his eyes, and yet he'd been a gentleman. Maybe...he really wanted the girl next door.

How awesome was it that he had been running this morning? Fate was definitely flowing in her favor.

A voice broke into Maura's reflections.

"Morning," said Sue Kolls as she walked past Maura toward the gym door. "Just so you know, I confiscated two DSes. They're on your desk."

Froggy Squats was an electronics-free zone, no phones or video games on the floor. Personally, Maura loved online gaming and had a list of favorites. But being at the gym made her want to get something out of the place that she couldn't get at home, so she'd readily supported the membership rules. Using electronics for music was okay, but the members—mostly parents—wanted their kids to unplug and exercise. Oftentimes it was the only physical challenge they received during the day. So her job was to think up ways to engage the kids and adults. Thus far the programs had been working well.

"Thanks. And good morning to you too," Maura replied with a chipper tone and an upbeat smile, even though she was still not ready to jump into the chaotic place. The gym was packed with early birds in mid-workout mania.

She flicked off a stray hair from her shirt and bounced toward the door. It was time to work.

Bosco Russo, a regular who looked as if he'd just stepped off the set of *The Sopranos*, walked out the door and nearly ran into her. "Hello, Maura."

"Hey." She smiled tentatively, then slipped past him and through the door he was holding open. *Right. Concentrate on the present. There's a lot going on. You're about to walk into your future.* There were more important things on the docket, like the gym…and the fact that she was officially about to take over. *Me! The owner of a giant place like this. Go figure!*

She resisted the urge to sigh over the list of worries and concerns that might have held her back. She seriously did not want to mess up this opportunity.

"Bob? Where are you?" Maura walked along the edges of the mats. Her eyes scanned the expanse, searching for the current owner. She was actually doing it. She was taking the plunge and buying the gym. She just had to make it through the next six months.

The idea to purchase the place had come from her brother Michael. The owner, Bob Lepke, was Mike's college roommate, and he wanted to move to the East Coast. Seemed like a good idea when she packed up her whole life and headed out this way. As a child, teenage, and college gymnast, she'd spent most of her life in and around gyms. She knew she could handle it.

"Hey, Maxwell, the keys are in the office. Good luck!" Bob didn't even give her a chance to object. He was leaving the gym in her hands for six months, half of a year, while he and his wife drove to Florida to visit her grandparents. Some kind of family reunion, though why they would be gone so long was beyond her understanding. This was her test run, and if she could handle it, the place was hers at the current asking price. She just wanted to be sure before she took the plunge.

"You've got my cell." With a final wave, Bob Lepke went out the door.

"Wait!" She coughed out the word, choking on her own indecision. She didn't know whether to be excited or scared. Her dad preached the concept that courage requires a leap of faith. Could she be brave for five minutes, long enough to watch Bob leave?

The gym had been up for sale for a year and a half, and Bob had inherited it from his uncle, who had been killed in a surfing accident in Mexico. Did that mean this place had good karma or bad? Did it matter? Not really.

If she was being honest with herself, she really liked this place. Endlessly easygoing and laid-back, people here smiled a lot. Also, its California Art Deco decor, spare and sparse with a multitude of heavy mats, and a black-and-white color scheme with bursts of color here and there pleased her aesthetically. Yes, her solace was here on the West Coast.

Besides, she'd found community here. The members liked her programs, and most of the single gym rats had brought in more friends, which had meant more business and more classes for all the instructors. Plus, she could play retro music softly in the background, indulging her love of '80s music.

The gym's perpetually upbeat attitude jibed with hers too. It felt good to hang with people of a similar ilk. Maura was looking forward to chatting with a few of the kids before their next class. As she drew closer to the group, one of the kids separated and ran toward her.

"Miss Max'ell, Miss Max'ell, I have a new trick," said Tats, a small charmer who'd recently lost his two front teeth. "Want to see? It's really super."

"Yes! Please, show me, Tats," she replied, following him into the center of the gym, where the heavy-duty, triple-lined mats were stacked.

Tats did a backflip. This trick had eluded him for weeks.

She was proud of him. "That's amazing! How did you learn it?"

"I practiced with the harness, and yesterday Joe helped me work it out. I know just the right amount to torque and tuck." He beamed with pride.

She hugged him. "Do you think we should add it to your superhero chart?"

"Yes!" he said.

They walked over to a wall where there were pictures of kids, teens, and adults—all shapes and sizes—and each person was dressed in a superhero costume. There were names such as Super-Genius, Heroically Happy, and other unique heroes created by individuals. Underneath every picture was a list of their superpowers and another list of their super accomplishments, everything from walking ten steps to ten miles, skipping rope, walking the balance beam, and so on. The superhero concept had been her brainchild, and over the past four months, it had transformed the gym into a superhero league and quadrupled their memberships for families.

The kids' program was her favorite, and Tats was a regular. She watched him write down his accomplishment and then decorate the achievement with stickers.

"Maura?" A woman tapped her on the shoulder. Mrs. Bolijier, Tats's mom, asked, "Can I talk to you a minute in private?"

"Sure." She patted Tats on the back. "Good job, buddy. Take your time with the spiffy decorations. I'm going to the office to chat with your mom."

"Okay!" The happiness radiated from the kid as if he'd just won the Olympics. Who knows, maybe someday he would.

They walked the few steps to the glass-enclosed office. The desk was mostly clean, but as everyone tended to use the space, it could get cluttered.

"What can I do for you?" Maura gestured to a chair and they both sat down.

"I can't afford to pay for Tats to come here anymore." The woman wouldn't look her in the eye, and her hands were shaking.

Maura touched her fingers to the woman's hand. "What's going on?"

A tear-filled gaze held Maura's. "I cut everywhere I could. Beni left, and with Tats and Simi to care for and no job, I cannot hold it together."

"Do you have a place to stay?" Maura didn't dare move. She didn't want to break the connection, but maybe, just maybe, she could help.

"Yes, we own our apartment. You know it is only two blocks away. It was my mother's." Her bottom lip shook. "But I can't get work."

Maura wracked her brain. "What do you do again?"

"I do bookkeeping and accounting, and…"

"Accounting! Really?" Maura tapped a finger on the desk, did some mental math, and came to a conclusion. She could still keep herself solvent and hire Mrs. Bolijier. It meant a pay cut for her, but for now it would work. "I could pay you for accounting on a temporary basis, or we could barter your accounting services for membership."

Mrs. Bolijier was out of her chair and hugging Maura. "Thank you. I had no idea you would say this. I will work hard. This will get us back on our feet. I will take the first option with a hope of moving to the second by the end of the year."

Maura hugged her back. "No worries, and promise you'll keep looking for work. If something better paying comes along, take it, and no hard feelings."

"Oh, this is so much better. Thank you!" Mrs. Bolijier clapped her hands. "My Tats loves it here, and Simi has just started classes. I will make it work, and yes, I promise to keep looking in a little while. For now, I celebrate."

Maura still wasn't sure it was going to be enough money for three people to eat and pay bills with, but she was thrilled that she could help in some small way. The economy was a tough place right now; even the military was taking cuts. What would it mean for the future of their country?

Closing her eyes, she breathed in the aroma of the gym. She'd come to love the smell of running shoes and sweat. This was the scent that made her want to be a better athlete, to run and sprint faster and push herself beyond her comfort zone.

Maybe that was what the gym would do for her, push her to get past all of her limitations and to go beyond what she imagined for herself. Having Mrs. B. here would make her stick to that promise. She wanted everyone who came here to be part of a gym family and to be striving to become the best version of himself or herself.

~~~

At home in her apartment…so much for an enlightened attitude of going with the flow. Now she was being paranoid. Maura checked the blue polka-dot backpack picnic basket for the third time. She took everything out and then repacked it again to reassure herself that she had included everything important. Yes to the corkscrew, California Chablis, and wineglasses, along with plates, napkins, silverware, and the giant containers of food. She didn't know why she was so panicked.

She toyed with a plastic vase, putting it in, taking it out, and then putting it back in the basket. Would it be romantic to include a flower, or was that dorky? She picked up the single yellow rose she'd bought on her way home from work and breathed in its sweet essence. Mmmm. It smelled so good.

Was she overthinking this dinner? Was that her problem? She'd been known to do that. Of course, it had been nearly five years since she'd been with someone. That was enough time to throw a few doubts into a first date.

"Chill, Maura."

What would she do if Declan didn't like her choices? Did he eat meat? Who was she kidding? He was a SEAL. He probably ate...like a cow every day of his life! Was a whole rotisserie chicken going to be enough? She tapped her foot nervously.

She seriously needed to get herself together. She purposefully sat down, closed her eyes, and performed a relaxation exercise. It helped her feel centered. Her dear friend, Shannon, had taught her that trick in high school. Who would have thought she'd still be doing it today?

A sharp knock at the door made her jump.

Laughing at herself, she smoothed down her hair and walked calmly to the front door. Well, her heart was racing like a car in the Grand Prix, but Declan didn't need to know that.

She threw open the locks and turned the knob. And there was Declan, holding a bouquet of daisies and yellow roses. She couldn't stop herself from blurting out, "How did you know?"

He smiled, a slow seductive movement of lips that drew her attention to that sumptuous mouth of his. "I saw the pictures on the bookcase. Most of them have you with medals or trophies, holding bouquets of one or the other. I took a logical leap and put them together."

Maura took the flowers from him, walked to the kitchen, and heard him close the door. She hoped tilting her head down would keep him from noticing the hot flush on her cheeks.

Giving herself a little breathing room, she searched through several cabinets before she chose a vase to hold the lovely flowers. Then she unwrapped the bouquet, snipped the ends, and placed them one by one into the vase.

When she finally looked up at him, he was right there. He reached for her, tilting her chin up toward him, and he lowered his lips onto hers.

It was a gentle brush of lips. Such a soul-searing caress! It made her cheeks hot again.

His grin widened. "I did that on purpose. You shouldn't try to hide a response from me. I like seeing how"—he kissed her again—"I make you react."

She gave herself over to the kisses and the sensations as his arms wrapped around her tightly. Her height made it easier for her to reach him. On tiptoes, she wrapped her arms around his neck and held him in the perfect position for her response, a truly mind-blowing kiss.

His hands molded their bodies to each other. The fit was extraordinary. Where he was hard, she was soft, and where there was need, there was a definite want. Hearing him moan made her smile. She could stand here all night.

An alarm sounded on her phone. She pulled back and looked at him. "That's my phone. We have to go."

He looked taken aback. His eyebrows lifted. "Are you sure?"

Nodding her head, she calmly turned away from him and picked up the phone, her purse, and the picnic basket. "Absolutely! It took me ages to get this appointment. It's a surprise. C'mon, let's go."

He pursed his lips. "Just…uh…give me a minute."
He leaned against the counter, obviously unhappy about
her choice. Taking a few deep breaths, his eyes bored
into her head as she walked around and headed for the
front door.

She laughed softly to herself. Now, that *was* cool. It
was Declan's turn…to take a little time…to meditate.

Chapter 4

STANDING ON THE SHEER CLIFFS AT THE TORREY PINES Gliderport in La Jolla was humbling. This place made her feel like a tiny pebble among giant boulders, and she had to shake off the queasy sensation in her stomach when she looked down. Maura knew she wasn't a woman who gave in to the fear of heights, but this was seriously high. It wasn't a backflip off a balance beam with foot-and-a-half pads to land on.

Below her, she could see people playing volleyball, like ants in the dirt. Their small dot-like representation was probably better suited to her sensibility, as that was a nudist beach. So if she plunged to her death while paragliding, she guessed the view would probably be good, or at least amusing.

She pulled on the sleeves of her long-sleeve shirt. It wasn't that she was hiding her scars. She'd long ago made peace with that. Rather, she was preparing for the temperature to drop as the sun set.

"Maura, are we paragliding?" Declan walked over to where she stood and slung an arm around her shoulder. "Why did you choose this activity?"

"It's on my bucket list. And since yesterday's experience, I thought I should stop dithering and start working on it." A nervous feeling surged through her, and she wondered if she should rethink this evening's entertainment. When she made this appointment, she'd been being brave; something about being in danger had spurred her to be more adventurous. Now, actually faced with the task, her stomach roiled. Maybe she should leave it on the list and they should go do something else. "But only if you want to…"

"Sure." He shrugged his shoulders. "Let's go glide before we eat. No fun blowing chunks at altitude."

"What an image…" She rolled her eyes.

Declan took her hand and led her up the hill. "It's not that bad. Paragliding has its moments."

"That's all you're going to say? How about giving this experience a little more enthusiasm?" Maura said flatly. She'd put a lot of work into this date.

"Hooyah!" he said with a half smile and a wink.

Maura sighed and shook her head. Was it good or bad that this man could be just as annoying at times as her brothers were? She trusted her family; they had never led her astray. And upon reflection, she realized she trusted Declan too.

He gave her hand a little squeeze, and she relaxed. Her gut agreed that Declan was a good guy.

Of course, there was still the paragliding to get through. Should she admit to him now or later that she was just the slightest bit afraid that the flimsy contraption would smack into the cliff wall and plunge them to their deaths? Later was probably better.

A squat man with broad shoulders and a ready grin stood in front of the sign-in counter. "Hey, good to see you, Master Chief."

Declan shook hands and grinned back. "Hi, Chad. How's it hanging?"

"Flying high, as usual."

Maura watched the exchange with shock. "You know him?" She had argued for ages with this manager about getting an appointment tonight.

Chad looked at her. "Are you with the Master Chief?"

"No," she said. "He's with me."

"Well, I can't give you carte blanche, but the Master Chief is a certified instructor. He can take you out if he likes. No charge."

Maura couldn't believe her ears. If Declan only knew how much trouble the man had given her.

"Just give me ten minutes. I have to take care of one thing first." Chad patted Declan on the arm before disappearing into his office.

Declan leaned down and whispered in her ear. "Don't get angry. That's how Chad is with most people. He's different when you're a friend."

"So, he's a friend."

"Yeah. For the most part. His son is going through BUD/S right now, and he's pretty stressed about it. I think it's harder on parents than the kids—the waiting part, at least. And the training, well, that's all up to the trainee. A tadpole has to be determined to become a frog, or in this case, a frogman/SEAL. Now let's go suit up."

—∞—

Declan looked at Maura as they stood before the paraglider. "You look awfully cute in that outfit."

She had a steel grip on his arm. Half excited and half sick, she wanted to get this event over with. All of her brave resolutions had flown away already, and if she was going to die, she wanted it to be swift.

He put his hands over hers. Gently, he released her

fingers and showed her where to hold on. "Now," he said, "I want you to take three deep breaths, and then we're going over the side of the cliff. The minute you see we're in the air, take in a slow, long breath. You'll feel better. Okay?"

She nodded, not trusting herself not to either cry or squeal like a three-year-old.

"One, two, three."

Declan pushed them off, and the paraglider lifted into the air.

Maura felt as though she were riding on a kite as they were lifted high over the cliff. Her eyes drank in the beauty of the water, the luxurious estates below, and the breathtaking view.

"Breathe," Declan told her.

She gulped in air. She'd forgotten and was holding her breath.

"Are you okay?"

"It's amazing," she said. She knew he could hear the wonder in her voice. "How did you discover this?"

His smile warmed her, as if he were heating her insides. "I never liked heights as a kid. So, after boot camp, I had a few weeks before I had to go to BUD/S—there was no pre-BUD/S training when I went through—so I came here and learned. Between paragliding, parachuting, and taking glider lessons, I got comfortable in the air, and it put me ahead of the learning curve when it came time for training."

"That's very insightful of you."

"Well, most SEALs are self-starters; we're pretty reliant on ourselves for anything we want or need to do." Declan pointed toward the ocean. "Do you see the pod?"

Maura craned her neck. "Are those dolphins?"

"Yeah, about eight of them. Looks like they're surfing."

The ocean sparkled with light as if someone had thrown a handful of diamonds onto the water.

Maura pointed farther out. "What's that?"

Declan turned the paraglider. "Looks like a gray whale. Yeah, I heard something about a few grays coming through this area."

"No way!" She was delighted. She'd always wanted to see one in person. Now here she was, with a bird's-eye view. "Can we go out any farther out or even lower?"

"No. We need enough lift to get back to the gliderport. So we'll just hover for a bit. Out there, the wind currents can get dicey."

"You sound like a man that's landed in the drink before."

"I've done quite a few things that might shock you."

"I'll bet!" Maura replied. Had she known paragliding was this much fun, she never would have had a case of nerves earlier. Talking with Declan was so easy too. Maybe her nerves were gone for good now.

"Ready for some tricks?" Declan waggled his eyebrows.

Maura was game, and used *his* word just so he would know. "Sure."

The paraglider did a loop. Then another. With two more in succession, she squealed with delight. "Do it again!" And he did.

Dinner was going to be anticlimactic after that incredible paraglider ride. As lights popped on below and the air horn sounded, Declan brought the paraglider back into the port. The landing was smooth, and Declan and

Chad talked for about a half hour while they packed the glider and gear. She was glad they had time to "shoot the shit," as Declan would say it. That gave her time to set up the picnic dinner.

Getting the basket from her car, she laid out the blanket and all of the accoutrements. She was so hungry after that enormous adrenaline rush that she couldn't help sneaking bites here and there. When Declan finally arrived, she'd already popped the cork on the wine and was almost done with her first glass.

He sat down and handed her a bottle of water. "You might want to drink some H$_2$O before you down any more wine. You don't realize how much hydration you use up in the air."

She looked at him sideways. "I have California white. I think I'll be fine."

"And you'll have a California headache if you don't drink some water." Declan stared at her for a moment, then opened his own bottle and downed it in several gulps.

She shrugged. *Why not?*

As she put the bottle to her lips, she took a small swallow and then, realizing how great it tasted, drank three-quarters of it before pausing to breathe. Looking over the top of the bottle, she could see him smiling at her.

"Thanks for believing me."

She finished the bottle and put it down next to his. "It's not that I didn't believe you, I just never thought of it before. I guess being in the air is like any other activity. It uses up energy."

"Yep."

"Why don't you dive in?" she invited.

He opened the container of chicken and plowed

through it like a linebacker at a football game. It didn't even look like he was stopping for air.

"Hungry?" she asked.

He picked up a napkin and wiped his mouth before depositing it back on his lap. "Always." After topping off her glass of wine, he filled his own. He raised the glass to her and then tasted it. "Nice."

"Yeah. It's a bottle from a tour."

He looked at the label. "Ramona. Interesting."

"I like visiting vineyards and collecting their best bottles of wine. It's fun."

"I'll keep that in mind." He lifted the half-empty container of chicken. "Would you like one, or is that container for you and this one for me?"

She picked at her drumstick. "I think they're both for you. I'll only eat a piece or two."

He stopped eating. "You're not one of those ladies who only eats two bites and wastes her meal, are you?"

She laughed. "Oh, no! I'm definitely an eater." She lifted her drumstick and took a giant, dramatic bite.

His laughter tickled her, and she laughed more.

"Good," he said. "Because I have a long list of restaurants that I'd love to share with you."

She reached for her wineglass, took a sip, and smiled. Another date. Multiple dates, even. She knew she shouldn't be so excited, but she was. Spending time with Declan was refreshing, enlightening, and flat-out exciting. She couldn't remember a time she'd enjoyed herself so much. She just hoped that it would continue, because she knew she was already falling for him.

Chapter 5

"You're the only woman in history who can survive paragliding, only to trip over her own feet on the way to the car. Such an innocent-looking rock too. And to top it off, you dislocate your shoulder. What are you doing for an encore?" He was teasing her.

"Ha, ha," she said flatly. "We don't know that it is truly dislocated." She knew why he was being a pain in the ass. There were too many males in her family who played the same game, and oddly enough his taunting *was* helping. It was sort of comforting too. Humor had distracted her from the painful ride in the car and the walk into the hospital.

"I do. I've seen hundreds of them. I don't know why you won't let me reset your shoulder. I've had plenty of experience in the field. I've even reset my own." Declan wanted to help so much; it was endearing. But it wasn't doing much to hide the fact that it was going to be ages before she got in to see a doctor. At the Torrey Pines Urgent Care Center, it was standing room only.

"That explains a lot," she quipped back. Maura wasn't thrilled with the idea of anyone bumping into her shoulder. Thankfully, Declan was like a walking wall, and as long as she stayed in his proximity, no one seemed to jostle her.

After two hours of waiting around, she was almost

inclined to take him up on his offer. The waiting room was the pits.

"Maxwell. Is there a Maura Maxwell?" asked a health care worker in heart-emblazoned scrubs with a name tag that had RN on it.

Maura spoke up. "That's me."

"The doctor will see you now."

Maura moved slowly to the door. Once through, she was amazed at the amount of activity; it rivaled that of a busy beehive.

The nurse had held up a hand, denying entrance to Declan. "It's a tight fit in here. If you wouldn't mind waiting outside."

Maura had to endure getting her vitals—blood pressure, heart rate, etc.—before she was escorted back to a tiny corner with two chairs and a curtain. Again, her heart sank. This was going to be another waiting game.

Gritting her teeth against the pain, Maura sat down slowly, but it didn't help the jarring motion from setting off the nerve endings in her shoulder. A hand on her good arm made her eyes spring upward to take in a mountainous man. He could have been a twin to Declan.

"I'm Dr. Singer. I'm going to examine you." He examined her fingers and fingernails and checked her pulse points against the other arm. "It's lucky I was in the building. Orthopedic docs are not usually here on weekends, but I had an emergency surgery and stayed to catch up on paperwork."

"Okay." She let the one word out on a strained breath of air. Luckily, it was not the arm that she'd had all the surgeries on as a teen. She didn't want to answer a million questions for this doctor about her scars and the injuries she'd sustained in the car accident almost a decade ago.

"You look pretty good. The blood flow isn't impeded, but there is no doubt you popped the shoulder out." His fingers poked and prodded. The pain was excruciating! "How did you do it?"

"Fell on a-a-a rock." It took everything she had to get those words out. She wanted to pass out from the pain.

Gently, he pried her fingers away from the death grip she had on her limb. "You need to let go. Give me control of your arm."

Dr. Singer bent her elbow, forcing her arm into a ninety-degree angle, then lifted up.

"Owwwwwwwww!" Maura couldn't stop the scream of pain from leaving her lips as the shoulder slid back into place.

A commotion from outside the curtain arose.

"Hold still while I fit this sling around you," ordered Dr. Singer.

The curtain slid back and Declan was standing there. His eyes were burning with a bright fire, and he looked like he was going to take out half of the urgent care center. Three nurses surrounded him, and they were calling for security.

"He's with me," said Maura.

One of the nurses gestured for Declan to get inside.

With two men of such large girth, Maura felt like a tiny flower. She'd never been the delicate type, and the idea made her grin.

"You'll need to keep this on for at least two weeks and follow up with your primary care doctor within that time. Just let him or her know that you've been to the urgent care and you will get in faster. Between us, it doesn't appear that you've torn anything, but just to be sure, you should get an MRI to confirm it. I'll list all of this in your file." Dr. Singer finished securing the sling. "Let's prescribe you an anti-inflammatory and get you on your way. I'll be right back."

Maura looked up at Declan. "Next time, you have my permission to put my shoulder back in."

Declan smiled. "That bad?"

"I'm sitting in a corner with two folding chairs, talking to a doctor who happened to be here by chance. Yep, I'd rather have saved the hours waiting out there and sitting in here." Maura scratched her neck. "This sling itches."

"I'll show you how to make it comfortable. I have a few tricks up my sleeve." Declan pulled a bandana out of his back pocket and looped it around the back of sling where it touched her neck. Then he made a few minor adjustments to the sling itself.

"I'll bet." Maura let out a sigh of relief. "Okay. You've got the position as my chief health care man. Consider yourself hired." The pressure was off and she felt significantly better. Declan really was a man of many talents.

A nurse opened the curtain and handed several pieces of paper and a prescription to Maura. "Follow the instructions. Heat and ice. Don't use that arm for any reason, and wear the sling until further notice from your primary care. Understood?"

Maura nodded her head.

The nurse looked Declan up and down. "I assume that you have a ride home."

Smiling to herself, Maura replied, "Yes, thank you."

Declan put his hand under Maura's uninjured elbow and helped her stand up. "She's in good hands."

One of the other nurses walking by said under her breath, "I'll bet."

Maura laughed softly as she worked her way out of the busy place, aided by her bodyguard. Declan didn't seem to mind being her buffer, blocking anyone who might bump her or obstruct her path. Most people who saw him got out of the way automatically. If they didn't, all he had to do was clear his throat.

Yes, there were advantages to having this giant hunk of a man by her side. And she was enjoying it.

Walking through the doorway of her apartment had never felt so good. Maura was relieved to be home. The car ride had been painful, regardless of how carefully Declan drove, and she was still a little tense.

She steered herself toward her bedroom. An arm blocked her way.

"Hold up, Miss Maxwell." Declan appeared adamant as he guided her toward his place. "We are going to my house."

"No offense, but I'm tired and sore, and all I want is to lie down."

He stopped pushing her toward the glass door and their shared balcony. Laying his forehead against hers, he said, "I know. Trust me. Okay?"

She didn't want to. They'd picked up the anti-inflammatory on the way home. The effects were already kicking in and she wanted to sleep.

"Back at the urgent care, you said you'd trust me with your well-being. Do you still?"

She wanted to deny it, but she did trust him. "Fine."

He winked at her. "Good. C'mon." Taking her by the elbow, he gently guided her out her glass door, onto the balcony, and over to his place.

"Earthy," she said as she walked inside. His apartment smelled clean and a little salty, like the sea. She liked the warm colors—beiges, red clay, sage greens, and creams.

"I find the colors soothing…as if I'm outside." He whisked her through the rest of the place, not leaving her much time to take everything in. Soon enough they were in his bathroom. It looked nothing like hers.

"How did you get a Jacuzzi tub in here?" That thing could have fit five guys the size of Declan.

"I own my apartment and when I remodeled, I put this beauty in. I wanted a hot tub outside, but the balcony would never have held the weight." He turned on the taps full stream and then turned to her. "This is the place I wanted to bring you after your paddleboard accident. I didn't know how you'd feel about it, though."

"You saved me that night."

"Maybe. If you'd held on through the storm, you'd have been able to save yourself. The storm blew itself out in a short time," Declan reassured her. "Don't give up your love of paddleboarding."

"I won't." She licked her lips. "You always seem to do that."

"What?" he asked.

"Empower me. Make me feel better about myself, like I can get through any situation no matter what it is, if I just give myself a chance to work through it." Maura smiled. "That's a gift, Declan, that you're like this."

"It's the SEAL in me. We never quit." He pointed at the top of the tub where the tiles made a shelf. "Why don't you sit on the edge of the tub, and I'll help you undress."

Maura's eyebrows shot upward. "I…uh…"

"Now you're getting shy? I've seen you naked. Don't lose that uninhibited side of yourself. I admire it."

"Ah, thanks." Maura swallowed the lump in her throat. The truth was…she wanted to soak in a hot tub. Her body was sore from all of the tension and pain, and she could use the relief.

When the tub was full of water, he turned off the taps, checked the temperature, and added something from a purple bottle of…yummm…lavender and eucalyptus.

Declan reached for her. Maura didn't pull away. He started with her shoes, and then removed her shorts and panties. Then he slowly reached under her shirt and unclipped her bra. From beneath her shirt, he maneuvered the bra off flawlessly before he picked up her— shirt and sling—and placed her into the tub.

"What are you doing?"

"You'll see." He stripped off his own clothes in record time and crawled in beside her. "I want you to lie on your back. I'm going to support you with one hand and use the other to finish undressing you."

Maura sighed. "My sling is wet," she grumbled. "I didn't think you were supposed to put these things in water."

"Relax," he said, leaning over her. "I have about ten of them in the linen closet. I even have them in camo and different colors. You can take your pick after the bath."

Maybe it was the warmth of the tub or his joking

nature, but she finally gave up and relaxed. The water felt blissful on her skin, and her muscles finally started to relax. "Go for it." She floated onto her back.

"You're a natural. I don't even need to hold on to you," Declan remarked as his fingers moved over her, taking off the sling and working her shirt slowly up her body and over her head.

Maura closed her eyes, trusting him completely. As the shirt and sling were wrung out and slung over the side of the tub to dry, she took several long, slow breaths.

The soothing scents and the Epsom salts were working magic on her. She could fall asleep right here and now.

Arms pulled her closer. From underneath, a strong, hard surface rose to support her weight.

A voice whispered in her ear. "I'm here. Rest. Sleep. Relax. Whatever you need to do…"

With her good arm, she reached up a hand and nestled it beneath her cheek, registering the fact that she was lying on Declan's naked body.

Mmmmm…naked. She smiled to herself. She finally had him all to herself…

———

Waking up in his arms was amusing and embarrassing. She must have been batting at the hairs on his chest, because there was a towel between them now. She vaguely remembered scratching at them.

Yes, he had lifted her out of the tub, dried her, and placed her onto crisp, cool sheets. That part had seemed like a dream. She remembered the twinge of pain in her shoulder as he secured a brace around her, and then she was out again. Now, here she was lying naked in a bed next to the one man who had captured her attention since she first moved in next door.

"I know you're awake."

"Rats!" she said with a smile. "How long have you known?"

"Since the sound of your breathing changed." He shifted his position so he could look into her eyes. "What are you thinking about, Maura?"

She lifted the sheet and looked down at herself, and put the sheet back down again. "Um, that we're naked." Her cheeks heated. His body was lean, hard muscled, and very, very well endowed. It looked like a kickstand down there.

She pursed her lips and blew air out in a soft sigh.

He leaned down and kissed her. "Yes, and…"

When life gives a woman a gift, it's worth enjoying it. Her hand moved to capture his. "I want more of those."

He squeezed her hand and then let it go. Trailing his fingers up her arm, he caught her chin.

Her fingers twined into his hair.

"Kisses?" he asked between the long, lazy play of lips.

"Yes. And more…"

"What about your shoulder?" Declan looked genuinely concerned. "There's no rush, we could…"

"Wait until my next accident." Maura searched his eyes. Was Declan being a chivalrous guy or was he playing with her desire?

His fingers traced the arch of her brow and line of her cheeks. "I want you to…enjoy it."

She smiled. He was a good guy. Down deep, she'd known that. "If you do your job right, then I will."

"Oh, it's up to me…to do a good job. I see. No

pressure." Declan laughed. The deep baritone sound slid through her senses in waves, tickling something inside her.

"Declan," she said, beckoning him to kiss her again.

He obliged as his hands moved over her body. Just like the experience in the tub, she gave herself over to it.

His lips trailed kisses down her neck, down the valley between her breasts, and down her stomach to the place between her thighs. As his lips and tongue explored her, she allowed the explosions of pleasure to ignite one of her wildest fantasies about him: being stranded on a desert island, with his giant bed as their oasis.

Her fingers from her good hand and arm dug into the sheets, attempting to get traction as he caressed that most sensitive part of her. Over and over, his tongue played a magical dance that made her breath shudder out and her body crave more.

"Declan!" she begged, needing and wanting him to give her that final pleasure.

His tongue changed angle, lapping at her body in a rhythmic pattern that lifted her higher and higher until she felt herself on the pinnacle of such incredible pleasure, she never ever wanted it to end. And just as she was about to leap down, his fingers played over her body, lifting her even more as her climax climbed two more notches and she finally leaped, crashing down once, twice, three times in a climactic crescendo of joy.

He looked up at her, his body shifting seductively as he leaned over.

Tears streamed down her face. She'd never felt such intense pleasure. Her body was still alive with the energy and vibrations.

Tenderly, his fingers wiped away the wetness from her cheeks. "Are you okay? Did I hurt you?"

"No," she said, looking up at him with enormous wonder. "I've never experienced such...completion."

He looked relieved. He smiled at her and gently kissed her lips. "Then hang on, Maura, because that is only the tip of the iceberg." His body shifted away from her head, and she watched him move all the way down to her feet and her painted petal-pink toes.

Oh my goodness, she thought. The *tip* of the iceberg. What *was* she in store for?

He grinned at her like a man delighted with what he was about to do.

Chapter 6

IT WAS ONE HELLUVA GREAT MORNING, JUST LIKE ALL the mornings Declan had spent with Maura for the past few weeks. Time passed quickly with her by his side.

He stepped out onto the balcony to breathe the fresh morning air. He'd never felt like this with anyone but her.

"Yo, Swifton, what's up?"

A voice from below caught Declan's attention. His eyes located the perpetrator and he waved. "McCullum, you jackass! What are you doing in this neck of the woods, Mac?" Declan leaned on the railing of the balcony and chewed the fat with his favorite Team THREE puke. They'd been close over the years and had hauled each other out of some tough jams. Now that Dan McCullum was Team THREE, Declan took pleasure in teasing the hell out of the man.

"Had some extra time. It's Aria's Ladies' Event. She's hosting the wives." Dan wiped the sweat from his face with his shirtsleeve.

"Sounds like fun," Declan said sarcastically.

The Chief Petty Officer laughed. "You'd think, but Aria's been panicked and is running through the house barking orders to anyone within earshot. I just dropped Jimmy off at a friend's house and decided to get some extra miles under my belt. I'm sure the walls can give her better answers than I can."

Declan chuckled. "You want to come up?"

Dan checked his watch. "Another time. I need to make an appearance in forty-five. I'm pretty sure I'll catch hell if I look like this." He gestured to his own sweat-drenched body in the ubiquitous yellow Navy shorts.

Declan nodded. "Probably right."

"Rain check," said Dan, turning around and taking off like a devil who had the Heavenly Host hot on his trail.

Declan shook his head. He didn't envy the man. Marriage and family were big steps, though Dan had seemed to adjust okay to it. His mind sped ahead. Maybe if he had someone like Aria. Nah, she wasn't his type. But Maura… He could see himself getting serious with her. The idea caught him by surprise, and that was a feat, for he was a man who had contingency plans for his contingency plans.

Spying Maura's notebook on the ground, Declan leaned over and picked it up. Paging through it, he was fascinated by the sketches. She had written equations and drawn figures in motion, jumping, turning, and twisting. Alongside each picture were notes explaining how high the jumps were, when to turn, and how to twist in a timely manner. Never in his life had he seen anything like this. *This must be for her parkour stuff*. Declan had been intrigued when she had told him about the gym and her parkour activities. She was definitely a woman who enjoyed physical activity and really seemed to have found her niche.

He closed the cover, walked the few remaining steps to her glass door, and knocked. When Maura didn't answer, he left the notebook on her patio chair and headed back to his own apartment. With one last glance back at her door, he smiled and headed in. The lady had certainly piqued his curiosity, and the more he got to know her, the more he wanted to know about her.

In his apartment, he stripped off his running shorts, throwing them into the open closet that contained his sack of sweaty laundry. The soothing earth tones of his apartment made it a real retreat for him, from the cream leather couch and mocha recliners to the warm, dark wall colors. This was his haven, surrounded by the stuff he'd collected through the years: ancient bows and arrows, books on strategies and languages, an assortment of framed handmade knives, and a large screen TV with a stack of his favorite movies.

He flipped on his CD player preloaded with The Who, the bass beat sounding in his gut. The band reminded him of his childhood, his mother playing the song "Behind Blue Eyes" and his three-year-old self learning to dance, mimicking her steps. He could still smell the honeysuckle thick in the air and almost hear the lilting sound of her laughter as they spun around in circles and did the box step. He always wanted to be her "little hero," and he'd like to think she would be proud of him today.

It'd been hard having no one there to represent family at his BUD/S graduation so many years ago. Picking up the picture of her he kept next to the stereo, he studied her image. "I miss you, Mom." He wondered what she'd think of Maura.

He put down the picture, the only familial object in his apartment. The rest of pictures consisted of collages from BUD/S training and graduation and places he'd been between missions.

Looking in the giant circular mirror—inlaid with real gold chunks dug up on a trip to Julian, California, and hanging in the hall near the door—he wondered what was next. Right now he was living his greatest dream, and he had done pretty much everything on his "frogucket"/bucket list, including making love to ladies in exotic, if not erotic, positions. Ahem, places.

A second alarm sounded from his phone. Damn, he was going to be late if he kept dithering and daydreaming. Work didn't stop, and he had a meeting with the CO this morning. Granted, it was two hours from now, but he had to prep.

He grabbed a coffee drink, popped the top, and took a long draw of the thick, rich brew, then headed straight to the shower. As heat pelted his skin, he smiled into the stream of the water. He was a SEAL, a Master Chief in Team FIVE, and dating a very hot lady. Life was good.

~~~

Spending hours and hours on paperwork was not Declan's idea of a good time. As he dressed in a pair of tan slacks and a navy blue solid silk Tommy Bahama shirt for dinner with Maura, Declan mulled over his day. He knew how important reports were for the brass and posterity as a whole—it helped Spec War trace the success or failure based on men, resources, terrain, difficulty, the enemy, etc.—but he knew he'd be thrilled if he could dump that side of his life for good.

The timer buzzed on his phone. He only had five more minutes before he was due next door.

At least he could spend the rest of this bland day focusing on Maura. He longed to wrap his arms around her again, to hear her laugh. And he was especially eager for the soft moans she made as she came. The way she looked at him, with a cross between slumberous exhaustion and complete satiation after they made love, did a lot for his ego.

She was so free in bed, with every emotion clearly written in her body language and on her countenance. He liked that. Most women hid such things…whether it was for control or for their own ease, he didn't know. Maura was honest, refreshing, and beautiful.

He scratched his chin. Damn, it was a little rough. Stubble was not a way to endear oneself to a female, especially to those tender female fleshy parts. He needed to make a pit stop to handle this.

As Declan took care of the stubble, he thought about how this woman had turned his world upside down in such a short time. Had it only been four weeks since he hauled her out of the ocean? SEAL Team had been his sole focus for so long—women had merely been a distraction—but Maura was becoming as much a priority as his work. He had to tread carefully. He didn't want to screw up a good thing.

Putting his wallet in his back pocket and his cell phone in his front, he checked to make sure he had his keys and headed out the door. He'd had the good sense to pick up flowers, and he scooped them up from the table near the front door.

Opening his door, he stepped outside, walked precisely five steps, turned, and knocked.

"Who is it?" asked the voice from the other side.

"The Roto-Rooter man," he replied.

"Oh, I'm not decent," said the female voice, laughing.

"Just ignore my unkempt state." The door opened and Declan's breath caught. Maura was a vision. She was clad in a skintight sea-green dress, and her eyes looked like the sea on a warm day. "Well, aren't you looking handsome? Are those for me?"

Declan had lost himself for a few seconds. He pushed the bouquet into her arms and pulled his libido together. He was acting like a lovesick teenager. He cleared his throat. "You look beautiful."

"Thank you," she said. "The flowers are gorgeous. Let me just put them in water."

He watched every move as she sashayed away, those hips beckoning him. He tilted his head to the ceiling. *Oh, good Lord, I'm not going to make it to the restaurant.*

Maura came up to him and tapped her fingers on his chest. "Hey, I'm down here."

Declan captured her gaze and was relieved to see that she was just as "inspired" as he was. They kissed, tenderly at first, and then it turned into something hotter, more delicious.

"No," he said, pushing back from those sumptuous lips. "We have all night. Let's…"

"Go eat," she finished. "I agree. I'm hungry."

He rubbed his hand over her hip just as her stomach rumbled. "I can tell."

She blushed. Those sweet cheeks pinked for him.

Smiling at her, he asked, "Do you want to take your vehicle or my Harley? We're going to the Brigantine."

"If you hold me tight…your Harley. My mother had a Harley and I rode it for a while when I was of age." She pointed to a leather biker jacket on the chair. She'd invested in a well-padded one just last week so that she could ride safely with Dec. Maybe she'd send for her old gear too. Mom would send it in a heartbeat. "Just don't stop too suddenly. Remember, I'm still sore."

"Dislocated shoulders take a while to quit hurting, but in a few more weeks, that shoulder should be as good as new." He picked up the jacket and held it so she could ease her arms in, and then he zipped her into the soft leather. Touching her chin, he tilted her face up to his and kissed her. "I have precious cargo. I promise, I will be very careful."

Escorting her from the apartment, he locked the door for her and aided her down the stairs. He liked playing the knight in shining armor for her. Maybe it was the fact she didn't ask for it, or that he just enjoyed being with her so much. Regardless, he was pleased that she beamed…for him.

The ride to the restaurant was relaxing as they sailed down the Strand and made their way into Coronado. Traffic was heading the other way as duty stations released for the day, and the other side was bumper-to-bumper with vehicles. He and Maura zipped down pretty much unimpeded, admiring the beach and sea on one side and Glorietta Bay on the other. He pinned her arms under his, wrapping her even more tightly against his body to make sure she felt safe.

As they pulled up in front of the Brigantine, there was even a parking spot, as if he'd somehow reserved it. He set the kickstand, turned off his Harley, pulled the key, and helped his date off his Fat Boy.

Arm in arm, Declan and Maura walked inside and he gave his name. They were whisked away to a darkened corner with the very private and out-of-the-way table he had specifically requested. The Brigantine was known for its cuisine. Though he tended to be a surf-and-turf guy, he knew he'd be going for the rack of lamb tonight.

"Maura, would you like wine?" he asked.

"Sure." Her nose was buried in the menu. "What's good?"

"Everything," he said, letting his emotion into his voice. They had been on over a dozen dates in the past four weeks, and in that time, they had shared quite a bit. They'd been bike riding, enjoyed concerts in the park, seen movies, taken day trips into the mountains and the desert, and gone out to numerous restaurants. Maura had learned about his life in foster care and hadn't balked at his frustration with the social services system in California. Instead, she had listened intently and agreed with his wish to adopt kids as well as have ones of his own. It was the first time he'd ever been so honest about his innermost thoughts with a woman, and he knew that said a lot about how much he trusted her.

She looked up from the menu and smiled. "Really? So what should I choose first?"

"Besides me?" He laughed. Learning about her large family, her parents, and their support of her dream had been refreshing. Her ability to rally no matter the occasion contributed several points in her favor. Her effervescence was contagious too. He often found himself smiling just because she was.

Maura put down her menu. Her near-side elbow connected with his stomach and he let out a soft *oof*. "Stop looking at me like that. We're in public. Be good."

He cleared his throat. "Yes, ma'am." He suppressed the smile tugging at the corners of his lips. Maura was

a riot when she put on her no-nonsense hat. "Fine. I'll
order. I'd like the lamb."

"Okay, how about I order the salmon, and we share?"
she asked, taking a sip of her water. He usually disliked
it when women ate off his plate, but with her it was different. There was a seductive quality about watching his
food go into her mouth, and he liked sharing what was his.

"That works," he replied and signaled to the waitstaff.

The waiter hurried over, and they placed their order.
Settling on a bottle of Chablis, they toasted each other
as they took their first sip. The crisp white wine was dry
and pleasing on his palate.

He moved closer to her. What did one need to say
when you had a gorgeous lady on your arm? Nothing.
When there was a lull, it was funny how easy it was to
be together. They didn't need to make small talk to be
comfortable; they already were. As Maura chatted about
her day at the gym, Declan naturally shared his experience of being a SEAL.

Just as he reached the climax of one of his million-
and-one Leaper Lefton comic savant stories, a commotion at a table around the corner interrupted him.

"I won't take this! I don't have to! Don't you know
to whom you are speaking? I'm leaving this date, you
big baboon!"

Unfortunately he knew that woman's voice.

The lady peeked around the corner. "Thank God!
Declan. I wondered if anyone I knew was here. You'll
do. Of course."

"Olivia," he said flatly. It was none other than Olivia
Fenwick—the twenty-six-year-old, blond, slim woman
with a fortune at her fingertips, and also a former lover.

She was not the person he wanted to see right now. He'd broken things off with her over a year ago by leaving a voice mail and leaving town. True, it wasn't the bravest maneuver, but this lady had claws. None of his liaisons had lasted very long, but Olivia's personality, or lack of actual depth of heart and soul, kept turning fun time into run time.

Maura's eyes turned to him. Her eyebrows went up.

"Let me just get my salad. No sense wasting my marvelous meal." Olivia disappeared for a minute, only to return with a giant bowl and the largest martini he'd ever seen—and that was saying a lot, because he'd been to a lot of bars around the globe.

She sat down next to Declan, scooting very close to him and planting a red-lipped kiss on his cheek. He knew there would be a mark. There always was with Olivia—tacky or not.

Olivia waved at Maura. "Hi, I'm Olivia. Declan's girl."

Declan frowned. "No, you're not."

Olivia threw up her hands. "Okay, fine. I'm your former girl."

"We didn't date." Declan physically pushed back from her, invading Maura's space. "This is Maura, my girlfriend, and we'd appreciate it if you left us to our dinner."

Olivia nibbled thoughtfully on her spinach salad. "Interesting… I guess I'm stuffed." The bowl was three-quarters full, and half the ingredients were pushed to the side. "I know when two is company." She stood and walked over to the other side of the table. "Honey, can you give us a minute?"

Maura looked at her as if the woman were a door-to-door snake oil salesperson. "No."

He couldn't have been prouder, watching Maura stand her ground. Olivia was not the type to back down, but here she was…actually backing away from Maura's death stare.

Olivia fished into her purse and pulled out a picture. It was of her naked. She placed it in front of Declan. "In case you need a reminder of what you have. This is a choice between her—a woman wearing off-the-rack clothes—and me. You know how lovely my skin is, encased in silk. I only wear natural fibers. They show off my naturally gorgeous form."

"Natural, my ass! Only Barbie has boobs that high. Do you keep upping the amount of silicone, hoping no one will notice the mileage? Now," said Maura, picking up her fork and going back to her meal, "take a hint, and get lost."

"Well! I never!" exclaimed Olivia, outraged.

"Somehow, I doubt that," remarked Maura. "I'm sure you've 'nevered' many times."

"Oh!" screeched Olivia as she grabbed her bowl of salad and tossed the contents at Maura and Declan before stomping out the door.

They looked at each other and burst out laughing.

"That was a rather comical scene," said Maura, picking spinach and bacon off Declan.

"You seriously held your own. Good job!" In turn, he was pulling clumps of mushroom and onion out of her hair. "I'm sorry about that. Olivia was probably the least stable woman I ever hooked up with. I should have never let her into my world. I make mistakes occasionally."

"I see. Well, um, I think we should go," said Maura, the humor melting from her lips.

"Why? You've barely eaten. I've eaten a half a rack

of lamb, a salad, a baked potato, and I still have room for more." Declan couldn't believe the woman would eat four bites of food and consider dinner done. When he ate, his body craved the sustenance like a starving man. He'd already had to slow down his intake several times to speak. "Let's order Black Forest cake. What do you say?"

Maura shrugged, wincing.

"Your shoulder is bothering you again?"

"Yeah. Do you mind if we go?" She seemed so earnest, how could he deny her?

"Sure."

He got the check and paid. His eyes were on her as she moved from the table. Her actions were not stiff or pained. Was there something else going on?

Outside, he directed her toward a bench. "Let's sit down for a moment."

She nodded her head.

"Tell me the real reason we left. Did you object to me calling you my girlfriend?"

"No, I liked that. I'm honored. Truly, I am, Declan." She looked at him earnestly, then quickly shifted her gaze away. Her fingers fidgeted with a thread on her skirt hem. "I just…"

"Maura…"

Finally, she exhaled and turned toward him. Her green eyes locked to his. "At first, I thought the situation with Olivia was funny."

He rushed to speak. "It was."

She put her hand on his arm. "Hear me out. Then I remembered all of the women going in and out of your apartment. It made me worry that I'm…" She couldn't finish the sentence, and her eyes welled with tears.

"That you would become one of them."

Maura nodded her head and wiped at her eyes. Her lips shook as if she were going to cry.

"Hey, that's not true. It's different this time. You're special, Maura. Okay?" He pulled her close and wrapped his arms around her. Burying his nose in her hair, he breathed deeply. He loved the smell of her. Being with her was just different than being with the others. How could he reassure her? "I never dated any of them more than a few times. It's been weeks and I still feel the same excitement with you as I did the first day."

"So, the others were what? Bed buddies?" Maura squeaked out. "And what happens if you tire of me? If I bore you?"

"You never could, Maura," he replied, then instantly regretted his quick agreement.

"Never say never, Declan. You're a grown man." She pulled back from him. "What makes me different? Will you treat me like Olivia when you're done with me? What's to stop you from kicking me to the curb when this is over?"

"This isn't the same situation, and you are definitely *not* Olivia...or more accurately, Olivia is not you, and never could be." He held her gaze—those beautiful watery sea-green eyes. "Everything is different. I could spend years exploring all the fascinating things about you. I haven't wanted that...ever. Maura, there is something so special about you. I can't put it all into words right now. But I think about you so much during the day, and I wonder how you are and what you're doing, and I can hardly wait to share things with you." He shook his head. "Man, I'm crap at expressing myself."

"Don't feed me lines…or excuses." She pushed on his chest. "This is just another conquest."

"No," he said, his voice very serious. "This relationship—you and me—is very important to me."

"I…I don't know, Declan. I need to think about this. It's a big step for me to get past, well, your history with women. Please…please take me home." Maura stood and walked to the Harley. She carefully got into the jacket and zipped it up. Putting on her helmet, she waited for him, looking miserable.

There was no doubt in his mind that this was a misunderstanding, and that they'd get through it. She just needed some time to reflect on everything they'd shared and the kind of future they could have together. Regardless, he was going to keep proving himself to her. He wouldn't give up.

He nodded his head and got up from the bench. Slowly, he mounted his Harley and inserted the key. The engine roared to life. He secured his own helmet and pulled into traffic.

This time, Maura didn't reach around him as they rode. She held his hips, clearly regretting that she chose a mode of transportation requiring physical contact.

He sighed. His visions for this night were going down the tubes fast and furiously. This was not what he wanted to happen. Not at all.

The lights in the apartment next to his were off. Nary a sound issued from its darkness, either.

Standing on the balcony, Declan turned his gaze to stare out at the ocean. Stars filled the sky. The crescent moon hung low, as if it were attempting to hook a fish.

He scrubbed his fingers over his scalp until his brain released its hold on the events of the night. He couldn't let this frustration hold him stagnant. He needed motion; movement was the core of his life and his happiness. He needed motion to relax himself.

He stripped off his clothes, going down to his boxer shorts, and then dropped to the sand. He did a series of exercises, warming up his muscles, feeling his heart rate increase, and his blood... Well, hell, that was already pumping, and in places it didn't need to be right now.

Getting to his feet, he looked up at the night sky full of brightly twinkling stars and said, "I need some help here. A little guidance would be useful."

Nothing was forthcoming. What did he expect? He shrugged and studied the waves, looking for the sweet spot where the current would draw him into the ocean. It would be easier to do laps and swim hard out there.

Besides, he hadn't really done anything wrong, had he? It wasn't as if he could erase his past. If she were meant to be his, she'd come around to his point of view. And if not...

Man, he didn't like thinking about not seeing her. Not kissing her.

Damn! This was not the mind-set he wanted right now.

His swim buddy was right when he said, "Women are an enigma and very unpredictable."

Catching sight of the perfect spot to enter the ocean, where the rhythm of waves would pull him straight out, he moved quickly. Digging his toes in, he jogged down the sandbank and dove into the churning waves.

The cold ocean water shocked his system for a second or two, but he ignored it. Feeling his body slice through the buoyant water brought a calm satisfaction and his own version of peacefulness as the current pulled him deeper and deeper into its briny darkness.

Chapter 7

"MAURA," DECLAN SAID LOUDLY. HE KNOCKED ON Maura's front door again. A night alone had brought him more than enough clarity, and he hoped the same would be true for her. "C'mon, I have to go. Please open up."

He'd tried the balcony glass door. Calling her cell phone didn't work either. When was this woman going to cut him a break?

"Maura." He waited for her to answer, but she didn't come to the door. Damn, he didn't want things left this way. Taking the note from his back pocket, he slid it under the door. Simply enough, it said, "I'm sorry. Will be gone for a few. Be well. Talk when I'm back. Declan." He couldn't say much more. This was the painful part of a mission situation; one couldn't say jack shit to anyone.

Maura would either be cool with him and his life, or not. He knew he was providing her with the optimal opportunity to drop-kick him into the ocean. He just hoped she'd want to hang on to him.

Shit! This fucking sucked. The timing for this Op could not be worse. The call had come a few hours after he'd gotten in from his swim. His brain had been completely at peace after the salt water soaked away his stressors, but he knew that was a temporary situation, because Maura was under his skin. He'd get laughed off the Teams if he'd ever admitted that about any woman.

Teammates knew how to push buttons—at least the good ones did.

Girls like Olivia made him nuts, because they liked to taunt and tease in a negative, manipulative manner. But Maura had an honest passion, and having her wrapped around him was addictive in the best of ways.

He grabbed his pack and headed down the staircase. He didn't want to be thinking about her or that kiss or the way they made love together, laughed, and talked, but it was hard to get her out of his mind. Something about her manner and personality caught his attention. Until he could figure it out, she was like a puzzle to him. Intriguing women always garnered his attention.

The best thing he could do was concentrate on his work and let the female thing work itself out. He believed in the universe's capacity to sort things out and man's ability to screw it all up.

He checked his watch. They'd be cutting it close. His eyes scanned the road, looking for his swim buddy, Leaper Lefton. The plane was taking off in fifteen minutes. There wasn't much time. He'd only had an hour to get organized and grab his gear.

"C'mon, Leaper, where are you?" They'd gone through BUD/S at different times—Leaper had been two classes ahead of him—yet they worked together as if they had known each other all their lives. It was like that with most SEALs. They became your brother, your friend, and your family. Training tended to weed out those who weren't suited to the demands of the job as well as the roll-with-it lifestyle.

A Mustang cornered the street with a screech. It was a twenty-five-mile-per-hour zone, and Leaper was going to get nailed if he wasn't careful. The man had luck, though, because there wasn't a police officer in sight. They'd have to keep hustling if they were going to get to Naval Air Station North Island (NAS) on time.

The car skidded to stop and the door opened. "Hump it."

Declan put his pack in the back and was barely in the door before the car started moving. He was used to it. Buckling his seat belt, he closed his eyes. *Think about the mission. Run through it in your head.* As he repeated the directive, his brain finally gave way, and he was moving through the drills at top speed, ready, prepared, and primed to go.

~~~

Maura watched the waves rush in, climb up the shore, and then slowly slide back into the ocean. The rhythm was soothing, and she lost herself in the push and pull.

The irrational fears rattling around in the back of her mind had played out in real life when she met Olivia. How horrible it must be to be thrust aside and treated so callously. Of course, Olivia hadn't seemed like a wilting flower, either. The woman had some balls, barging in on her date with Declan. And that was the thing...it was possible that Maura had accused Declan wrongly, that Olivia was one of those nutty, obsessed types and Declan had avoided things going further with her for just that reason.

She hugged her legs to her. She wasn't getting any answers sitting there, so she stood and wiped the sand from her long cotton skirt and cardigan. She needed to talk to him.

The sun was high in the sky. She had been out here

since sunrise and the time had flown. She had the evening shift at the gym, so there was no need to rush. But she did want to talk to Declan before the day was through. No sense in stewing over the incident for days. She really liked him.

She knew it was true. The way he spoke to her when she was upset, the cajoling kindness that helped her face tough moments, and his kisses... Secrets were uncovered about a man when he made love. She knew the depth of his passion and tenderness, and she wanted more. Their time together made her want to know everything about him.

She headed back down the beach toward home. "I guess that's my answer," she murmured.

She was stuck on him. Regardless, today she would give him a chance to explain about Olivia, and she'd apologize for her temper. She knew anger was anxiety and fear amplified. She just didn't want to be one of those souls ruled by emotional outbursts; that wasn't who she was. Rather, she'd prefer to define herself as strong, capable, and independent. She'd proved she was different than Olivia.

———

Riding in a C-17 was like willingly sticking your ear next to the loudest air conditioner you've ever heard for hours on end. Declan had flown in the belly of these aircraft for years, and it never got better.

The Team was packed into the belly, along with the support staff, gear, and additional mission specialists. It was a tight squeeze.

Miller was reading off his clipboard. "Packs, check.

Money, check. Communications, check. Miller Roth—that's me and I'm pretty sure that I'm here. Harvey Wilson, Hayes Johnson, Declan Swifton—please don't roll your eyes. Leaper Lefton—nice bird! I think that fingernail needs a trim. Tyler Kidding—if the flight crew catches you spitting tobacco chew on the ground, we're scrubbing this place, so quit it. Bunks Fox—you've got some nerve popping pills! Oh, it's Dramamine. And Sobbit Dahl. We're eight for eight, and we're loaded, and everyone that's supposed to be aboard is…so we're good to go."

Pulling a sound-canceling headset and his iPod from his pack would give Declan the few hours of the peace he craved, not to mention save his battered eardrums. There was only so much shouting he could listen to from his Teammates, especially when they involved Leaper's dirty joke collection. Telling the same jokes every time seemed to be part of his superstition.

Donning the headphones and dialing up a mix of Placebo, Queen, Beck, Bowie, U2, Bush, Foreigner, and Creed, he closed his eyes and zoned out. His mind was immediately transported to a state of complete Zen. His muscles loosened, relaxing, as images danced through his brain: family, friends, and women. When it finally settled on a vision, he smiled knowingly.

Maura Maxwell bit the tip of her perfectly rounded fingernail with that sultry smile. He could hear her voice beckoning him. Watching her disrobe, revealing that silky smooth skin, made him lick his lips. He craved to hold her, touch her, and make love to her.

He walked to her, but she was always half turned

away from him. Why wouldn't she face him? "Maura? Why do you keep moving away?"

She laughed, throaty and deep. "I'm not. You're just not fast enough to catch me."

"Yes, I am." He heard the dare in her words and liked it.

Then she disappeared, and he was alone.

"That's not fair," he said, getting frustrated with her.

"I'm here now." She appeared again, but one hand was behind her back. Something was hiding there. She stared at him with her terminally smoky, sea-green gaze. "You make me yours."

"How?" He shook his head. He didn't do games. He needed to hear the words from that gorgeous mouth, feel those lips that would be so delectable on his body. "Enough!" he shouted.

He grabbed for her and reached her shoulder.

As she turned toward him, he was surprised to see Maura crying.

"What's wrong? How can I fix it?" he asked.

"Invite me," Maura said, standing there in some prim, high-necked black dress one second and completely naked in the next as she twirled in circles.

He felt he should turn away, but he couldn't stop staring. His hands caught her and pulled her toward him. She was so very, very real.

She opened her arms and her soft skin rubbed against him. "I'm ready. I'll let you in," she whispered. "I promise. Just be mine now."

As their bodies were about to touch, he kissed her, becoming lost in her intoxicating touch. His choice this time, as his lips devoured her sweetness, was to have all of her.

*Her murmurs beckoned him to hurry, to make love to
her before the chance slipped away.*

*He reached a hand down to pull off his own clothes,
but he was already naked, his clothes disappearing
before the thought had even fully formed.*

*They were flesh on flesh now, hands stroking and
caressing, bringing such electric pleasure that it was hard
to contain himself…to wait for her to be ready…to…to…*

Declan jolted awake. He pulled off his headset and
looked at the man next to him. "What the hell!"

Leaper was shoving his shoulder. "Dude, we're here.
Time to hop."

Turning off the iPod and stowing it with his headset,
Declan rubbed his eyes and gave his mind a few seconds
to clear. His body was set to another function and he had
to dial back his, ahem, need and get into warrior mode.
His conflicted libido was going to have to duke it out
some other time.

Miller was shouting again. Most likely, he was saying
something along the lines of…*Move those asses*. Declan
was guessing at that as he followed his Teammates, lifting his pack and grabbing the rest of his gear. They were
getting off the C-17, and the blast furnace of midday
heat bathed him in an instant sweat.

Images were still dancing at the edges of his thoughts,
of a woman that intrigued him and made him want to
hold her again, to definitely know more.

—◈◈◈—

Maura read the note for the tenth time. She sighed and put
it on the coffee table. Placing a heart-shaped glass weight

on top of it so the wind from the balcony door didn't accidently blow it away, she stared at the piece of paper.

She threw her hands up. *Why did I bother going for a walk? I should have gone over to his house first. Now, who knows if I'm going to see him again!*

She shook her head. "Don't think like that. He will be fine."

But the worry rolling around in her gut didn't make her feel better. It was akin to accelerant thrown on a fire. She didn't want to believe the worst, lest it come true. So she'd have to pretend that everything would be fine. Faking it until she made it had worked when she was younger. She would try a jump or new gymnastics trick, pretending she could do it. The pretending eventually worked, or she got hurt. Either way, it was somewhat effective.

Moving from the couch was necessary, if she was going to stop thinking about him. So she went to the kitchen closet and pulled out her cleaning supplies. She'd put her anxiety to work and clean her apartment completely. She just had to keep busy, keep moving.

In an undisclosed city in Syria, Declan and the Team were utilizing their favorite segment of SEAL training, evasive driving. Parachuting and playing with the latest tech and guns was pretty cool, but zipping through the streets really got their blood pumping. It added to the moment, when the enemy was chasing them. It felt like something out of an action and adventure movie, except this was real time.

They'd been tasked with retrieving intelligence, and half of their mission was complete. The *when* and *where* the Taliban were hiding their latest stronghold had been uncovered. Unfortunately, their contact had died as he relayed the details. The Syrians had recently captured the additional source, a double agent who was going to lead the SEALs there. That was a serious problem.

Now, with Leaper droning on in his ear, Declan gunned the car's engine and took a hard turn, with Sobbit and Tyler shooting out the back. This could have been labeled a little dramatic, except this shit happened more than anyone would believe. In reality, it was just another day in his blessed life. Being a SEAL meant he was doing some cool-ass shit, if he survived it.

"They're peeling without the squealing," said Sobbit. The Combat Medic had a wicked sense of humor. Probably went with the territory; patching guys up couldn't be easy.

The rest of the Team had taken a different car and an alternate route to run decoy. Normally, they probably wouldn't have split up, but they'd run into problems with the locals, and it had been optimal to ditch and dash.

Whoever got clear first was going for their safe place (SP). Not a house, but a place where there was better cover and good escape routes. They had a few more contacts tucked around there too.

"Understood," said Declan. Taking the corner on two wheels had Tyler hooting with laughter and Sobbit holding on for dear life. Declan knew he'd nailed the turn, which gave them an advantage as they sped down the alleyway and made it back out onto the main thoroughfare, losing themselves in the cover of traffic.

After driving a few extra blocks, he was pretty

confident no one was on their tail. It'd be worth going to the SP now.

"I'd have preferred a stretch," teased Leaper as he scanned the area around them too. Declan's gut told him to hit the SP and get out of Syria.

"You know how I like to hide in plain view," said Declan. There had been nothing extraordinary about the car they'd lifted. Instead, he'd purposefully chosen one that would most likely run well, but looked like a POS, with its peeling paint and dented fenders. Contrary to what most folks knew, in this part of the world, having any car was like owning a Bentley, and those who were so privileged kept them running in top shape. This was his fourth Op to this place, and he knew the streets pretty well. He could even tell what the temperature would be within a few degrees.

"My friend, the wallflower," said Leaper.

Pulling the car into a small parking lot, Declan waited at the designated rendezvous for the rest of the Team to join them. He knew he was pretty laid-back for a Master Chief. He hadn't gotten this far by cracking the whip; instead, he gave his Teammates room to be themselves. Ranks didn't matter much in the Teams, especially on mission. Everyone had his own specialty. The only time they really toed the rank line was when they wore formal uniforms.

Sunlight heated the car's windows and interior. It'd be reaching a hundred soon. In the meantime, Declan watched the mirrors. He had two different routes in case someone spotted them and they needed to drive around again, though it was doubtful. He preferred having several contingency plans, just in case.

Leaper pulled a granola bar from his pocket. "Well, it's not a beer, but it'll have to do."

Declan scratched his nose. The dust was pretty fierce in this part of the world. He was blessed to not have any allergies. His first swim buddy, Larry Tars, had rolled out of the SEALs after four years because his nose leaked like a faucet. It was hard to be on an Op for ten days and be sucking down phlegm because you couldn't blow your nose and risk making too much noise. As a matter of fact, they hadn't been far from here. "There's a place, somewhat of a bar, around the corner. No stout, but there's a decent ale."

"Ha, ha, ha," added Tyler, briefly checking the ammo in his 9 mm. He was young, had only been in the Teams two years, and you could still see the shiny newness on him. "Damn, I'm hungry too. Leaper, toss me one of those."

"Eat your own," replied Leaper, taking a big bite. "Yum!" He was a character to be sure, and the best guy Dec knew to have at his back. There was no doubting his ability, with the amount of action he'd seen.

"Pussy," said Sobbit, pulling a bar from his shirt and handing it to Tyler.

"Dickless," said Leaper, opening his mouth wide.

"What a symphony," mumbled Tyler as he stuffed half the bar into his mouth, chewed for ten seconds, and swallowed. "All we need is a trumpet and trombone. Wait, we have Leaper… He can be the resident baboon."

"Bassoon, ladies. The word you're looking for is *bassoon*." Declan chipped into the snark pot.

"Gesundheit," blessed Leaper.

Declan smiled. This was a good time to banter. Best

part was, he adored these guys and could go to hell and back with them without a second thought. He wouldn't have it any other way, and neither would the rest of the Team. Being in battle bonded them. They could anticipate each other's moves and comments, and half the time a single glance said it all. Declan believed this was what family was like, except that he was closer to his Teammates.

The Teams were a tightly bonded group of brothers. Miller coordinated everything; as Intel Officer he was one of them, and he understood how all their personalities worked together best.

In the other car, Miller was driving. Dec was pretty sure that with more officers on board, things were pretty quiet and rather tense in that vehicle. There was a lot of brass and rank on this mission, because it had been a volunteer Op. It was good to get away from desk work and coordinating crap. Besides, they'd all backed each other at different times, and this Op needed a certain kind of extra decisiveness.

If he'd had his way, he would have filled the Op with enlisted personnel. Something about working your way up the ranks gave experience that school couldn't.

In this mission, Hayes and he tied for the paternal role. Hayes had no funny bone, but he was a dead shot in the trenches and he settled all disputes.

Declan liked to think he was an asset too, as he could anticipate stuff well. SEALs, regardless of rank, tended to all have opportunities to lead at times, unlike other branches of the military.

"I see them," said Declan, spying the car he'd known would come. He supposed he was more like the

partygoer uncle who often had to pull people's heads out
of the toilet or their ass out of the fire. If he'd gone to
college, he'd be an officer—a cake eater—and pretty far
up the food chain, but that wasn't who he was. Declan
Swifton was an enlisted man through and through who
pretty much wanted to stay enlisted. He had no interest
in going to the dark side. As Master Chief, this rank let
him be himself.

A reader. A warrior. A philosopher. An athlete. A
sailor and a SEAL. There's a philosophy that says if you
visualize what you want, you get it. In his mind's eye,
he'd seen just this moment and prepared for its result.

"The locals?" asked Tyler.

"Nope. Our brethren." Declan smiled. The driving
had been textbook. Squeaky clean! Ah, how he loved a
good "carpool."

Chapter 8

LOOKING OUT THE CORNER OF THE WINDOW, DECLAN managed to stay hidden as he scoped out the street below. They'd holed up in an abandoned house, and he was on the top floor, attempting to take in the neighborhood and gain an understanding of its rhythm. He didn't like the fact that this contact had been a no-show. That didn't bode well for their mission.

The whole Team still used Frogman Swepston's Rule of Three. When three aspects went sour, the Op was over. So far, Declan was uneasy. It had been hell to find this place, and if this rendezvous went bad too, they'd be using the Rule of Three to ditch the Op and get out of this place. A fourth problem was one too many, and Syria was not a country that any of them wanted to be caught in, dead or alive.

Screw the denial capabilities of the United States government. The hostiles that could potentially capture the SEALs would torture them and/or kill them on the spot. The environment here was more than volatile. Even the innocents—women and children—hid from the hotbed of the political scene, and if the United Nations truly knew how bad it was, they would be singing a different tune and changing their strategy in helping these folks.

His eyes caught movement across the street. A little girl was sitting in the window. Her mother pulled her away quickly, admonishing her—no doubt for the risky behavior of being visible in the window. *It's a sad day when kids cannot even take a breath of fresh air without worry of being shot or worse.*

So far, their hideaway appeared safe. He gestured to Leaper, who headed down the stairs. Gathered Intel would be relayed, and hopefully his swim buddy would come back with news of the contact's arrival.

He put his attention back on the street and the buildings around them, scanning for trouble. He caught sight of a man who was moving quickly through the street, then paused.

Declan could see blood on him. "Damn," he swore softly.

Miller stepped up next to him and looked through his own scope. "I'll let them know." He headed downstairs.

Standing on the top floor alone, Declan knew the situation couldn't be good, not with two operatives out of the game. The first contact was dead, and now the second…well…he had clearly been shot and was most likely dying in this particular hellhole. Did that mean the Intel was sound or that it had holes too?

A noise to his left had Declan sneaking a quick glance. It was Leaper, who gestured with his head for Declan to go downstairs. The men exchanged places and Declan headed down to the second floor.

The informant was sprawled out on his back, his blood-soaked shirt in tatters as Declan's Teammates tried to stanch the bleeding.

"No. I…won't…survive. Take…the information. Make my death quick. And…go." The informant struggled to get the words out. He pushed a piece of paper into Miller's hand, and before they could deny the wish to take his life, he died.

The two Teammates who had been working on the informant made swift work of cleaning up the man, carrying his body down to the first floor, and staging him just inside the battered front door as if he had been shot in the street, stumbled into the abandoned house, and died. That was common enough here.

Miller and Declan pored over the map. They looked at each other.

"No way," said Miller.

Declan shook his head. "Could this Op get any more fucked? The headquarters is in one of four mountain ranges: Jabel ar Ruwaq, Jabal Abu Rujmayn, Jabal Bishri, or Jabal al-Druze. Given the time constraints, we've got to find out which one is the most viable. We can't lose any more American lives." Several eyes connected with Declan's.

"There's always some kind of immediate threat. We shouldn't act out of fear," said Miller. "Even though the informant died, we've got the info. Let's hop and see what Command wants to do with it. I could go either way on the Rule of Three. We've hit too many roadblocks to make me want to go any further, so we'll bounce the decision up the chain." Miller spun his finger in a circle. The men gathered their gear.

Declan nodded his head in agreement. He wanted to get out of here. His gut was twisting, and that meant they were in a bad position and it was time to move quickly. "I'll get Leaper." He took the steps two at a time. At the landing, he signaled to his swim buddy as he pulled his pack on and grabbed Leaper's. They'd stashed a car out back.

Now they needed to find out what Command wanted to do next. They'd have to find another place to go where they could set up the radio. Staying safe in Syria, with all of the violence, was easier said than done.

—◦◦◦—

It had been a week since Declan left. Maura missed him. That was a big negative on her emotional scale, but on the positive side, her shoulder continued to feel better and get stronger every day. She'd continue to do light rehab but decided to hold off on the extra arm work until she fully healed.

If only that pleasant feeling of getting better carried through to this moment. Standing at the entrance of the gym, she couldn't believe her eyes. Froggy Squats was in ruins. Equipment was on its side and the insides were spray-painted. Mats were torn, their insides spilling out.

She wanted to cry at the sight of it. But that emotional release was not going to get this place cleaned up.

"Wow. That's a shame," said Bosco, one of the regulars. "This is third time the gym's been hit by the same gang. I came in early too, to get a workout in before my meeting."

"I didn't know that gangs were a problem here. They're not going to win," she said, going into her office, dumping her bag on the desk, and coming back out. "I'm going to put this place back into shape, and we're going to change our relationship with these gangs."

"Good luck on changing them. I'll help you clean up the gym and put it right," said Bosco.

"Thanks," she said, giving him a nod.

The two of them were joined by several more staffers

and members, and together they righted the equipment, carried out the mats, and gave the spray paint a coat of primer. Maura was exhausted, but the gym looked better by the time they were done.

"I got my workout today," said Bosco as a parting comment.

"Hey, I appreciate the help, Bosco," she said, wondering how long it would be before she could head home and take a long, hot bath with a large glass of chilled white wine.

"Uh, could you do me a favor?" Bosco hemmed and hawed, looking embarrassed.

She put her hand on his arm. "What is it? What can I do to help you?"

He looked at her with large, doe-like brown eyes. "Be my date tonight? I'd really appreciate it. I have this thing to go to…and…"

She sighed. "I'm sort of seeing someone…" Not that she had clarified it with Declan, but she did feel loyal to him.

"We could go as friends, you know. Colleagues, or stuff like that." Bosco had a whiny tone in his voice.

She could see how important it was to him. After everything he'd done, she couldn't deny him. "Fine. Turn left at the last road before Main Street/Beach Street dead ends. I live in the last apartment complex on the beach, the second-to-last apartment on the second floor. Apartment 2B."

He dipped his head like he was going to kiss her. "I'll be there at seven. Thanks, Maura."

She pointed a finger at him. "As friends. Just remember."

"Sure." Bosco walked out the door in a hurry.

Maybe he was worried she'd change her mind. In truth, she probably should. But she owed him, and this seemed like a small favor in return. Besides, she trusted herself. Nothing was going to happen, and everything would probably turn out just right.

What had possessed her to agree to the date tonight? After a whole day of cleaning the gym? Her shoulder was throbbing and all she wanted was a hot bath and a glass of wine. She sighed. A promise was a promise.

Getting ready was making her nuts. She was on her third coat of mascara, and over half of it was on her cheeks and eyebrows. Dating had never been high on her list of favorite events.

"I look like a clown on a binge." She sighed and threw the applicator and its small supply tube into the bathroom trash can. It landed with a thunk and all she could think was *Good riddance!*

It wasn't that she was nervous. The fact was that she'd rather be with Declan right now.

Picking up a wet washcloth, she scrubbed her face until the black smears were gone. Then she looked in the mirror, shrugged, and put on her sheer lip balm with the hint of pink. Why change how she looked? Her regular makeup routine was perfectly fine.

Standing back from the reflection, she surveyed her cotton print dress with the tiny white-and-yellow daisies and her matching white flats. The outfit screamed "friends" for sure.

Brushing out her hair, she tried to pile it on her head with several bobby pins, which sprang out in all directions, looking like lost kittens waving for help. Unraveling that mess, she tried one hair clip. The static from all the hair wrangling made her feel like an elec- troshock patient.

Wishing she could do more with her hair, but frus- trated beyond belief, she grabbed one of her bulky sun hats and plopped it onto her head. Good enough. She was not a woman who primped. She thought about rein- forcing her sore shoulder by going back to wearing the sling for the night, but discarded the idea. She'd be fine.

Maura picked up her small purse with her wallet, keys, and cell phone and hurried to the front door. Outside waiting was a man most women would call an excellent specimen of the human body, though he was certainly *not* her type. "Hi there. Sorry I took so long."

"Yeah, you look good enough. Unless you want to show more skin."

She balked. "No. I'm good."

"Okay," he said as he grabbed her right arm and practically hauled her out of her doorway, slamming the apartment door behind of her. The sound stood her on her toes.

Walking to the staircase, he was partially lifting her off of the ground with each step. She felt as if she were a lopsided trolley car.

Fearing for her own safety, she said, "Hold on a minute." She untangled herself from his grasp, returned to her front door, and locked it before returning to Bosco. "I'd rather walk down in front of you."

"Why?" He looked baffled. Did other women like to be pawed like this?

She smiled patiently up at him, though he was losing

88 ANNE ELIZABETH

brownie points with each and every Neanderthal move.
"Uh, why? Well, you can, uh, watch the swooshing
of my dress. It'll be fun." *Oh yeah, like that comment
didn't play into the situation. You're not helping yourself, Maura.*

He frowned. "What's a swooshing? Where on the
dress do I look?"

Her mouth was open as she stared at him. *Seriously,
man! Have I totally chosen a meathead? Please someone come down and help me with this date. I'm in over
my head.*

She closed her mouth and didn't answer him. But she
did manage to walk down the stairs unaided. That was a
small victory. "So tell me about this party."

"It's an engagement party for my fraternity brother."

"Where did you go to college?"

"MIT. We have meetings out here. A bunch of us
landed on this coast." He straightened the lapel of his
shirt and resettled his shoulders in his jacket.

*Holy smokes! Talk about jumping to conclusions.
This guy is probably a bona fide genius.* She swallowed
her shock. "What did you study?"

"Molecular physics. Lately I spend a lot of time
in an experimental lab, and the gym." He flexed his
muscles. "Hey, my biceps like ya, and my delts are
digging ya."

She smiled at him and knew it fell flat. Ugh! Smart or
not, Bosco was definitely not a match for her. This was
going to be a long, long, long night.

Maura climbed into the largest pickup truck she'd
ever seen, trying not to flash her underwear to the entire
world, and then closed the door. Buckling herself in, she

looked longingly at her apartment front door. What she wouldn't give to be staying home, baking brownies or painting her nails or watching a movie.

—∾∾—

"Drink, drink, drink!" shouted the men in various state of preppy uni-dress. Khaki pants, white or pin-striped shirts, and blue or red ties with a navy-blue blazer appeared to be the fraternity uniform, or perhaps that's what preppy guys wore on semiformal occasions. But as much as she wanted to say they looked nice, their behavior was not the best she'd ever witnessed.

"Suck it down, you pussy!" shouted Bosco at the groom-to-be, who'd already downed four shots and two beers.

Maura checked her cell phone. *Yep, we've only been here forty-five minutes, and I'm ready to bang my head against the wall.* She'd politely rejected several drinks, going for the hors d'oeuvres table first. After the cleanup and the long day, she was starved.

The energy bar she'd eaten for lunch had long since disappeared from her system. Loading her plate with vegetables and dip and grabbing an unsweetened ice tea from the bar, she found a somewhat quiet corner and sat down. It wasn't long before a woman joined her, a petite redhead with very dark skin and brown eyes. Maura swallowed the morsels in her mouth hastily and extended her hand. "Hi, I'm Maura."

"Mimsey Blakely," said the woman briskly. "You can call me Minnie or Mims." Ironing wrinkles out of her beige linen dress with her fingers, she asked abruptly, "Are you sleeping with Bosco Russo?"

Maura choked on her own shock. "What? No!"

"Okay," said Minnie, uninterested in her now. "I guess we can talk longer then. Just so you know, he is mine. I'm going to marry him someday."

Maura had no idea what to say in return. This tiny woman was blunt.

"I used to date him," she sniffed. Minnie took a tissue from her purse. "And I still love him."

Was she really crying? Good heavens! Maura leaned in close. "I'm seeing someone. I'm not interested in Bosco in any way. This is…a favor, so he didn't have to come here alone." She hated ratting him out, but the woman seemed to need the reassurance.

"Thanks. I appreciate the info." Minnie dabbed under eyes and blew her nose. "I was a little sister of his fraternity, and he was two years ahead of me. I worshipped him. Cleaned his room. Washed and folded his laundry. Made his favorite protein drink every day. Do you know what it's like when you like someone and no matter what you do, you cannot get him out of your mind? Every time he has a new girlfriend, I fall to pieces."

Maura listened patiently, indulging in the food, which was surprisingly good. When she could finally squeeze a word in edgewise, she asked, "Why don't you tell him?"

"I did, sort of. I moved out here to be close to him. I got a job at the company he works for. I even joined the gym he works out at." Minnie turned to face her. "That's where I know you from. I've seen you there."

"I thought you looked familiar. Stop by the office sometime and say hello."

"That guy you're seeing. Do you love him?" Minnie

tapped a finger over her heart. "Does the thought of him keep you up at night?"

Maura felt heat rise in her cheeks. "Yes. I like him a lot." She stuffed a piece of broccoli in her mouth and chewed determinedly. *Please don't ask me any more questions.*

"You more than like him," Minnie said with a grin. She seemed satisfied with Maura's response. She lifted her drink and toasted Maura. "To unrequited love."

Unable to chew and drink at the same time, Maura swallowed the lump, feeling it scrape her throat as it made its way down. Lifting her glass, she smiled weakly at Minnie and then drained the glass, giving her the ideal excuse to get up and leave the table—and thus the conversation—for the rest of the event.

<hr />

When the highlight of the evening was walking down the street, it was an unfortunate night. Maura was just happy to be away from the loud party.

Sitting on a bar stool, rubbing her feet, was not how Maura thought she would end her experience with Bosco. Being groped, having drinks spilled on her, and having drunk guys hit on her had pretty much sucked sewage water.

Maura was glad she'd followed her instincts and walked away from the event. So she'd hoofed it as far as McP's Pub and then gone in for a stiff belt. The smell of alcohol surrounded her like a heavy perfume.

A rather handsome older man with a thick mutton-chop mustache was behind the bar. He smiled at her, a friendly sort. "What'll you have?"

"Whiskey. Something good and old," she answered,

knowing that she might regret it in the morning, and yet there was no way she'd make it home without it. She was too frugal to pay for a cab.

He raised his eyebrows and then grabbed a bottle from the top shelf. He poured three fingers into a glass and placed it in front of her. "Tough night?"

She put her shoe back on, picked up the drink, and sipped it, allowing the fiery amber to burn a path down to her gut. Relief flooded her veins, and she looked up at the bartender. "Confusing," she admitted. "I went out on a date that I didn't want to go on, just to have something to do."

"Nice to meet you, Confusing. I'm Gich." He shook her hand. "Doesn't sound like much fun."

"It wasn't," she agreed. "Strange name for a bartender, Gich."

He tossed back a belt of whiskey and came around and sat down next to her. "I'm not a bartender. Just watching the place while Ken hits the head—uh, visits the facilities."

She laughed. "Thanks for the good stuff. What do I owe you?"

"Nothing, until he comes back, that is." He tipped more whiskey into his own glass and topped hers off. His arms were as thick as tree trunks, and his beefy frame was slightly smaller than Declan's, yet Gich reminded her of him. "What brings you out tonight? Don't think I've seen you around here before."

"I'm not much for visiting bars or clubs." She tossed back the entire shot. Her throat screamed in protest as she tried to make her lungs work. Finally, she let out a few shallow breaths and coughed.

"So I see. Though you're obviously changing that tonight." He went to pour her another shot, but she covered the glass.

"Water, please."

He signaled to one of the passing waitresses, who brought two glasses of water to them.

After she'd drunk a half of a glass and cooled her throat off, she said, "I'm a social disaster waiting to happen."

"How so?" His large hands cupped his water glass, playing with the condensation on the outside. "What are you running from?"

"Myself."

He nodded his head. "Makes sense."

"It does?" Maura looked at him curiously. "I often talk before I think, I'm impulsive, and I don't like being ignored."

"Who isn't, at times? We're human. No one is perfect. But there's a trick to understanding emotional action." He pointed to the spot over her gut and then to her heart. "You have to know the insides of yourself—your gut instinct—before you can do any act of importance. It's not going to serve your world to just run about haphazardly when you can actually have a definitive direction. Make each action count. Slow down and take your time. Then, when you act, it comes out a logical and instinctual choice rather than a knee-jerk emotional reaction."

She smiled. "Good advice. I've never heard it explained that way. My coach was a lot like you—steady and stalwart."

Gich nodded his head. "What kind of coach?"

She took another sip. A warm pathway heated toward

her tummy. "Gymnastics. I was on the short list to compete in the Olympic trials."

"Interesting." He said the word slowly and without sounding impressed.

It was the greatest experience of her life, competing at that level. Not that she ever talked about it, or her wish to win Olympic gold. She hadn't gone down that road with anyone for a long, long time. Here she was opening up, and he all he had to say was "interesting"!

Her eyes snapped to his. "No, it's not just interesting. It was my everything!"

He lifted the glass of whiskey to his lips, took a long sip, and said, "Tell me about it."

Man, I seriously unloaded. Poor guy! But Gich took it all in stride.

The night ended in a friendly manner. It was what she had hoped the date with Bosco would be, and yet it was Gich who walked her all the way from Coronado to Imperial Beach. They talked companionably the whole way, and she hadn't realized how much she missed talking in-depth with someone. Declan hadn't been gone that long, but she was already anxious for his return. She missed the closeness, and if she was being honest, the physical intimacy too.

Gich, like Declan, had a vibe that reminded her of her family, and he'd been a gentleman the whole time. Never once did Gich sneak a grab or grope her, make unwelcome innuendos, or make her feel weird; instead he kept a comfortable and respectful distance.

Before he left—grabbing a cab back into town— she'd asked him, "Why is it I can talk to you…like this?"

"I'm a stranger," he said and shrugged.

She grabbed his arm, breaking the unspoken no-contact rule between them. "No, you're not. You feel familiar to me. Tell me something about yourself, so I understand why I am at ease with you."

"Because you don't want anything from me," he said bluntly.

"That's...that's true." She didn't believe that was the reason. There had to be something else.

"And you don't see me as a threat either. So you're willing to be honest. Personally, I like the fact that you're on the reserved side. It's classy." His cell phone buzzed. He checked it and scratched his chin. "I have to go, my daughter needs me."

"Lucky girl, your daughter. Thanks for a nice night, Gich." She gave him a quick hug.

"Hey, I'm around, if you want to talk again. Just come to McP's." As he reached the bottom of the staircase, he said, "Don't be too hard on Swifton. He's a good guy."

"How...how did you know about my neighbor Declan?"

"I'm retired from the Teams. I keep in touch with Teammates that come through my life. When I saw where you lived, I put two and two together." He pointed to Declan's door. "Him, I know very well. He's a good guy. One of the best I know."

Her mouth was open wide enough to catch fireflies, and she couldn't say a single word. She watched Gich walk down the street and hail a cab before going into her apartment, closing and bolting the door, and then picking up Declan's letter. The edges were so worn from reading it that she held it gently. Her eyes scanned over the few brief lines, and then she put it back in its place of honor on her bookshelf.

Stripping out of her clothes, she pulled on her worn white cotton nightgown and robe and walked to the window, where she could watch the ocean waves coming up the shore. She unbolted the balcony door and the ocean wind blew hastily in.

It's a good night for kite flying. A memory popped into her mind. A month after she moved in, she had looked out the window and seen Declan show two little boys how to work their kite. The instruction included gaining lift, getting their kite into the air, and making it go higher. This wasn't a few minutes of instruction; he spent hours showing them different techniques to make it move. *That's when it happened*, she thought. *That's when I started to fall in love with you.*

Her skin prickled with gooseflesh as she fought the wind and was finally able to close and lock the door. Then she lay down on her couch and listened to the wind battering the furniture outside. It might get a little scratched up, but it would survive. Like her, it was made of sterner stuff.

—∿∿—

The phone was ringing. It pulled her straight out of her dream. She sat up in bed and reached for her phone. "Hello?"

"Maura?"

"Declan." She sighed his name, relieved to hear his voice. "I'm so sorry. I was on the beach. I wasn't avoiding you. I was wrong…"

He chuckled. "As much as I love hearing how you are

wrong, I only have a few minutes. I want you to know that I look forward to seeing you when I get back."

She nodded her head.

"Are you there?"

"Yes!" she shouted into the phone. "I'm here. I'm looking forward to seeing you too. Be safe."

He replied, "You too."

The line went dead.

She hugged the phone and wallowed in the pleasure that surged through her body. Declan had called. She was so thrilled, she couldn't bring herself to close her eyes. It was true her feelings for him were greater than she would admit, but evidently so were his.

Chapter 9

THE LUCKY LADY THAT TEAM FIVE WAS TAKING TO the dance was the Jabal al-Druze Range. Thanks to several Teammates in the area, they'd been able to scope out all of the viable options. Drones had helped too, though the Syrians tended to use them for target practice if they spotted them.

According to their Intel, this particular stretch of mountain range housed several missile-launch sites and was heavily guarded. The topographical pictures looked fairly normal, but the thermal scans lit up like a Christmas tree. It would have been their last choice of a place for an Op, because the chance of capture was quadrupled there.

His Team had been instructed to locate and penetrate the Taliban headquarters. The rumors that top rebel leaders were having a "meeting of the minds" in this wasteland had been confirmed twice, via CIA chatter and through their Syrian contacts. Intel placed this area as the spot where a major attack on the U.S. was being masterminded. That was good to know…if they could find the damned place!

Declan barely had any saliva left. He wanted to cough, to spit the dust and dirt out of his lungs and drink from his water reserves, but the enemy was just over the rise. Though these tangos were not their mission target, they could pose a threat. Very soon they'd see whether these particular bad guys lived another day or not.

The taller man, the tango in charge, squatted down, jabbering about the new guns.

Declan wished they could take these guys and learn what they knew, but it would hold them up and possibly ruin the mission. His Team was after bigger game: the headquarters of the Taliban stronghold.

Leaper was rubbing his finger over the edge of his gun, itching for a fight. He knew better than to engage without the go-ahead, but Leaper had his own quirks. The man lived for mixing it up with fists, guns, knives… you name it. His nickname was Leaper because he liked leaping into trouble. But when it came to work, Leaper had a more even keel. Declan trusted his life to him.

One of the tangos was pointing toward the desert. The others were talking over each other. Something about gold now… Declan knew enough of the language to get by if he needed to.

He only knew one good gold reference: "Go for the gold," as that was what his instructor had repeated a hundred times in training. "You do that by following the plan, thinking on your feet, and sticking with your Team. The Teams means Together Everyone Achieves More Success." He'd never forget those words; they should be on a bumper sticker as much as they were branded on each SEAL's heart.

"Cache." Declan knew that word. The enemy spoke rapidly. Declan could only catch a few phrases, something about action in the desert. He watched them move off, running down the hill and disappearing over the next rise.

The SEALs were careful as they worked their way across the path the tangos had recently vacated. The mountainous terrain was tough and slow going at times, but they were patient as they climbed ever upward.

Declan checked the compass several times, but the magnetic pull of the mountains was playing havoc with his equipment. Fortunately, Miller knew this area better than he wanted to and took point, bringing them through a narrow pass and down into the desert.

They had less than an hour of night's cover and needed to find an optimal place to dig in. Miller pointed at a few places where the shrubs would work, and Declan and Leaper tucked into a higher vantage point under an outcropping of rock. They each took different points to scan and burrowed in for the day, bringing up branches, stripped bushes, and other types of foliage to shore up their hidey-hole.

Declan pulled a small scope from his pocket and scanned the horizon. It picked up several infrared signatures in the distance. As the predawn light hit the edges, he pocketed the scope. No sense blinding himself. A few minutes from now, he could watch them through the scope of his rifle.

He rubbed his eyes, thinking about the trip out of the city. It had been dicey. They'd almost been discovered a few times, but Sobbit sounded like a native Syrian when he spoke Arabic and had talked their way out of trouble. Hiking was another story—they'd had to retrieve their packs, ditch the car, and take a roundabout path through the mountains to avoid being spotted.

Declan shaded his eyes, letting the light filter in slowly so they could adjust faster. The sun lifted into the sky and he knew the heat would soon follow, bone-chilling cold being replaced by heat so intense that it could fry eggs to a crisp. But this was why they trained: so they could manage the terrain, deal with the environmental shifts, and achieve their goals.

If only this Op was going to be as easy as the training ones. Well, they could hope for it. Reality, Declan decided, was going to be much tougher. So far, the base they were looking for was supposed to be only a few miles out from their position. Why hadn't they been able to see it? Or catch people going in and out?

There was only so far into the desert they could trek without being visible. Declan tried to thrust away his concerns. This plan was a monster. The brass might be optimistic about what they'd find, but the gnawing in his gut was getting worse, telling him something was not right. Like it or not, his Team would do their duty, but they only had one more strike before the brakes went on and they scrapped this version of the mission and had to start over from scratch.

―――⁓⁓――

Night fell on the desert in stages. As the sun sank behind the mountains, the desert was covered in splotches of darkness until the light was all eaten up. There was no moon tonight, as the cloud cover hung low.

This…being in the right spot at the right time…was what they'd been trained to do: infiltrate, gather, shit, and git. Their advantage was that they'd worked in this type of terrain for months and were prepped for heat, sand, and whatever or whoever faced them out here.

Still, they'd spent the entire day watching this area and they couldn't locate the stronghold.

Squinting his eyes, Declan briefly checked his

footsteps. There were still IEDs around here. He'd seen animals set off a couple of them now and then. As long his Teammates traced each other's paths, they'd be good.

None of them were fond of the idea of walking through the desert, trying to find a hole in the ground or some kind of entrance. It made Declan's stomach ache just thinking about it. But they'd agreed as a Team, this was their only option. They couldn't sit in hiding for weeks on end waiting to either find the answer or be discovered.

Hayes Johnson glided forward with fluid movements. He was like the wind, in sync with his surroundings, neither too slow nor too fast. As point man and Commander, his motions were pretty flawless. In another life, he probably would have been a ninja or a Zen master. Most likely, he'd be an Admiral someday, teaching the junior officers at JOTC.

The Team had eyes on the vast expanses around them, but their gaze constantly returned to Hayes.

They'd been stashed since sunup, lying low during the light and heat of the day, and Declan was ready for movement. Standing in place, he quietly stretched his limbs.

Checking the sky and then his watch, Declan saw they had about nine solid hours until dawn. That was a decent amount of time to figure out the lay of the land.

Hayes had just reached the edge of the small rise when he slowly sank down, simultaneously lifting his fist. He pointed two fingers to his eyes and then held up five fingers and pointed ahead.

The entire Team got eyes on where Hayes was indicating. From nowhere came a group of tangos. Each team member took up a different vantage point while monitoring the group.

Declan knew that they had the strategic advantage of a small sand dune between them and the bad guys.

Harvey, Miller, and Declan joined Hayes just below the peak, spreading out along the rise. Leaper, Tyler, Bunks, and Sobbit protected the sides and rear.

It looked like the enemy was arguing. They smoked several cigarettes and then entered the hatch to the underground complex again, securing it behind them.

The Team had previously circled this spot at least three times without connecting with it. Any guerilla would have been proud of that hidden entrance.

Hayes made another hand gesture, calling the outlying men in: circle up.

"We could call in an air strike," said Declan. "We know where it is now." Something about this place was making his skin crawl. There were a lot of unknown elements in that bunker. Could be twenty guys or could be two hundred. Who knew if there were booby traps and tripwires, gas, or whatever else?

"I'm with Dec. Let's mark it with flares and hop," said Leaper. He could be sitting perfectly still, and yet it seemed as if he were in constant motion—his eyes were going, his fingers made minute movements, and his whole body was primed like a spring. He could lay anyone out with a single strike regardless of the size; he just always knew where to hit, where the glass spot in every jaw was.

Tyler and Sobbit spoke together. "In."

Bunks and Miller looked at odds with each other, but finally nodded and said, "In."

Hayes and Harvey were going to tip the scales. "In." Two-steppers had a different view at times. It could be the officer in them or the sword strapped to their hip.

Teammates turned to Leaper and Declan, waiting for acknowledgment. They had to be *all in* to go forward.

Declan didn't like the unknown part of this. He liked being as prepared as possible for a mission, but he would support his brethren one hundred percent in what they took on. He nodded.

"Yeah, I'm not turning over so easy. Lay it out for me," said Leaper, giving Declan a dirty look. "My feet are itching, and when that happens, that means...split."

"Or your athlete's foot is acting up," said Bunks.

Leaper flexed his hand and gave Bunks a steady look, but Hayes put his arm between them. "Hang it up." He eyeballed the brawlers and then said, "I'll send coordinates and a message. Let's dig in and wait for a chance to get in there. If no one's come out in two hours, we blow it. Otherwise, we pop the cork."

One hour and forty-seven minutes later, the trapdoor in the sand opened, and three men left the underground bunker. They were heading straight for the Team. Declan recognized one of the men from up on the mountain. Declan held his spot as Hayes, Miller, and Bunks took the three tangos down and slit their throats. They placed their bodies on the far side of the small sand dune and covered them with sand. Any cat would be proud of the job they did, burying the rubble.

Leaper, Tyler, Sobbit, and Declan descended down the ladder. The concrete walls dripped with moisture from the water pipes above, the echo keenly evident in each drop. Declan shook his head at the waste of such a precious resource as water in the desert. He would have thought they'd care more about fixing a leaky pipe.

As silently as possible, they worked their way down the hall, moving in time to the drips.

Sobbit, the point man, had been a Marine in EOD (Explosive Ordinance Disposal) before becoming a SEAL. He set a brisk pace even as he marked the path. Declan was a similar creature, as he had studied EOD too. Men who held both SEAL and EOD—Twin Pins, as they were called—were few and far between. This label meant you were a seriously impressive overachiever. Hell, if Sobbit were an eagle, he would have stripped the valley clean of prey in an afternoon.

Declan quickly rubbed at his left eye, trying to chase the dust from the corners as Sobbit flagged spots where trip wires had been rigged or pressure caps were buried, allowing the rest of the Team to pass quickly without mishap. Hayes and Miller stayed above, protecting their six.

Coming to a four-way fork, they listened. Following the most worn path, they came to a door, behind which they could hear voices. A lot of voices.

Declan pulled a device from his pocket that could be slid under the door and would give them a bird's-eye view of the room. As the device slipped underneath, it climbed the door to the peak. There were over two hundred men in the room, and the number six terrorist on America's watch list was running the meeting. The device took pictures of everything in the room.

Going deeper into the lair, they discovered that it was a warren of tunnels beyond. It was possible that this place ran the whole length of the desert in this valley. Made sense, since this land was a honeycomb of caves.

Reinforced with concrete and structural supports, it was the ideal place to work from.

They doubled back to the meeting room, once again checking on the inhabitants. The men looked restless. Several of them began to stand. Declan signaled to the rest of the Team. They needed to blow this place. Setting C-4 with triggers and timers, they hoofed it back to the opening.

Noise was filling the tunnels behind them, so they blew the first one as they were climbing out. Tyler called in an air strike and helos, while the Team double-timed back over the path they had originally traversed. Dec's mind automatically clicked off the head count. Hayes. Wilson. Miller. Sobbit. Tyler. Bunks. Himself. And Leaper bringing up the rear.

Someone was saying something to Declan. Yelling. They called in their coordinates to the incoming helo. They needed to be extracted ASAP.

Sounds exploded around him. Too loud! Then, all he could hear was this sharp, high-pitched ringing and everything else was muffled. Distant.

As his body hit the desert floor and sand filled Declan's nostrils, he attempted to get to his feet. His legs wouldn't stay under him. He kept falling.

Crawling forward, Declan felt hands pulling on him. He pushed them away, but they were adamant, pulling off his pack and his gun.

No way was he giving up his SIG Sauer. He fought them and they finally relented.

Bunks, the senior Combat Medic, was barking orders. Declan could see his buddy's mouth moving.

Sobbit and Hayes held him down as pain seared his

body. Declan couldn't pull away from them or make the pain stop.

A needle pierced him, and a blessed release zipped through his body, the pain floating away. Suddenly, sound burst like a bubble. He could hear it now. A helo was laying down suppressor fire. Explosions shook the earth.

Miller slid down a bank and Leaper grabbed Declan, yanking him up. They carried him together as desert sand collapsed into the ground behind them like a drowned ant farm.

Declan watched the desert turn into a giant sinkhole as bombs blew from under the ground.

Bunks pulled him into the helo, the whole Team tucking around them. A needle was pushed into his arm and fluids were being pumped. It made Declan want to puke.

Whup. Whup. Whup. The sound of the helo lifting brought his eyes open.

Someone was trying to get a second needle into one of his veins. It wasn't working.

"Quit," he managed to say.

"You need fluids," said a short, broad-shouldered, blond PJ (a United States Air Force Pararescue Jumper) that looked too young for such a job. "Hey, the SEAL's awake."

Going in and out of consciousness, Declan felt intense, hot pain. He punched out with his left arm, landing a shot on the PJ who was drilling an IV hole into the bone of his right humerus.

"Crap!" said the PJ, losing control. "Help me out here."

Another pair of arms held Declan down. A brunet guy with a bristle of whiskers on his face braced his body so Declan couldn't move. "We're the good guys, Master Chief Swifton."

The blond handed a kit to his partner. "See if you can get a line on the other arm. He definitely landed a shiner on me."

"It's in," said the other PJ. "Let's get those fluids moving."

Adrenaline pumped through Declan's body, making him want to move, making him anxious to get off the helo. He knew he needed to stay here and let them take care of him, but it felt like he was climbing out of his own skin.

"Easy does it," said the blond PJ. "We've got you. We're almost to the field hospital. Just stay with us."

"Hang in there, Dec." Leaper's face appeared before Declan, and then everything went black.

Chapter 10

THE SOUND OF AN AIR CONDITIONER WAS BLASTING IN Declan's ears. *Someone turn that damn thing off! Don't they know my fucking ears hurt!*

Not an air conditioner. That wouldn't make sense. *Am I in the desert?* The sound reverberated in his brain, forcing him to open his eyes.

The world was blurry and there was a cot above him. *Why am I here? I shouldn't be here. I'm supposed to be with my Team.*

Pain ripped through his body.

His eyes tried to focus and take it all in. There were bandages and tape on his neck, chest, and face. One side of the lower half of his body was searing with pain. His arm was partially bandaged around the shoulder, and there was an IV in his arm pumping steadily. Blood slid down the tubing at an alarming rate, and there was a smaller bag, probably an antibiotic, dripping liquid.

Turning his head to the side, he saw more cots. *A C-17.* His brain sped through the conclusions. *Air Force plane. Hospital. What the fuck happened?*

Turbulence sent his body into the air, but the safety straps held him suspended, and then the plane was through the air pocket, restoring gravity and shoving him back into the fabric of the cot, sending waves of intense pain throughout his body.

He groaned. Then the world divided into individual

round blotches, like a series of odd-sized dots converging at once, until everything went black.

Light. A cool hand was on Declan's forehead. He wanted to smell her perfume. He bet it was sweet. He tried to sniff, but there was a mask on his face. Rubbing his face against his shoulder, he tried to pull it off to tell her she seemed familiar.

"Don't move," she chided him. "You need to stay still, Master Chief."

"I know you. Don't I?" he asked. His voice sounded gravelly, but he grinned anyway, and then he lifted his head slightly. His throat hurt and his skin itched.

She yelled over her shoulder. "Who gave him codeine? He's allergic. Someone get me some epinephrine."

A gorgeous brunette with tanned skin, kind brown eyes, and a gentle way walked up and handed a needle to the blond. "I didn't see it on his chart."

"Yeah, I don't know why it isn't in there. I know him."

"You do?"

"Yes, Declan and I met years ago, three days after he finished Hell Week. He'd broken his arm racing motorcycles in the desert, and I had to treat him. He caught hell from his CO about his actions and was put on report. The Navy tends to hold its sailors to a pretty tough standard."

The brunette tilted her head. "Fascinating… Were you and he serious?"

"Not really. Bad timing, mostly." The blond stuck the needle into the tubing and pressed the plunger, pushing the medicine in. She leaned over. Her face was hazy. "Hang in there, Dec. You're not going to like this ride, but I'd rather you have a long and healthy life."

Declan's mind put the pieces together like a puzzle, finally remembering her and their brief sojourn together. "Cam...Camilla?"

"Yeah, I'm here." She squatted down so their eyes were level. "You okay?"

"I liked you too, for a time."

She held up her hand. "You're sweet, Dec. I married the man I love. I wasn't too straight with you back then. I was dating a Seabee at the same time we were together. We have a baby girl now. Her name is Lidia."

"Happy for you..." He couldn't hang on to the rest of what she was saying. "Can't stay...in my body."

Convulsions filled his torso, and he heard shouting in the background. His mind drifted, first hovering over his apartment, and then switching to Maura and her maddeningly lovely visage.

———

Sunlight streamed into the open windows. Maura stood in one of the beams, bathed in the golden glow. She knew the next few minutes were going to be challenging.

"This way." She directed the group of people to her office and didn't say another word until she was seated behind her desk.

"You know this place is for the community. It is the only gym in all of San Diego that accepts barters such as time or babysitting or maintenance help in exchange for use of the equipment. We teach gymnastics to aspiring athletes and have a full parkour gym. Your acts of vandalism stole from your community, so this is your chance to give back." Maura kept her tone even, no matter how badly she wanted to yell at them.

Here she was, facing a parole officer and the four gang members who had totaled her gym. The kids couldn't be more than fourteen or fifteen. How hard it must be, to have such a challenging life at a young age? She wanted to bring this situation to a pleasant resolution.

"Let the judge know I will accept these four young men into the gym as part of their probation if they agree to follow our rules." She stared each of them down in turn. "There are no gangs in here, only individuals."

A couple of the boys shifted uncomfortably.

"This is your last chance. If the gym is hit again, I will press charges. This is your opportunity to change the conversation and start a new relationship with this place. If you play by our rules, you might even like it."

The parole officer looked at the kids. "She's cutting you a break. If you don't do right by this lady, it's off to juvenile hall for each and every one of you. Listen to her and do as she says. Got it?"

The sullen youths nodded their heads. They didn't look too thrilled to be there, but Maura was pretty sure it would work. The place was fun, and belonging to something as unique as this gym could work miracles.

"I will be checking on you every day to make sure you all are following her direction." The parole officer stood up. "You have my card, Ms. Maxwell. If you need anything, don't hesitate to call." He looked each kid up and down and then left.

She stood up and walked up to the kids. "You are going to start your time here by painting the walls you vandalized. I don't want you interacting with the members or playing on the equipment until you've earned that right. It all begins with doing a good job on each task. Got it?"

They nodded their heads and then followed her out to the janitor's closet. Inside the kids found paint, brushes, and a tarp.

"It ain't going to be as much fun painting as it was tagging," said Martin, the smallest of the bunch.

"Who knows, if you do a good job, I just might give you a tagging wall outside," said Maura, remembering a street she'd walked down in Paris that had an ever-changing wall of graffiti art. She'd been intrigued by the concept. "Inside the gym, this is for athletes. Now, get to work."

The boys moved slowly, pushing each other and joking.

She cleared her throat and they looked over their shoulders at her. Straightening up, they hustled to the wall she'd indicated and got to work.

———

Declan's body jerked. He opened his eyes, but couldn't speak. His tongue felt large and dry as he tried to swallow; it felt like cotton balls were stuffed in there.

Looking down his body, all he could see were bandages on the lower part of the right side of his body. His leg throbbed.

Camilla stood over him. She brushed back his hair with her cool hands. He wished she would put those cold hands on his body and relieve his skin. Too hot.

She leaned down and kissed his forehead. "This is where you get off. Be well, Dec." She paused, her eyes traveling over him.

He couldn't make his vocal cords work to say thank you.

"I'll try to check in when I'm back in San Diego

next." Her eyes held his. There was something there. Sadness, yes. Pity, maybe? She smiled at him, contrary to what was in her eyes, and then she gestured, calling people over.

What the hell's going on?

Two burly corpsmen leaned over his cot. When they moved it, pain ripped through him. This time he willed darkness to come, but it didn't. Instead he was consumed with endless heat and throbbing pain.

"You're at Walter Reed now. You must have slept through the stopover at Germany. They stabilized you there and sent you here. I'm Fitzpatrick with SOCOM. Master Chief Swifton, can you hear me?" A gruff voice pierced his brain.

A wave of smells penetrated his senses: disinfectant, urine, sweat, and apple juice. None of the scents appealed to him. He frowned. Why didn't any of this make sense?

Declan cracked an eyelid, staring into the image of a somewhat overweight, balding, barrel-chested Army Master Sergeant. The man's hazel eyes were bloodshot and the lines on his face looked permanently etched. Looked like this guy had had a rough day.

"They finished your surgery yesterday. They say you'll be on your way back to San Diego in a month or so."

"What? Why?" Declan was alarmed. "When did I have surgery?"

It was the Master Sergeant's turn to look shocked. His mouth gaped and then he stuttered, "D-d-don't tell me no one has talked to you yet…about your injuries or the surgeries?"

"No." Declan's brow furrowed. *What the hell?* He

shifted his shoulders and hips trying to sit up, but pain split through his leg and torso, halting the movement. "What happened to me?"

"Damn. That's not how things usually work. Uh, let me get the doctor."

Outside the door, which hadn't completely closed, Declan could hear voices. "Why hasn't anyone done a drill down? You should have told him that he lost his leg! This is unacceptable. We're here to help these guys, and it's impossible for us to do our job if you haven't done yours."

"Don't go down that road, Fitzpatrick. You know how things go. Patients heal at their own rate, and we respond as they need help or healing, not by your timetable. We assumed he was briefed in Germany." The female voice with the soothing tone got firmer. "The surgeon will make rounds this afternoon. In the meantime, we'll make him comfortable and answer questions as they arise. This is the first time he's been awake."

Declan didn't like people talking about him. He wanted to know the truth ASAP. He sat up fast, waves of dizziness swept his head, and he didn't care. He threw back the covers and swung his legs over the bed.

Cold tiles stung his toes as they reached the ground. His left foot flexed as he noted the rough texture.

He looked down. Something was wrong.

He stared. Incomprehensible. The lower part of his right leg was gone, from the knee down. Mounds of bandages covered the stump.

His hands rubbed over his thigh and the stump. His mind couldn't make sense of it.

The SOCOM guy's head popped back in right then. "Someone will be in to talk to you shortly."

"Get the hell out! I don't want to talk to anyone." Anger punctuated the spitfire barrage of words. Bubbling under the surface was an overwhelming pit of bile waiting to spew. A part of his brain didn't recognize the depth of the emotion. He'd never been one to be angry. Instead, Declan had always prided himself on being steady. In this very moment, there was no way to pull back from the edge. His leg. His passion for being a SEAL, for being outside and doing a zillion athletic things, and his entire identity—everything was wrapped up in his good health and physical abilities.

The Army man paled and withdrew. The door closely completely this time, clicking shut.

"Whiskey. Tango. Foxtrot." He breathed out slowly through his clenched jaw, trying not to scream at the top of his lungs. There were no words to describe this moment, his anger, and the pain.

"He what?" asked the nurse. More angry voices came from outside, but Declan didn't give a shit right now. Brain overload was mashing his capacity for communication.

His hands moved down his body, running over his torso and then going down his leg again. "This can't be real." As his hands reached the rounded wad of bandages, the pain told him it was more than true. It was a fucking horror story that he was never going to wake up from.

Touching the stub a second time didn't change anything. It just fueled the questions. *What happened? Where are my Teammates?* Now he regretted asking the SOCOM Liaison to leave. *This wasn't his fault. He was probably a good guy. And I'll bet he had some answers.*

Declan slammed his hand down on the railing and felt it give under the pressure. The plastic cracked all the way down the railing, splitting it wide open. His fingers throbbed.

He lay back on the bed and tears stung his eyes. He pushed his fingers into his eyeballs, but it didn't stop them from leaking. He wanted to punch something so bad, hurt someone, anyone, and most of all he wanted to know where his Teammates were.

A nurse entered the room. "I need to give you this."

He took a deep breath and steadied. "What?"

"This will ease the pain." She pushed the medicine into his IV tubing. "The doctor's in surgery and will be with you at 1600. He'll have more answers than I do." Checking the IV monitor, she placed another bag onto the stand. "I'm sorry…for how this happened. You shouldn't have learned about it this way." She paused at the door. "Is there someone you want us to call?"

"I'd prefer to do it," he stated flatly. He picked up the phone and put it on his chest.

She nodded and left the room, closing the door behind her.

Images slammed through his brain. Maura. How could he ask her to love him now? He thrust the worry aside and dialed Leaper's number.

The phone came alive on the other end. "Go for Leaper!"

Emotion released in his chest. "Man, it's good to hear your voice."

"Hey, guys, this is Swifton. Dec, how's it going?" His Teammates yelled into the phone as one, talking to him like nothing was different. They chewed the fat for ages, each one checking in. They were fine. He changed the subject when they asked about his leg. He didn't want to talk about it, and quite frankly he didn't know what the next step was going to be.

He hung up, relieved the Team was secure. Scrubbing his hands over his face, he wanted to scream, both in happiness and in pain. Balling his hands into fists, he pulled his anger inward. He knew, even with one leg, he could rip this whole room to shreds.

Medication flooded his thought patterns. The pain-killer took away his needs, his concerns. The subconscious part of his brain though…well, that had a lot of fucked-up, disjointed things to say to him about himself, his manhood, and worst of all, his place in SEAL Team.

———— ∿∿ ————

Waking up to two women lifting him was a somewhat welcome and yet unnerving experience. He'd never been a deep sleeper, so the idea that someone could be touching him and moving him was disconcerting. Not that he could have done much about it, with the amount of drugs swimming in his system. He felt no pain…anywhere. Probably the optimal way to handle a special-ops guy, he supposed, without those knee-jerk, hand-at-throat experiences.

"Look who is awake. Good to see you." A soft voice teased his ears. "We're giving you a bath."

They reached the section he was worried about and it stirred to life.

"Thank God." He sighed.

"Hi, Master Chief Swifton," said one of the nurses. "I'm Doris." She smelled like vanilla sugar cookies, a pleasant scent. Her red hair was twisted into a bun and her makeup around the eyes was heavy with streaks of pink shadow. "You might ache a little. You've been catheterized, so give your private parts a day or two to recover, okay?"

"So nothing permanent."

"Not that I'm aware of, though extreme pain can turn off pleasure receptors pretty quickly. Again, give yourself some time. Your meds should wear off in an hour or two. Let us know if you need another dose."

He nodded, though he already knew he didn't want more pain medication. He'd seen plenty of buddies drop down the slippery drug slope, and he didn't even want the temptation. His preference was to gut it out.

The other woman chimed in, the tone mellow and low. "I'm Valerie. Nice to see you awake, Master Chief. After your bath, we'll get you some food. Chicken noodle or tomato soup?"

He cleared his throat. "How about a steak and a Caesar salad with a large ice tea?"

Doris laughed. "Not quite yet. Your stomach isn't ready for food that heavy. Go…"

"Slow," he finished. "Got it."

Valerie put a straw to his lips. He drew deeply on the water. *God, it tastes amazing, almost as good as frozen stout. Pure heaven!*

"Slow down. You'll want to take small sips," said Valerie as she lowered the glass to the table next to him.

—⁓—

The days blurred together. He jerked awake. He felt like Rip Van Winkle, lost and clueless upon waking.

Right now, two nurses hovered over him with sheets.

"What's going on?" His voice was a little rough, though he could still make himself heard.

"You've been out for four days with a fever caused by your wounds, but now you're responding to the new antibiotic marvelously. Just relax while we put some new bedding down. You've been sweating up a storm."

That didn't make sense. Germany. DC. The flights back… Hadn't I just gotten off the plane? Wait, something happened to me. He struggled to sit up.

"Move slowly. Your temperature spiked at 104.5. You're going to feel some residual aches and light-headedness." The nurse's eyes were gentle as she rubbed the towel over his arm.

As the memory of the SOCOM guy flooded back, he pushed the helping hands away. "I can do it myself, thanks." He moved into a propped position on the bed. Looking down, he said, "Thought I dreamed that."

"Many of my patients say that," Doris said as she finished washing him and then began drying him off. "That it's a nightmare. Hard to take it all in…in the beginning."

"What? People get used to it?"

She shook her head. "No one gets used to trauma. But they often find a way to make peace with it." She smoothed a blanket into place over him. "We can see about getting you some other clothes. You're going to need to get up and moving, and I don't think you're going to want your tail hanging out."

He felt a smile tug his lips. "Yeah, I don't want to invite anything I'm not prepared to follow up on."

She smiled back at him, but she didn't engage him further. That was fine by him. He wasn't into chitchat.

Finally, he watched her go. In another time and place,

he might have admired the way the cloth clung to her behind, the swing of her hips, and the movement of her hair. Today…he was facing the crap he wouldn't have wanted his best friend to have to see. He knew he was luckier than most, with a lot of years under his belt, but it still ripped his guts out.

He lifted his forearm and placed it over his eyes. The battered arm protested. Ignoring the tenderness there and on his head, he concentrated on his leg, trying to desensitize it. He forced himself to take it—the mental backlash of what-ifs, should-haves, and what-nows—so he could face what was coming. *Who am I without the Teams? Without my brothers?*

He'd held brothers—Teammates—in his arms as they died, and faced their families and their widows. Why was he griping? He was alive. A tear sped down his cheek. He wiped it away quickly. *Christ, if only I could go run the emotion out of me.*

He knew there'd be tears in private—to let the pain out. But he wasn't going to let anyone publicly see him cry; he'd deal with the emotion and force it to go eventually. No damnable feelings would master him.

Those bastard terrorists out there could try to take his life, but they were not going to break him. He was tougher than that, and he was going to damn well stay that way.

Now he had to call Maura. Or should he wait until he knew more about his medical condition? Either way, he had no idea what to say, so maybe radio silence was the best move.

Chapter 11

His body wrapped protectively around hers.

She felt safe.

He was reaching for her, caressing her body and her scars.

She was showing him everything perfect and flawed about her form.

He celebrated everything about her as he stroked his hands over her and kissed her flesh, igniting her passion and making all her senses come alive.

Thrusting her breasts against his chest and using his shoulders for stability, she took control. Climbing onto his hips, she lowering herself ever so slowly onto his manhood.

Her body wanted to protest, but she was so wet that as he slid inside, all she felt was intense pleasure, an electric firing that made her whole body tighten and stretch.

Feeling the breadth and width of him inside of her, the pulsing, the passion, the heat...she couldn't stop herself from taking exactly what she wanted. She took it again and again and then changed the rhythm, thus denying him his pleasure until he was saying her name, pleading for his own release, "Maura. Maura. Maura."

Maura awoke in stages. She was sexually frustrated and seriously wanting. Her dream might have been coitus completus, but her life right now was nothing but never-ending interruptus or complete denial until Declan got home.

Tossing the covers off her sweaty body, she stretched and then stood.

She unlocked her balcony glass door and stepped out onto their shared balcony. Even the balcony didn't smell right without the scent of his skin and that horrible stout he drank. In her opinion, it stunk worse than regular beer. She was most definitely a lager girl, if it had to be beer.

She checked her watch. Nine o'clock on a Saturday, and the beach was already filled with sunbathers. She could go down there and join them, maybe make a new friend, or she could stay here in her oasis, protected from the rest of the world. Her hair blew into her face. As she tucked it behind her ear, it was difficult not to look over her shoulder at Declan's apartment. Flashes of their time together made her close her eyes, reliving those images. She arched her back, wanting it to happen, wanting him…wishing she could kiss him and make love to him all over again.

Standing on the balcony, Maura couldn't resist looking into Declan's apartment. She hadn't heard from him since that night many weeks ago, and she was worried.

Her apartment was so sanitary you could eat off any surface, and she needed to use up more energy.

Maura jiggled the handle of his glass door and it slid open. "No way." It figured, Declan would leave it open. Only a SEAL would think that crooks wouldn't break in. Then again, it was California. Didn't most folks leave their doors unlocked? She'd never get used to that concept. They locked doors where she came from.

She stepped inside and her nose wrinkled. The air in here was stale. She opened the door wider and took a look around. It wasn't messy per se, but the place did look lived in. Mentally, she made a list. There were dishes drying next to the sink and half-open bottles of stout perched on the coffee table, and his bed was unmade. Declan must have been in a hurry to leave.

The worst part was the kitchen floor and refrigerator. Seeing the fridge open a crack, she noticed a pool of water surrounded it, and everything inside had gone bad. Looking at the side, she saw it was partially unplugged. It was a fire hazard for the whole apartment complex. She pulled the plug.

Spying a towel on the counter, she mopped the floor and wrung the water out in the sink. Unable to find any kitchen cleaner in the cupboards, she went back to her apartment, grabbed her cleaning kit, and thoroughly scrubbed out his refrigerator, his oven and microwave, and the rest of the kitchen. Making a list of what had previously been in there, she stood in the doorway and smiled.

Putting her hands on her hips, she surveyed the rest of the apartment critically. "This place could do with a little more work, a woman's touch."

She flipped on the stereo and listened to The Who as she picked up clothes, ran several loads of laundry, changed the sheets on the bed, and dusted. Pretty soon the apartment smelled as fresh and clean as hers.

As the stereo switched to the next CD and the Pretenders joined in on the musical parade, she felt her spirits lifting. Maura admired his closet, the neat rows of uniforms, shirts, pants, a suit and blazer, along with jeans and various casual all-weather jackets. She could see Declan did indeed have some order in his life. The shoes were polished and all lined up appropriately to match the clothes above.

Taking one of his hats off the shelf, she slipped it out of the plastic and tried it on. Going back to the mirror in the hall, she looked at herself. "Looks good." She laughed as she danced around. Maybe she should have gone into the Navy. The uniform would have looked great, but there were parts of her life she was pretty sure would be barriers to the military system. She had difficulty following orders. Returning the hat and closing the closet doors, she went back to her tasks.

Humming to herself as she sanitized the bathroom with the strongest cleaners she owned, she actually finished in record time. Only took ten minutes longer to clean his than hers.

"Okay, so I'm a little OCD about cleanliness, but you have to admit this place looks perfect now." She smiled.

A knock sounded at the front door.

The smile melted from her face. She froze. *Should I answer it?*

Slowly, she made her way to the door and peeked through the peephole. *Goodness! It's her.* Olivia Fenwick had been in the newspaper practically every week, hosting charity events or being seen on someone's arm, and here she was at Declan's door.

"I can hear you breathing," said the voice in a short, high staccato.

Flipping open the locks, Maura opened the door wide. "Hi, Olivia." She was holding her basket of cleaning supplies.

Olivia walked past her and into the living room. "Oh, it's you. Well, you've certainly done an adequate job. I guess you can go now." Seating herself on the couch, she arranged her skirts. "When do you expect him home?"

Maura didn't close the door. She left it wide and stalked into the living room. Who was this stuck-up cow to "dismiss" her? Taking a deep breath, she slowly exhaled and decided to play nice rather than upbraid the uppity woman on her lack of etiquette. "I'm *not* the cleaning lady." Of course, she didn't know exactly *what* she was to Declan, but the maid she was not!

"Oh?" Olivia's eyes were sharp as they swept up and down Maura's body, stopping at the basket of supplies. The look in those eyes was not admiring. "Enlighten me."

Growing up with brothers had made Maura tough, and she had played several withering games with her brother's girlfriends before. Blood was, in most cases, thicker than lust. "I live here."

Not quite the truth, but the woman made it impossible not to respond to her cattiness.

"Fascinating, I thought he preferred them...young." Olivia looked away. "I guess men are fickle at times."

Was that a dig? Maura's eyes narrowed. "Why would he need a girl when he has a lady?" She might be shy around men at times, but she could hold her own with any woman. Competing in gymnastics for most of her youth had taught her to psych out many a competitor.

Olivia sniffed. "Precisely." She stood and walked to the counter. For several seconds, she seemed to search in her purse for something, and then she withdrew an elegant envelope. Making a show to kissing it, right over his name, she placed it on his counter and walked out the door. "Enjoy your grunge work."

Maura was so mad she wanted to spit. Instead, she ran to the door and slammed it, but Olivia was a fast little minx and was already in her car, revving the engine. The gesture was lost, however juvenile it might have been.

Leaning against the closed portal, Maura slid to the floor. She threw her hands up. She had played right into Olivia's game, and Declan didn't give a rat's ass about her.

Pushing herself to her feet, she took one last glance around the apartment, trying to ignore the envelope on the counter, and then closed the balcony door behind her, making sure she locked it.

As she traced the steps back to her own place, the cool ocean breeze blew against her skin. Sunbathers were wrapping up their blankets and heading for home. She'd spent her whole day cleaning Declan's home. Initially she'd done it to blow off steam, and now she realized it was an act of love. She really cared about him.

Sunset would be coming very soon. Maybe wishing on the green flash, the light that streaked across the sky at the exact moment the sun set, would help her wish come true.

As she watched the green flash split the horizon, she whispered, "Come home soon, Declan. Come home to me."

———

The gang teens had made tremendous progress at the gym. Not only had they painted walls, repaired mats, and cleaned equipment without a single grumble, they'd asked permission to work out on the parkour course.

Maura granted it eagerly and was delighted to see them working out and assisting the younger kids.

American Ninja Warrior had made its mark on the southwest corridor of the U.S., and the trials for the show usually started in Venice Beach. Several of the regular contestants called San Diego home and used her gym as one of the home training spots.

Among her new clients was Minnie. Maura spied her on a treadmill near the window and walked over. "Hi, Minnie. Nice to see you again."

"Hi, Maura." She beamed. "Guess what? I came here with Bosco." She slowed her pace from running to a brisk walk. "We're dating now. Thanks for the advice you gave me. It turns out he likes me too."

A male voice cleared his throat behind her. "Hi, Maura." The awkwardness at seeing him at the gym over the past few weeks seemed to melt away as he stood before her smiling and so obviously infatuated with Minnie.

She looked over her shoulder and smiled at Bosco. "Hi, Bosco."

"Uh, listen. Sorry for how things turned out with the date. Though, I, uh, appreciate your kindness to Minnie. I've known her a long time. She told me what you said." Bosco nodded his head. "I appreciate it, ya know."

Maura nodded her head and smiled. She was happy for them both.

Bosco's cheeks reddened. "She's my girl and I'm her guy."

"That's great. Friends should always be happy for their friends when they find joy, and especially love." Maura patted his arm.

Minnie said, "Thanks, Maura."

"Anytime." She left them and headed for her office. On many levels, she was relieved. The friendship boundary was clearly in place, and she could move on to other matters. It was nice, though, that Bosco had apologized. He had gone up a few friendship points in her opinion.

Mrs. B. was in her office working on the calendar when Maura finally arrived. She sat down behind the desk and decided to join in on the effort.

"Hey, Mrs. B., did the gymnastics coach leave her schedule for the next set of practices?" asked Maura as she held the general calendar in her hand. "I want to make sure that we don't have any competing events during the tryouts for our squad."

"Right there, in your top box." Mrs. B. pointed to a stack of plastic shelves on the desk. "I believe the four-to-eight-year-old parkour group wants to have a show for their parents too. Don't forget to add that to the calendar."

"It's already on there," confirmed Maura, setting the calendar down. "Practically every day is filled. We've gone from a small community group to a bustling gym with the superhero kids groups, the gymnastics competitions, and the parkour, not to mention the regular workout crowd. I can really do this, can't I?"

Mrs. B. smiled. "I knew you could. And look at all of the jobs you've created. I'm especially grateful for mine."

Maura returned the grin. "I'm glad you're here. Okay, back to paperwork or no one is getting paid. I can hardly wait until we have the new payroll system loaded on your computer. No more outsourcing! That's going to save us at least four hours a week of reviewing the records. Pretty soon, employees can punch in, and automatically it will link to their paycheck. It's brilliant. Thanks for the suggestion."

Mrs. B. nodded. "Oh, Maura. I forgot to tell you, a man came by the gym. Asked if you were here. I told him you were running late."

"Can you describe him?" Was it Declan? Was he home? Why wouldn't he come over to her apartment first?

"He was lean and blond, but strong looking."

"Oh," said Maura, disappointed. "Well, you can give him my cell phone number if you like." She checked the clock. "Okay, let's get back to the accounting."

As Mrs. B. ran through the figures, Maura tried to keep her mind on the issue at hand, but it was difficult. All she wanted to do was run home and see if Declan was back yet. Though in her heart of hearts, she knew he wasn't.

Chapter 12

DECLAN WATCHED NURSE DORIS SAFETY PIN THE RIGHT leg of his sweatpants up over his thigh. She looked like she had done this a million times, and still she smiled. The staff here was remarkable, buoyant, and their optimism truly lifted a patient's spirits.

He knew his lips were set in a grim line, though he managed to mumble, "Thanks, Doris." Today it was his own frustration getting the better of him. He wanted to be out of this bed and off the East Coast completely, back home in the sunshine with his Team and Maura.

Looking down at himself, he couldn't remember the last time he'd dressed in sweats. Maybe when he was a kid, with his mom. She had been his world. Foster care had been hard for him when she died as he moved from home to home. His possessions had been few: a couple of pictures and his memories. The only permanence he had ever known was the Teams. They were his family, his brothers, and his entire world.

He couldn't complain. There had been a lot of kind gestures since he was wounded. The sweatshirt, T-shirts, and pants were from Jack and Laurie Roaker, a Team ONE bud and his wife. Dan and Aria McCullum from Team THREE had sent a trident blanket, a bunch of comfort items, and a dozen Team FIVE challenge coins—round metal coins that often denoted a branch of the military, a unit, or an individual. The practice of exchanging challenge coins originated in World War I and is still in practice today. They are given as a gift to thank or honor someone as well as to show who you are. Gich had sent a bottle of twenty-year-old scotch, a SEAL hat, and a bunch of truly ugly socks in addition to well-fitting Saucony sneakers.

The Teams always took care of their own, though SOCOM had tried to help out. People outside the community just felt…like strangers. Hard to explain to outsiders, but most military folk, family, and friends that got the combat connection could understand. It didn't stop him from being polite. "I appreciate it."

"Anytime," the nurse said brightly, helping him to pull the sweatpants over his left leg and then tighten the drawstring at his waist. "Don't know why you won't let me fetch you a pair of boxer shorts. Those things come untied, you're going to have a world of embarrassment."

"Nothing down there ever embarrassed me," he said, pushing his body upright.

She blushed beet red as she handed him the crutch. "Just one, right?"

"Yep." He had his center of gravity down, and though he wanted to move on to the prosthetic phase, he'd had two surgeries and wasn't allowed to try it until the stump healed. His one-month stay had bloomed into two, but he was looking forward to getting on a plane heading for Coronado…soon.

The sweet nurse stood by while he rose. "I got it." He kept his vision forward and moved toward the bathroom.

"Great." She opened the door wide for him. "I'm not supposed to tell you, but the doc will be by in an hour to discharge you. You'll be flying back tomorrow."

"I look forward to it." He grinned at her.

She hesitated, leaning again the door frame. "I want to thank you for the advice you gave me about Larry. Being honest, telling him how I felt about his ex and my dogs and where I wanted our future to go was the heart-to-heart we needed." Nodding her head, she beamed as she said, "We're getting married at the end of the year."

That stopped him in his tracks. It took a few moments to maneuver around, but he turned to face her. "Really?"

"Yes." She smiled. "No more sniping at each other. No more subtext. We flat out tell it like it is. I'm so relieved."

He smiled back. "Hot damn. Glad it helped. Thank you too. For help with all of this."

"My pleasure," she said.

Turning back around, he went into the bathroom to shave. He could have done it in bed with a hand mirror, but he wanted—no, needed—to stand to illustrate that life hadn't changed that much.

His gut twisted in a knot. When he got back on the West Coast, he'd learn more about his fate. *Please, let me stay in*. It wasn't the money that made him send out that prayer. It was the fact that being a SEAL was all he knew and what he had been for most of his life.

He reached the sink, propped the crutch up against the wall, and spread the foam over his jaw and cheeks. He scratched the razor over his stubble.

A beeper sounded. "Declan, I have to go. Catch you later."

"Okay," he said. His eyes stayed with her, watching until she was out of view. Nurse Doris Niccly had been a gift to him these past few weeks. She'd been company, even on her days off, coming by to check on him, making him laugh, and generally answering questions. Her brother had died in Afghanistan, losing three limbs in the process. She would have given anything to be there, she'd told him. Any family member would be honored and grateful to see their loved ones again before they were gone.

Rinsing his face off, he dried it with the paper-thin white hospital towel and grabbed his crutch. Going to the bedside table, he took a Team FIVE coin, put it in the pocket of his sweatshirt, and went to the door. Heading down the hall, he stopped at the room of a kid, not more than nineteen, and entered. He sat in a chair and waited.

His eyes studied the young man who slept so soundly. He'd met Private Kellogg Lesterman on his second week. He'd started out in Declan's room and then had been moved down the hall as complications arose. The kid had lost both legs up to the hip and both arms below the elbows. His family had been in and out constantly. There were seven Lestermans on scene and twelve waiting and praying at home.

Big families were an advantage, one he'd hoped to have someday. Now, well, he'd have to see how things went before he tackled the female hurdle again.

Checking the clock, Declan figured the Lestermans would be back from lunch shortly.

Declan had watched this kid struggle to be upbeat in front of his family and cry when he was alone. He wished he could ease the young man's load. The kid had a significant journey ahead of him, and every day needed to count.

He wondered if other people felt that about him.

No, he didn't want anyone to ever feel sorry for him. *I'm damn lucky and know it.*

It was obvious that every soldier or sailor housed on this floor had injuries that provided different challenges. Didn't the brass know that *one* protocol did *not* fit everyone? But, hell, despair had to be the greatest crusher. Keeping that beast away was priority one. For individuals who took their problems to the track or the pool or some other kind of physical expression, problems got worked out fairly readily. When he couldn't lick his issues with a workout, he knew he could often run the hamster wheel of doubt and frustration. Without the physical offset, the sitting around was tough on the psyche and sometimes even a killer.

The kid must have heard Declan thinking. He twitched and blinked his eyes open. "Master Chief," breathed Kellogg, the delight radiating in his words. "Good to see you."

"Declan. Or you can call me Dec." Declan pulled the chair closer. "I brought something for you." He held the coin up for Kellogg to see. "This is my Team coin. I want you to have it. If anyone ever gives you any guff, tell them you got a buddy that will do right by you."

"That's cool, Dec. Thanks. Can you put it on my tray so I can see it?"

Declan nodded and did as requested, placing the trident side up.

The kid took a shaky breath. "You're going home soon, aren't you?"

"Tomorrow." Declan pursed his lips. He had so much he wanted to say and no idea where to begin. "Do you have time to talk?"

"Okay." Kellogg licked his lips and looked at the tray table in front of him.

Declan grabbed his crutch and stood. He lifted the glass with a straw sticking out of it to Kellogg's lips. Watching the kid take several long sips seemed to ease him.

When Kellogg nodded, Declan put the glass down. The private was breathing in short gasps now.

"Do you need me to get someone?"

The kid shook his head. "Don't want anyone. Hate needing help."

"Me too. But it doesn't make you weak to ask for help. Actually it makes you stronger, because then you know your strengths and weaknesses, and you know for sure what you can learn from others. One of my BUD/S instructors used to say that."

Declan almost lost his balance, and then he steadied. He wanted so desperately to leave the private with a feeling of hope. "I know…they're telling you stuff here in the hospital. Like it will get better. I don't know whether it will or not." He took a deep breath. "Here's what I do know: every day you have to find happiness. Laugh. Find joy. Love the people that love you. This is what we got—all we got is today."

Kellogg's mouth pinched tight, and then he hung his head. "I want out of this bed. I told my family that. I won't spend the rest of my life in one."

"Good for you," Declan agreed. "Go out there and live. There are some honeys to catch and kiss."

Kellogg smiled briefly. "They're working on getting a chair that I can control with…with what I have." The last part of the statement was flat, as if the heart was willing and yet the spirit was already defeated.

Declan didn't know any way to alleviate the burden. The best thing he knew to do was tease someone out of an emotional spot.

"Don't go over fifty-five miles per hour," Declan joked, holding Kellogg's gaze for a long time. "You got my number. Call me anytime. They told me your voice-activated cell phone would be here tomorrow. And I'm here until 1200, if you want to catch the game on TV or just want to talk."

The young man nodded and then looked out the window. "I don't want to listen to that thing drone anymore. I want to get on with...everything." His eyes welled. "I need to feel the Montana air on my skin. See my horse and my dog." He gulped back the emotion. "I'm afraid I won't...make it back there in time."

Declan put his hand on the kid's shoulder. He wished he could transfer his strength. "Hang in there."

"Yeah." As if he'd flipped a switch, the kid brightened in an almost maniacal manner. "Did I tell you I have a sweetheart? I met her at basic training. We write letters. I have a stack of them. My sister has been reading them over and over again. I even wrote one back to her two days ago. Hope she likes it."

"Charlotte." Even as he said the name, Declan couldn't stop the cringe. He had overheard Kellogg's mother and father talking. Apparently, the girlfriend had dumped him when she heard the news, giving the message to the family rather than telling her boyfriend herself. They couldn't bring themselves to share this with him.

"My Charlie. I can't wait to see her. Bet my parents will love her." Kellogg coughed several times. He took a couple of shaky breaths. "Need to get rid of this cold first. I was never one for being sick. Rather be outside, doing things."

"Me too," Declan agreed. He could hear the Lestermans coming down the hallway. They were a loud and inviting group, the kind that pulled you out of your own quiet and into the fun. There was no doubt they'd keep a good eye on Kellogg, but still...something made him worry about the kid, as if his spirit wasn't going to hang on to the hope of life and the joys it could bring.

"Your folks are on the way in." Declan touched the private's shoulder again. "Good meeting you, Kellogg. Stay frosty."

"You too," said Private First Class Kellogg Lesterman. Then those gray eyes moved away...back to the window...and to whatever was beyond Declan's scope of vision that no one but Kellogg could see.

Back in his room, Declan dialed Maura's number. He was relieved when it rolled to voice mail.

He cleared his throat. "Hey, pretty lady. It's Dec. Just checking in. I should be home in a bit. I'll let you know the details when I have them." He hung up and lay down on the bed. What he was going to say to her? Maybe it was best to leave the decision in her hands. If she split because he lost a leg, he'd know her true motives for being with him. If she stayed, then most likely she really liked him. Either way, he'd have to be good with it.

Closing his eyes, he let his mind wander. It zoomed in on their day together at the gliderport and all the time they'd spent together, the sounds Maura made

when she laughed, or of them making love. He liked
that. He liked…her.

———∿∿∿———

The air flight from east to west was pretty calm. The
C-17 was filled to capacity and flew directly to Miramar.
He didn't know what he'd do from there…probably get
a cab. His Teammates were still away, and he didn't feel
much like talking to anyone anyhow.

He was still trying to put the pieces together in his
head. Closing his eyes, he focused on the Op.

"Hey, are you okay?" A Private First Class on his
left shook his shoulder with a bandaged arm. The look
of concern was fleeting as Declan's gaze settled on the
young Marine PFC.

"Yeah." Declan nodded, turning his iron gaze away
from the Marine. He thought he must have made some
kind of noise. If he had, he honestly didn't want to know
what it was. Otherwise, he doubted the Marine would
have dared. Declan knew how imposing his sheer size
and haggard look could be.

The plane hit its descent. The energy among the men
changed to one of anticipation.

Coming home was a good feeling and he couldn't
wait to be on the ground. He was sure the rest of the
varied souls on board were thinking the exact same thing.

Leaning his head against the headrest, Declan contemplated what he'd remembered. Surely, someone had
pulled the data from his camera for the CO. When he got
back to his apartment, he'd check his gear.

His mind drifted back to the hospital. A lot of the
West Coast SEAL community had checked in. They had

definitely geared up and the number and size of boxes they had shipped to him was slightly embarrassing. He loved them for it, but he left most of it behind for the guys on his floor.

He shifted in his seat. Their acts of caring made it harder to ask his buddies to get lost for a while, but he knew his psyche pretty damn well, and his priority was to deal with his injuries in his own way. He'd always needed to figure out stuff on his own before he asked for help or relied on others. Maybe it was a survival instinct from his childhood. Whatever the cause, he didn't relish putting the word out, but he knew he would.

As the soldiers and sailors began to deplane, he heaved his body up and steadied on his crutches—they'd made him take them both—and managed to somehow grab his pack with his less-needed hand. He must have looked pretty damned determined, because no one gave him crap about how slow he was going or offered him a hand with his stuff.

Sunshine beat down on him as he stepped outside. Blessed California. He turned his face up to relish it. There was definitely something special about the sun out here, as if it were medicine for all of life's miseries.

Putting his head down, he concentrated on making it into the building. The walk into the terminal was intensely slow, and though he managed it, he was still sweating like a trainee on his first day of BUD/S.

A gruff voice barked at him as he entered the door. "What took you so damn long? I heard they were letting the ugly guys off first."

It took Declan a few seconds for his eyes to adjust to the cool darkness, and then he was dropping his pack and reaching for the owner of that voice. His lips split into a cheesy smile. "Gich, you, son of a bitch, good to see you."

They shook hands, then the older SEAL slapped him on the back, nearly bowling him over before grabbing Dec's pack and swinging it over his shoulder. They made their way outside to Gich's giant truck and stowed the gear.

Once inside, Gich started the motor and pulled onto the road. "I need someone to do some stout tasting before I drop you off. Work for you?" That was code for stopping at McP's Pub or Danny's and drinking until someone blacked out. Declan had never really been a drinker and wasn't about to start now. Beer was his exception, though he'd gone nonalcoholic for several years. Made it easier when he had to hop or shove off at a moment's notice.

"I'm kinda tired…"

A hard look came from Gich, who studied him from head to toe. "Can't avoid the world forever. A lot of people want to see you."

"Yeah." Declan was noncommittal. "I, uh, want to be good with things first."

Gich nodded. "Understood. I'm not saying the rest of the community is going to get it, but I'll abide by your wishes…for now."

"Thanks," said Declan. Looking over his shoulder, he spied a case of his favorite stout. Alongside it was his bag from the Team FIVE cages. "For saving me a trip."

"Yep. Figured you'd need keys and stuff to get in. Not that I'm doubting your ability to jimmy a lock, just don't want you to have to go get a new one when you're done."

"Good call," Declan said flatly. The Commander

could break in anywhere, though the XO had probably given some direction. He nodded with his head. "Who's that for?"

"A friend. Thought he might need a drink. He's a stubborn asshole who'd rather be alone than laugh his dick off with his friends." Gich smiled and his mustache twitched as he held back the laughter. Before he pulled out of the parking space, he punched Declan in the shoulder. "Keep in mind we aren't a sum of our parts, or even a part of them; we're what we got inside. SEAL spirits are indestructible."

Declan nodded. He resisted the urge to dump his emotional load on the Commander, former BUD/S instructor, and good friend. Instead he listened to the man harp about a pretty lady described as the sweetest thing he'd ever met and how he never ever wanted to let her get away.

———

Stairs were a bitch and a half. Something he used to take two at a time now had him moving at a snail's crawl. Made him feel fucking frustrated! When did the little stuff become so tough?

"Do you need help getting it all inside?" Gich was shorter by several inches, but the man's power made him a giant.

Dropping the case and duffle at the door, Declan went back to the top of the stairs.

"No thanks, Gich," said Declan, proffering his hand instead. The faster he said good-bye, the sooner he could be alone in his apartment. Home. Something he'd been craving since this shitstorm happened.

Gich slapped it away and gave him a hug. Power that could snap a spine wrapped around his shoulders, and then Gich was thumping him on the back again. Damn, that man could dislodge food without the Heimlich. Size and strength just didn't change things when your core was fueled by belief and confidence. This man had taught him that, and so much more.

"Hey, how did you know…when I'd arrive?"

"Old Frogs & SEALs. A Team wife is in touch with a couple of the docs at Walter Reed and the Master Sergeant at SOCOM. She badgered them all until she knew when you were coming so you could be met and the community could roll it out for you. I added my dime about waiting on the fanfare. She deferred to me."

Declan nodded. "Please thank her. And I'm glad it was just you."

"I know." Gich headed back down the stairs. Over his shoulder, he yelled, "Stay ugly."

"You first." Watching Gich leave was bittersweet. Part of him wanted to invite the guy in and the other part just needed time alone. Sliding his key into the lock, Declan opened the door. It smelled clean and fresh in here, like bleach, ammonia, and glass cleaner. Must have been a Team wife.

He pushed the case into the entry hall, pulled the rest of his gear into the apartment, and closed and locked the door. Despite the fact he was being careful maneuvering over the pile, he stumbled and landed on his shoulder.

Crawling away from the pile, he pulled himself to his feet, got his crutch, and went immediately to the glass door. He stood there with his hand on the latch, wanting to open it and smell the fresh air. Craving the sunlight on his skin and the ocean lifting him high on the waves. He could get lost out there, forever. It'd be such a happy way to go…

Turning away from the temptation, he went into the bedroom, stripped off all of his clothes, and collapsed on the bed. His mind needed to shut off. His body was shaking with exhaustion. *Just a few hours… That's all I need*.

Cramps twisted and squeezed his stomach. Waking up abruptly, Declan was covered in sweat. He shook his head, trying to make the memory fade, but it was far more vivid and memorable than the sand in his pants during sugar-cookie drills.

Moving his legs toward the side of the bed, he groped on the floor for his crutch with his hand. Fingertips wrapped around the cold metal, and he pulled it closer so he could haul his body out of bed.

He headed into the other room slowly, grabbed a beer from the case, and fished his pain pills and antibiotics out of his pack. Gich's stout was the real stuff, no near beer here. He knew he probably shouldn't combine the two—the medication label was pretty explicit—but he didn't give a shit right now.

He slammed the edge of the bottle cap against the counter, and the top popped off and foam spewed out. He sipped, once, twice, three times, feeling the warm brew hit the spot.

Withdrawing the prescribed meds, he tossed them onto his tongue and chased them down with a long pull of brew. "Ack," he said, tasting the chalky film and bitter taste left behind by the pills.

He finished off the stout before heading back to his

bed. Pulling off the sweaty comforter, he tossed it aside and lay down on the cool, clean sheets.

There was one scene he was hoping to avoid, the thing he hadn't dreamed about yet, but that had lingered on the edges of his conscious and subconscious mind. He had successfully anesthetized himself, not realizing that he was unleashing the dam of his memories.

"Can you hear me, Master Chief?" The man was rubbing his knuckles on Declan's sternum. "I'm Dr. Walters."

That fucking hurt! "Yes," Declan answered. His eyes were slits because the light was so bright. He wanted to close them, to just go to sleep. Why wouldn't they let him sleep?

"Where does it hurt?" asked the doctor as he pushed on spot after spot.

"Everywhere," replied Declan. He was so tired... Too exhausted to do this.

"What about your legs? Can you wiggle your toes?" The doctor wore glasses and Declan could see his reflection in them. The eyes behind the lenses looked confident, kind, and concerned. "You need to move..."

Declan felt his heart squeeze as if something were crushing it. His mouth was open, but he couldn't ask for help.

"He's crashing. Hypovolemic shock. Get that blood volume back up. Get the paddles. Move!"

It was the strangest feeling, hovering over his body, looking down on himself and the doctors and nurses. Had to have been at least six of them working on him. There was so much blood. And someone was keeping pressure on his leg.

They ripped open his shirt. Laid paddles on his chest.
"Clear! Clear!"

The shock sent him back into his own body. Into his pain-ridden, bleeding body, which looked like so much red meat from above. The pity he'd felt was gone. Instead there was a sense of fighting. He wanted it, wanted to live.

"Got a pulse. It's steady. Okay, let's get him to surgery." The doctor was leaning over him.

Declan was looking into those bespectacled eyes.

"Stay with us, Master Chief. We're going to get you fixed up."

Leaning over the side of the bed, Declan grabbed the edges of the mattress and threw up. The entire contents of his stomach purged themselves onto the floor of his bedroom. The image of his body as tattered and torn red meat played over and over in his brain.

His body shook. Going down, stout tasted great. Coming back up was like barfing acid.

Seemed like forever before the heaving stopped.

Opening the nightstand drawer, he withdrew a pack of Extra spearmint gum and shoved two pieces into his mouth. It was ideal to stop the heaves and was a pretty good stopgap until he could get to the bathroom and brush his teeth. Thinking of the bathroom, though, made him have to do other things.

Why was it that bodily functions wanted to happen all at once?

He reached for his crutch and knocked the lamp off the nightstand. It crashed to the floor and he ended up in the same place. Just then his bladder let loose, and he started to laugh as relief and pain dueled in his body. In for a penny, in for a pound…

The balcony light came on. The glass door opened and Maura's voice was tentative. "Declan, is that you?"

"Yep! It's me. I was going to call you in the a.m." Declan didn't know if that was true or not. All he knew for sure was that he hated feeling helpless as a baby.

Lights snapped on in his living room and then in his bedroom. His eyes drank in the sight of her like a thirsty man.

"Declan? What on earth?" She stood there in a white cotton nightgown and robe, and from this angle, he could see her white panties with a small pink bow on top. She leaned down next to him. "When did you get home? What happened?"

"A few hours ago. I wanted to get a few winks before I came over and woke you."

"Oh." She bent down beside him. Her fingers touched his face. "What happened? Give me two minutes to call an ambulance."

"No," he said adamantly. "No doctors. No more hospitals. I'm fine." He had just gotten out; he couldn't bear to go back.

"Okay. Don't move then. Just give me a minute." She was gone less than a minute. When she came back from the bathroom with wet washcloths and dry towels, she also had his crutch. She didn't say anything about his leg, merely handed it to him.

She ran the wet washcloths over his body and then dried him. It was actually sort of nice, better than the experience at the hospital. From this position, his body joined in on the applause.

"Declan, let's get you back up on the bed."

"First, a side trip to the bathroom to clean up." He used his arms to pull himself up and onto the bed. Feeling her hands brush gently over his flesh brought a flood of memories. He used the crutches to get to the bathroom. While he rinsed himself off, he realized how starved he was to see her, to touch her and smell her. And he had denied himself that pleasure…why?

Smiling when she saw him, she propped pillows around him after he lay down. She gave him a glass of water and his toothbrush with toothpaste on it and then tackled the messes on the floor. As he brushed his teeth, he wanted to tell her that she didn't have to do it, but watching her touched something inside of him.

"Do you want to talk about it?" she asked.

He pursed his lips and shook his head.

"By morning it will be better. Why don't you come over to my place?"

Surprisingly, he wanted to. He wanted to smell the scent of her on her sheets and towels and wrap his body around her warmth. He pushed away the pillows and covers, grabbed his crutches, and got to his feet. They moved through his apartment slowly and then onto the balcony. The fresh air made his senses feel alive. He breathed deeply for several seconds and then followed Maura into her place.

"I can sleep on the couch or the floor. I've slept worse places." He really didn't want to put her out. She'd already gone above and beyond.

"No way." Maura stood like a militant nurse. The expression on her face was unreadable, and he would have given just about anything to know what was on her mind.

As he sat down, the bed sagged under his weight. Stretching out, he felt the cool clean sheets beneath him. Her scent enveloped him and he immediately relaxed.

Slowly, she lay down next to him. Putting her head on his chest, she hugged him. "I...I missed you." She stayed like that for a long time.

He cleared his throat; her tenderness had brought a sudden swell of emotion. "I missed you too." He stroked her hair and her nightgown-covered back, and then shifted her body so she lay half on top of him. "I'm terrible with words. They get in the way. I'm better at showing." He kissed her, putting everything he wanted to share with her in that touch of lips.

A moan escaped her mouth. It was his turn to take his time and explore the beauty of Maura Maxwell, and given her response, this was exactly what she sought.

Her needs rose to his. She was kissing him back as if he were oxygen. Her hands caressed his skin, playing along the muscles on his chest and stomach and then pulling on his biceps...wanting...asking for him to be on top. As he rolled over, he struck his leg and cried out.

"Sorry," she said. "I'm such a disaster."

"No," he said. "You're not. Come here." Pulling her on top of him, he settled her so that she couldn't tweak his leg, and then they began to play. There was no rushing as he cupped and caressed her breasts, first with his hands and fingers and then with his tongue.

The soft murmurs of pleasure coming from the back of her throat excited him. Her skin was so soft and beckoning, it was hard to keep his hands off of her. As she moved restlessly against him, he lowered his touch to that most tender place between her legs, and finding

the rhythm that made her breath race and her body arch
made him smile. Again and again he brought her until
she was so wet, his fingers were bathed in her essence.

Then he lifted her again, suspending her body above his.

She giggled such a purely feminine sound. "You're
so strong. You could probably do bench presses with me
all day long."

"You're lighter than my pack." He grinned. "Uh, do
you have a…"

She nodded and pointed to the drawer next to him.

The box was sealed. He ripped it open and put on the
condom, and then he lifted her back into position and
lowered her onto his waiting cock, watching as her eyes
went wide and her mouth opened.

When he was completely inside of her, she sighed.
"Declan."

Taking his hands from her waist, he said, "I'm all
yours. Do with me what you will."

The smile on her lips was wicked. She moved slowly
at first, finding her pace.

He relished the pleasure, something he hadn't enjoyed
for a long, long time. His body was so close, so primed,
but he held on, waiting for the moment when her back
arched and she cried out.

"Declan!"

His name was a call to battle. Grabbing her hips with
both hands, he increased the speed, driving himself
deeper into her, and then he came. His body shook with
the force of the climax. His arms vibrated with effort
and he almost dropped her on the bed as he lifted her off.
Instead, he managed to tuck her next to his body. God, it
was like a marathon.

Words tumbled unheeded from his mouth. "I was on an Op and it went sideways. One of the explosions caught up to us faster than we realized, and it blew my leg off. I don't know what it means, if I'll still be able to be active duty, though I'm pretty sure my operational days are over." He took a long, slow, deep breath and then let it out. "I'm not ready to face all the emotional baggage that goes along with this, but I do know that I care deeply for you. I thought of you often. I just…didn't want you to worry…and didn't know what to say…about this."

"You wanted to tell me in person," she added.

"Yes." He hugged her tightly. "Be patient with me."

She pushed herself up onto her elbow and looked at him. "Why wouldn't I? You're still the same man, the person I was falling for."

He grinned. "I thought I was the only one doing the falling."

Her fist struck his chest in a playful jab. "Ha, ha. Who wouldn't fall for you?"

"Don't underestimate yourself, Maura. The fact that you're unaware of your own strength, fortitude, and beauty…you're a gorgeous woman inside and out. Most of all, your tender heart…touches me." Declan felt emotions welling up inside. Maybe this was the time to put it out there, what he felt he had to say to her. "Just want you to know. I'm not the only fish out there. You can do better." He had to give her an out, as much as it hurt him.

"Declan, I'm not going anywhere. You're the only one I want." She leaned down and kissed him, teasing his upper lip until he joined in. "I've put away my fishing pole."

He nodded, his heart full. She wanted to be with him, even given everything going on. He was speechless.

He took his time exploring her body and listening to her moans and sighs before he brought her to completion. One thing was for sure, the passion between them had not faded, and neither had Maura's sweetness.

Chapter 13

HARD TO THINK OF MYSELF AS FALLING FOR THIS GUY, AND YET I am. Maura blew the suds off of her hands and dried them on a recycled paper towel. Tossing it into the garbage from where she stood, she said, "Two points."

It had hardly been twenty-four hours, and she was practically lovesick.

"Sorry, I didn't hear you," he said, patting his lap.

"Just considering telling the world that you've made me a sex addict." She settled herself instead next to him on the couch. She wanted him naked and available to fulfill her desires 24/7. *Is that normal?*

"Welcome to the club." His arm settled around her shoulders, and she snuggled into his warmth. "They say admitting the problem is the first step to wallowing in it or fixing it. What's your choice?"

"Wallow."

He grinned at her. "Good choice." His hands moved under her shirt, rubbing along her spine. "Can I ask you a question?"

"You just did," she teased as she rolled her eyes. "I'm kidding. Go ahead."

He lifted the back of her shirt and laid a kiss on the scarred flesh of her back. "You never talk about your scars, but you're obviously comfortable with them. Would you share the experience of how they happened?"

She nodded her head. She wasn't scared of showing

her scars, not anymore. But she was still uncomfortable talking about them.

Declan studied her, and then shook his head. "Sorry. If it's too much…"

"No." She patted his hand. "It's okay. Just give me a minute. I'm comfortable with myself and my body. The scars are part of my life experience. But I, uh, still have difficulty…talking about the accident. It brings me back to that moment like it was yesterday."

She took a long, ragged breath and let it out. "Okay. As you know, I began gymnastics at the age of three. I loved tumbling, and the beam—I couldn't get enough of it and would spend hours and hours practicing. So in middle school, my parents enrolled me in a gym about two hours from our house that was known for its competitive standing and for making great gymnasts. I competed for them throughout high school—my folks made me go to a regular high school so I'd have friends and a regular experience, but I was hardly there and nothing was normal about my life."

She shifted in her seat. "It was senior year. I was returning from a gymnastics meet with five friends. We were all piled in there together. None of us were wearing seat belts. We were celebrating, because we'd just slaughtered our nemesis, Knotch—a gym that had turned out two gold medal winners and one bronze—and we were pretty pumped."

Maura couldn't hold his gaze, so she looked at her hands. The memory came to life again as clear and painful as if it were yesterday. "Betsy was driving, and Elizabeth was in the passenger seat. I was behind the driver, Renee was behind the passenger side, and

Chassey"—she swallowed the hard lump in her throat as tears welled in her eyes—"Chassey was in the middle seat. I don't know what happened up front, but our SUV overturned. I can still feel it rolling—over and over. The metal twisted and we were screaming."

Wiping tears off her face, she continued. "I must have blacked out, and when I came to, I was pinned and my arm was trapped in the wreckage. A piece of sharp metal had cut into my back and I could feel the blood. But the hardest—" She swallowed and coughed, choking on her anguish. "The hardest part was looking up and seeing Chassey. My best friend's body was broken, and her face was turned to me. There was no life in her eyes; all of the energy that made her such a firecracker was gone." She looked up at him, sobbing. *God, after all these years, it's still hard to talk about it.*

"Chassey's head was next to mine for hours, while the firefighters worked to free me from the wreckage." She held his gaze as if he were a lifeline. "It was like she was hugging me…holding me…while the skin on my crushed arm died and I lost all feeling in my fingers and hand. And I talked to her. Trying to get her to talk to me, but she wouldn't. I knew. I knew the truth in my mind, but my heart wouldn't let go."

He reached for her.

She let him pull her into his arms. She wept. Declan was only the third person, besides her parents and her last boyfriend, she'd told. The potency was always there, in the periphery of her life, waiting to catch her. And she still missed Chassey.

He kissed her head and rubbed his hand over her back. "I'm here. I'm not letting you go."

She wiped her face on her sleeve. "Thanks."

"What happened to the other girls?"

"They lived. But I don't think any of us were the same. I left gymnastics, because of my arm. I had to go through a bunch of surgeries. They replaced the bone of my arm and I had a bunch of grafts on it and on my back." She leaned back so she could look at him. "I might not understand exactly what you are going through, but I understand some of it."

"I'm glad you shared that story." His fingers traced the scars on her back. "I like your battle scars. They are part of who you are."

"Thanks," she said. "I never thought of it that way. But I suppose if we live long enough on this planet, only the rare soul is without trauma and pain." She cuddled closer to him. "Are you going to talk about your experience?"

He nodded his head slowly. It was time to let the pain out. He couldn't hide forever. "Though I'm foggy on some of the details. We had planted several charges, ready to blow the place, but we made a mistake. We didn't take into account the type of explosives they had in this…uh, bunker." He sighed. "I'm sorry I can't be more specific…"

"That's okay. I honestly don't want to know the details that aren't relevant to you. Please…continue."

He gestured with his hand. "So we set the explosives and the timers and got out of there. But the enemy was on our heels, and when the explosives detonated, we were thrown. I couldn't make a lot of sense of it after that, but all I was worried about was my Team and getting away from the pain. At the hospital, I was able to check in and find out they were okay, and I had to face the fact that I lost my leg."

Declan was staring at some far-off spot. "Infections meant more meds and additional surgeries, and when I could finally go home, I didn't tell anyone. Of course Gich found out—he always does—and met me at the airport and brought me home."

"I met him. Gich." She waved her hand. "It's a long story, but he walked me home from McP's. He seems like a good soul."

Declan turned his gaze to her. "He is. I've known him for my entire career in the Navy. He's a Sea Daddy to a whole bunch of us."

"Interesting term…"

"Yeah, a combination of mentor, friend, teacher, nemesis, and a few guys add Antichrist into that mix. Gich can be a handful, though he's one of the best men I know. I trust him with my life, and obviously, now with my lady." He winked at her and then there was a long pause.

"You know the story I told you about my accident." She waited for his nod. "I only told that to one other person besides my parents, and that was my last boyfriend. He told me that I was too clingy and emotional, and he dumped me after that. I wouldn't do that to someone. I wouldn't do that to you. I have such strong feelings for you, Declan. As a matter of fact, I think… no, I know that I'm falling in love with you."

He drew her head toward his and he kissed her. "Me too." He placed his forehead on hers.

"Glad to know that I'm not the only one. What should we do now?"

"Get naked."

Maura sighed. Men did not make good patients. There were still bandages that needed to be changed on Declan's leg. According to the paperwork, he was supposed to take the entire dressing off and let his wounds air out. He was being stubborn.

As her hands reached for the edge of the tape, he stopped her. "Don't."

"I have bandages. We can wrap it later."

He sighed. "You read the paperwork on my counter."

"Yep," she admitted.

Putting his hands over his head, he held the edge of the headboard. "Go ahead."

She nodded. Slowly, she pulled back the tape and unwound it. Then she pulled off the first layer of wrapping, and then the second, until she reached the gauzy pads at the bottom. "They're stuck."

He leaned down and ripped them off. Blood oozed out.

Naked, she ran to the bathroom and came back with gauze and first aid wash. Gently, she cleaned the wound, put ointment on the bleeding parts, and then wiped all around the stump. Putting the first aid items aside, she withdrew a small amber bottle and then lifted his leg and propped it on a pillow. Tenderly, she rubbed vitamin E oil onto the healed parts and then started massaging his thigh. Up and down she went, rubbing the healing oil into his skin and muscles and occasionally raining kisses.

He watched her. His breath caught as her bare breasts touched his skin now and then. When she was done, she rubbed the rest of the oil on her breasts and belly and used herself to rub oil into him. It was sensual, and sexy. He reached for her.

She moved out of his grasp, wanting him hard and ready for her when she was done. "Not yet," she murmured as her teeth caught the tender parts of his inner thigh and toyed with him.

Teasing her way upward, she inhaled his essence — so male, so him. The musk was driving her wild and she wanted to keep going, but he lost his patience, pulling her upward and into his arms. He rolled her to his good side, his hands and fingers eager to touch her.

"I'm more than ready," she whispered in his ear as she tormented his earlobe.

He growled and pushed her thighs wide. His fingers assured that she was ready for him. Grabbing a condom from the bedside-table drawer, he pushed it on and was back in position. Kissing her, exploring her mouth with his tongue, he thrust into her.

She moaned into his mouth as he filled her. The pleasure was so intense, she couldn't stop herself from moving against him, needing more…

He filled her fast and furiously, increasing his pace as she kissed him wildly. Her nails dug into his shoulders as her first climax overtook her. Just as swiftly another built, until they were cascading and she could hardly catch her breath.

She broke the kiss, panting as he threw back his head and called her name.

Her final orgasm slammed through her system as her body sought to drink him dry of his seed.

Carefully, he pulled out, placing the condom in a tissue and dropping it in the wastebasket next to the bed. Then he gathered her close.

His voice was rough as he said, "Thank you."

"Always." She knew exactly what he meant. The words were not referring just to the sex; it was the whole experience—the acceptance. Her accepting him made it easier for him, and his accepting her made it easier for her—this was a two-way street. And she could feel the change. Their lovemaking had been more special this time, more intimate than last night. Emotion and openness changed things.

She snuggled her head under his chin and smiled. She loved this man. Wherever things went from here, she'd given from her soul and he'd shared his in return. "Always," she repeated, and in her mind, she said, "I love you, Declan."

Two hours didn't really count as sleep, but neither of them cared. She had taken a shower as he loaded a movie into the DVD player. "What did I miss?"

"Nothing. I paused the movie at the beginning."

"Why?" She laughed. "You could have started it. I would have caught up."

"A movie with battleships *and* aliens. They filmed most of it in Oahu. Love Hawaii." He sighed. "Yeah, I had to wait. This is something that has to be seen in order. There's no rewinding and fast-forwarding." His head tipped down to hers, touching their foreheads. "Besides, you made dinner and I provided the movie. Did I thank you for getting my packages while I was gone? If I had been deployed, I would have stopped it, but when I get called for a mission, I rarely have time to do more than get my gear."

"Sweet man." She laughed. "Yes, you thanked me.

Several times." Maura cleared her throat. "Speaking of mail, Olivia dropped off an envelope."

"Doesn't matter." He waved the notion away.

"It's not a love note, is it?" She hated to ask, but she was unwilling to let the idea take root and fester.

"Maybe in Olivia's mind it is. Her standard attempt to draw me back in is writing a check to Naval Special Warfare or NSW-Kids. That's my soft spot. They help SEAL families quite a bit. Another good cause is the Warrior Foundation too. And when I thank her for her donation or her efforts on the charity's behalf, she ropes me into a meal. Obligation, I suppose." He shook his head. "I've been very forthcoming that I'm not looking for a relationship or anything else from her. But she seems to be stuck on me. I wish she'd get over it."

"Sticky spot to be in."

"Not really. It's clear to me." He hugged her tightly. "Many things have been clarified in my life as of late." He nibbled on her neck and then tickled her playfully. "You are the only woman I want to spend time with."

She laughed and struggled to get out of his grasp. "Stop! Let me go."

"Never." He leaned in and kissed her neck, teasing the tender flesh until she turned toward him and gave him her lips.

"I'm not surrendering."

His eyes held hers. "I wouldn't want you to. Just be exactly who you are."

She laid her lips on his, getting lost in the kiss and the warmth of his arms. The primal urge lay just below the surface, willing and wanting, needing and craving his touch. "We just did it, and we'll miss the movie."

"I'll rewind it." As he lowered her slowly back onto the couch, the remote triggered the movie. Missiles fired as she pulled his shirt over his head. The sounds in the background became more distant as the kisses transported her, them, to somewhere special. It was a place where they were all alone, making love in the peaceful harmony of bare skin, titillating caresses, and breathtaking pleasure.

Chapter 14

MAURA STARED THROUGH THE GLASS DOOR AT HER boyfriend. He was holding vigil in his favorite beat-up chair on the balcony, staring at the ocean. Over the past month, their lovemaking had gone from several times a day to nothing. In her opinion that wasn't optimal, and though she was loath to complain about that fact, she *was* ready to nag him about his complacency. He needed to get out of his groove and leave the apartment.

His Teammates had stopped by to see him, but that didn't seem to change anything. She was so frustrated with him that she wanted to scream. Instead she opened the balcony door and went outside and calmly sat down.

"We need to talk," she said.

"God, I hate those words. Nothing good comes from that phrase. Can't you start the conversation with something else?" Declan took a long pull from his stout—this one was alcoholic.

She stood up, pulled the bottle away from his lips, and dumped the contents onto the sand. "Things have to change. I'm not going to keep making excuses for you. The coordinator of physical therapy services needs you to schedule your appointments, and you need to get the hell out of here and *go to them*."

Sitting down in her chair, she heaved a sigh of relief. "So much for not yelling." She turned her chair toward him. "Listen, I'm not trying to be the bad guy. I support you, and right now you are stuck in limbo. And it needs to change."

"I know."

"You know! Then why don't you do anything?"

He scratched his chin. "Because when you're in limbo, there's no rejection. No answers to the questions that could potentially rip your soul out. The more still I am, the safer it is."

"Seriously?" She could hardly believe her ears.

"Hey! Everyone gets depressed. Haven't I earned that right…to take a little time off from life?" Declan's eyes narrowed and the pulse at his temple throbbed.

"No," she said flatly. "Life is made up of a series of patterns. Once we *choose* to get in a rut, we stay in a rut. In order to avoid that, you have to fill your life with something. Anything. And your focus is to get better. What happens when you stop working out?"

"Your muscles atrophy," he said pointedly.

"Yes, and it will take you twice as long to get that movement back. You told me the other day that you were tired of hearing what handi-abled people cannot do. Well, damn it, show the world what you can do." She stood up. "I'm going to work. I'll be home at seven."

From inside the apartment, she added, "There's stuff I can show you at the gym, if you're willing. I'll leave the car." And then she left. She knew from their conversations that most SEALs trained themselves to use both left and right hands and feet, so they were never caught in the lurch if they should become hurt. Declan had boasted of his skill using alternate limbs. Now was the perfect time to gear up.

—ᴧᴧᴧ—

Declan watched her walk away from him. He didn't like the feeling, and he hated it even more that she'd just bitched him out and kicked his ass. The truth was…she was right. Gich used to say, "If you don't like something, fucking change it!"

And that was precisely what he was going to do. He could prove to Maura and himself that he had the same gumption inside of him that he'd always had.

Grabbing his crutches, he made his way inside. He called the coordinator of physical therapy and scheduled his appointments, and then headed for the bathroom to shower.

As he passed the mirror, he stared at his reflection. Five days of growth had produced a rather full, dark beard. It wasn't pretty. Picking up his razor, he started clearing the scruff from his face. A bigger question loomed as he lifted his arm and got a whiff of his armpits. *Ugh. When did I shower last?*

It was amazing what a shave, shower, and clean clothes—shorts and shirt—did for a person. His place was picked up and he'd eaten a sandwich. The prosthetic he had been fitted with before leaving the hospital was in place. He was healed enough to use it, though didn't want to. There were no more excuses. He was fueled and ready to move. Now he had to apologize to the woman who had had the guts to kick his butt.

He pocketed his wallet and Maura's car keys and headed out to visit the gym. Maybe he'd stop along the way and bring her flowers. Couldn't hurt. They were significantly nicer smelling than he had been.

Declan stood just inside the entrance at the large glass doors and attempted to take in the madness. His eyes adjusted quickly from the bright sunlight to the darker inside, but it was the sight that intrigued him. His eyes widened with delight.

"Miss Max'll. Miss Max'll." Kids flocked to Maura, grabbing at her for hugs and acknowledgment. She was in her element, pulling kids into her arms, laughing with them. Standing there watching her made him feel so proud of her. Maura was doing something special here.

"Did you bring us a new friend?" asked a little boy wearing a harness and brown leather airplane goggles strapped over his eyes. He pointed at Declan and took a few steps toward him.

The prescription of the glass was strong, making his eyes look huge. "I'm Henry."

"Declan." Maura rushed to him.

The kids shouted greetings and attempted to maul him.

"Good manners, boys!" reinforced Maura. "I'm pleased to introduce a new friend to play with. This is Master Chief Declan Swifton. Why don't all of you show Declan your routines?"

"Yay!" they shouted, rushing back into place.

At least three dozen adults helped kids of varying ages and needs climb onto equipment and get hooked into devices. Some children were missing limbs, or hands or feet or ears or eyes, a few children seemed very hyper, but here—in this wonderful place—they were just kids. Perfect in every way they needed to be.

"C'mon!" shouted a little boy, and then he and the others were moving through the most incredibly complex gym circuit Declan had ever seen. It could give the SEALs a run for their athletic prowess.

"What are they doing?" he asked curiously, moving closer and stepping onto the thick mats.

Maura spoke quickly, her excitement evident. "Parkour, a wonderful school of movement. The kids are taking themselves on and over or under obstacles using their bodies and the equipment to propel themselves forward. When I was healing, this is one of the ways I found my strength and my joy in athleticism again."

All the kids wore harnesses and gloves to help them move swiftly. "Amazing!"

"Yeah. It's like flying." She turned to face him. "Want to try it?"

"Heck, yeah!" he said and then stopped. He turned to her. "I need gloves."

She laughed. "I just happen to have a pair in your size in my pocket."

"You knew I'd come."

"Mm-hmm. I cannot imagine a Navy SEAL being beached for long. You have too much spirit in you to give up." She leaned up on her tiptoes and kissed him. "I'm glad you're here."

"Me too." And he truly was. As she led the way toward the mats, Declan knew he had met his match in Maura Maxwell—a woman who could hold her own going toe-to-toe with him—and he was grateful that *she* was in his life.

⸻

Declan slid into the passenger seat of Maura's car, buckled in, and let out a happy sigh. The afternoon had been one of the best in a long time. It'd felt good to have his heart pumping hard and his lungs straining for air. Granted, he was out of shape and had found himself panting in places, but he'd mostly mastered the course after a few tries. The fact that it was geared toward kids helped, and those angels had been right there with him. A couple of them were far faster than he was. He chalked it up to their proficiency on the course. He'd bet he'd catch them next time.

His prosthetic ached, and he longed to pull it off. He could too. Maura wouldn't care.

"What are you thinking about?" She pulled the car onto the main road and headed for the 5.

"I'm thinking about how to get faster. Those kids are speedy."

"Really? Well, if you think you're going to beat Tats and Kyle, I hate to burst your bubble, but they keep getting faster too."

"We'll see." He shifted in the seat, noticing their surroundings. She'd hopped onto the interstate and was pulling off onto the Coronado Bridge, driving them into Coronado proper. "This isn't the way home."

"Nope. I'm hungry, and the best way I know to top the word *fun* is with stopping here." She pulled the car up in front of the gelato shop that was around the corner from McP's Pub.

This was the last place he wanted to be. It made him more uncomfortable than he cared to admit. At least if they went to Danny's, they could eat a decent burger in the intentionally darkened interior. It was easy to be anonymous in there.

"Ready for an icy cold treat?"

No. I'd rather be going inside the pub for a beer than for some sticky sweet concoction. He'd never had a sweet tooth. He was more of a salt guy.

Looking down, he sighed. He'd prefer wearing pants for his first public adventure. Not that these clothes were going to change people's reaction or his reality.

A finger dug sharply into his ribs. "Move it, Swifton. I'm hungry."

He looked at Maura. How could he explain? There was just no getting around it. She had revealed herself and her trials to him. Couldn't he suck it up for a twenty-minute ordeal of ice cream? Hadn't he just dealt with a whole room full of kids? So why should it matter what anyone thought now? He muttered under his breath, "It doesn't."

"What?" she asked, completely oblivious to his internal debate.

"Nothing," he said in a sullen voice. "Let's go. There's no denying a woman her chocolate."

"You've got that right," she said with an overly bright smile.

Dang, is this woman continually chipper or what? It's darn annoying…and pretty admirable too.

He watched her get out of the car, and then he pulled the door handle and hauled himself out. It took a series of small movements, but he was standing, looking at her shapely bottom as she entered the shop.

Slamming the door behind him, he followed her. Maybe they had stout-flavored ice cream.

The door was open, and a small sign that hung from the uppermost point said, "Bring your appetite in, leave your contrition behind." He stepped inside and felt the cool air immediately slap his face and neck. Keeping his pace going, he didn't stop until he was behind Maura. His eyes scanned the room, assessing, making sure there were no threats, as he usually did.

A tug on his shirt had him looking over his shoulder. Nothing was there.

Looking lower, he saw a young girl with an older one trailing behind her. "Mister. Mister."

He turned to face her, unsure what to expect.

"Are you a cyborg?"

A smile tugged at his lips. "No."

"I'm three years old, and she's six."

"What's your name?" he asked. Where were the parents? These kids had to belong to someone.

"I'm Micki and she's Mary Lou." The six-year-old joined the younger girl, who was obviously her sister; their faces were practically identical, as was their shiny, wavy hair. "Can you add sparkles to that?" she asked, gesturing to his prosthetic.

"Sparkles?"

"You know," she said between licks of her ice cream cone. "Fairy dust and wings and pink feathers and… and…maybe some rhinestones to your leg. You need to have lots of diamonds."

"Ah…" He had no idea how to answer. Shock had frozen his brain.

"What's going on?" Maura leaned around his arm, tugging him slightly off balance, but he held his ground. "Hi." She grinned at the girls. "Yum. That looks good! What are you eating?"

"Mango," said the six-year-old. "It's my favorite. Want a lick?"

Declan couldn't hide his smile any longer. "No, thanks. I'm not an ice-cream person."

"Gelato," said the three-year-old as she stamped her foot. "I finished mine already. I think you should add tiny baby dolls and stuffed koalas to that. Feathers would look silly on a boy!"

Kids. They are so pure, and that innocence made everyone smile.

"Michelle. Mary Louise. What are you up to?" said a gruff voice from the other side of him.

Coming around them and stepping behind the two girls appeared Rear Admiral Richard King with his wife, Carly. "Swifton, good to see you." His arm shot out over the heads of the two girls, and the two men shook hands briefly.

"Rear Admiral King, I'd like to present Maura Maxwell." Here he was in public, with no choice but to deal with the situation. King was a hero in the Teams, a veteran of World War II and a member of the Scouts and Raiders, which were predecessors to SDV (Swimmer Delivery Vehicle), UDT (Underwater Demolition Team), and SEAL Team itself. Listening to the legend talk was like being transported back in time and dropped in the middle of the fight. So many life lessons…and a lot of generosity with that wisdom.

"Richard, please." The Rear Admiral wrangled the girls, wrapping a large hand around each of their small ones.

"Yes, sir."

"Nice to meet you, Richard," said Maura as she stepped up to stand beside Declan. "I think I've met your wife, Carly. She came in last week looking at programs for…these little ladies, I believe."

"Great-Grandpa, I want more," said the three-year-old, tugging on his hand.

"You've had two flavors and that's the limit, right, Declan?" said the Rear Admiral.

"Yes." Declan nodded in automatic agreement. "Though…I haven't had my flavors. Maybe they could split them."

"Yes! Yes!" shouted the girls as the Rear Admiral rolled his eyes.

"Come on then. Let's get in line. Swifton here is going to help you girls pick them."

———

The drive home was pleasant. Declan found it strange to still be smiling, but looking in the side-view mirror confirmed it. He laughed. He'd survived Maura's version of fun and walked around in public without having anyone criticize or ostracize him. Hell, even if they did, those jerks would be assholes. What were people with challenges supposed to do, live in a hole and only come out at night?

Awareness hit him. *Shit! Is that what I was avoiding?*

Hell, no, he was made of tougher stuff. Anyone who had survived spec-ops training knew worse. Sitting in your own excrement for four days topped the list. Way ahead of a fear of being seen in public. But the mirror showed the truth again. He was different now; his body felt foreign to him and he hadn't figured it out. He *was* nervous about going out without knowing how to handle himself. So he'd keep pushing himself until he could overcome that.

As they drove past the Amphibious Base, he knew

that all the crap in his mind was just a distraction. His real fear was not being able to be an active-duty SEAL anymore.

Looking down at his leg, he knew he'd be benched, and given the military's current policy of Reduction in Force, he would most likely get a medical separation from the SEALs or, rather, be retired with an honorable and/or medical discharge.

Bam! His hand slammed down on the door rest. He did *not* want to be RIFed, dammit!

"Hey, take it easy on the upholstery. I know it's pleather, but I'm fond of it just the same." She was teasing him.

Shit! I don't want someone to lift my spirits. I need a job. My job!

Maura pulled the car over to the side of the road and touched his shoulder lightly. "Declan…talk to me."

He looked at her. It was hard to hide the tears in his eyes. "I don't want to stop being a SEAL. This is it. This is all I ever wanted for my life."

"Then fight for it!"

"How?" He needed a path. "You make it sound so simple."

"I never said battling for anything would be easy. But you need to decide what you want and go for it with all of the gusto you previously had." Maura's eyes held such an earnest emotion, she obviously believed her words wholeheartedly.

He shook his head, but nothing could shake off his emotion or frustration. "Who am I without the Teams?"

"I don't know." She tilted her head to the side. "Isn't it a good time to find out?" She pulled the car back into traffic, and they were soon speeding down the Silver Strand.

She was right. Desire—true want—for something pure and real could take an individual to his or her goal. He'd seen it happen, and he'd done it when he joined the Navy, zipped through Boot Camp, and survived BUD/S training.

His hand stroked along the top of his leg and then touched the top of the prosthetic. *I'm still me. Right?* He realized that the biggest reason he hadn't engaged in contact with others had more to do with how other people's viewpoints challenged his own. He'd been reluctant to face his inner demon—*he* was the hurdle—and this giant frustration had to go before he could achieve anything, let alone happiness.

Chapter 15

DECLAN ROSE WITH A RENEWED HOPE. TODAY WOULD be different than the endless weeks he'd spent sitting in his apartment. This morning he was joining the physical therapy course, and he was oddly jazzed about it.

He grabbed his wallet and keys and hightailed it out of the apartment before Maura woke up. Needing to do this his way, he'd planned the whole morning without her. Though he appreciated her help and the way she lovingly cared for him, he had to face this battle on his own.

The ride to Rehab Center was quick. Interstate 5 was barely buzzing with traffic yet.

Pulling up in front of the center, he was surprised to see the place lit up and alive with activity. Several men in wheelchairs with service dogs were sitting outside. It looked like they were waiting for rides.

Declan got out and strode through the automatic double doors. His senses were assaulted by the bustle. Nurses, docs, men, women, animals—this place was hopping, and as he checked in, he decided he liked the vibe. The place smelled clean and he could see through to a large gym where individuals rehabbed on pieces of equipment.

It would have been so easy to go down the negative route as he stood here people watching. Instead he preferred to concentrate on hope and the ability to move on with his life.

"Swifton," said a man about Declan's size with a Marine Corps tattoo on his bicep. "This way. You're active duty?"

"Yes, and I'd like to stay that way." Declan stood and followed him through the maze of hallways to a consultation room. "Retired?"

"Yes. It's better than I thought it would be." As the Marine closed the door, Declan sat down at the chair next to a desk. "I'm Joe Logen. You can call me Joe. I have your records. Seems like you were reluctant to begin treatment. Can you explain why?" The Marine put down the manila folder with Declan's name on it.

There was nothing Declan hated more than having to give a reason. Still, this wasn't his program. He knew he had to play by their rules for a time, because there was stuff he sought to learn. "I had aspects of my home life to deal with."

"Is that handled?"

"Yes."

The Marine stared at him as if he was judging Declan against some invisible ruler. "You'll be expected to make all of your appointments, barring medical emergency, and in that case, your doctor will contact us directly. If you skip, we'll take that to mean you don't want to be here. Understood?"

Declan nodded. Those eyes were holding tough, and Declan resisted the urge to smile. That was the way Marines were, tough sons-a-bitches! And they knew it. Not that a SEAL wouldn't enjoy challenging him.

"We'll get you started. I'm going to make a list of exercises today. Ask me any questions you have while you're doing them. You will need to make progress to

stay in your slot. We have a long waiting list. Active
duty always jumps to the front, but that doesn't mean
you deserve it more than our retired or former military,"
said Logen. "We'll start with a tour and then you can
start sweating your balls off."

————

Damn, that Marine wasn't kidding! His body hadn't
ached this much since Hell Week at BUD/S.

Visions of sitting around for weeks on end recovering
from surgeries and drinking beer flashed across Declan's
internal View-Master, and he had to acknowledge that
he had a major hand in his current situation. It was going
to be a long slog to complete this program.

"Hold it, Squid," said Logen, teasing the SEAL.
They'd developed a decent camaraderie back at the
pull-up bar when the two of them had competed for the
highest score.

"I was just finding my rhythm, ya Jarhead," Declan
joked back.

"Listen, we're over our time, about a half an hour late.
Declan, you did significantly better than I thought. Good
work. I'll see you in two days. Remember to hydrate and
stay away from beer," Joe tagged on as he grinned.

"Crap! You could have said chocolate."

"Yeah, that too." Joe leaned down and added, "At
least I didn't take away the bedroom activities."

"Dude, my girlfriend would have been all over you
for that." Declan laughed. His Maura would have had a
fit. She was pretty feisty and frisky. Who was he kidding? So was he.

"There are tubs in the back of the locker room. Just

ask Gerry to walk you through the use. I'd like you to soak for thirty minutes, and then Jesse will be back there to work on your muscles and show you additional exercise before Dr. Howard checks the fit on your prosthetic." Logen stood up. "Are you going to move, or should I decorate you and use you as a wallflower?"

"I prefer to look like a daisy. It shows off my sunny personality," quipped Declan as he slowly moved his aching legs toward the tub. A hot soak sounded blissful.

"Wiseass." Logen shook his head.

Declan clenched his teeth as he lowered his body into the tub. His forearms and biceps strained. The water was blessedly hot, and the combination of minerals Gerry added to it made it feel like it was eating the end of the tender flesh on his leg, in a pleasant way. When his ass finally hit the bottom of the metal container, he sighed. Exhaustion hit him as he closed his eyes and sleep sucked him under.

He was running, willing his body to go faster. His Teammates were just ahead, turning to him, gesturing for him to hurry up.

The ground shook beneath him like the world had been toppled to its side. At the same time, heat seared the back of his clothes.

He was suddenly tossed into the air like a rag doll, but not before the lower part of his leg was ripped off. He could feel the ripping of his flesh and the rending of the muscle and bones.

It had been impossible not to look down and see his calf and foot left there behind, still in his boot. Who knew where it was now? He'd come home…and the foot hadn't…

The image of the torn and bloody flesh lying on the ground, abandoned, jarred him awake. His hands grabbed the side of the tub, and Declan knew he must have made a noise.

"Daymare?" asked the guy in the tub next to him.

Declan rubbed his hands over his face. "Yeah."

"I still have them too. I'm LT Ford Woollens." The man proffered his hand.

Extending his own hand, Declan clasped the other man's and shook. "Declan Swifton, Master Chief."

"Ah, a Navy man. Good. Me too. I've had enough Seaman jokes from here to last me a lifetime. How did you, ah, lose it?" Woollens pointed to his leg. "I'm EOD. Stepped on a fucking IED after dismantling a clusterfuck in the middle of a road."

"On an Op," Declan shared, though he still wasn't comfortable talking about it. "Shit happens."

"Yeah," said Woollens. "They tell us the shit will change, but you never fucking get over it. If you're lucky, you find a way to make peace with it and get on with your life. If you don't, you're a walking dead man just waiting around to die. I wouldn't dishonor my friends that way, or myself. I lost three people from my squad that day. The whole fucking car blew up, because I stepped wrong. The survivor's guilt is worse than anything."

Gerry came in. "Sorry to interrupt. Your wife and Dr. Howard are ready for you. Are you going streakers today or can we wrap a towel?"

Woollens gave Declan a big smile. "Let it all hang out."

With large arms extended, Gerry hauled Woollens out of the tub. Declan's eyes went wide. The LT was missing two legs, an arm, and there was chunk out of his side. One ball was gone and it looked like several surgeries had been in that area.

"Hey," said Declan as Gerry and Woollens went by. "Thanks for the talk. See you around. Okay?"

"Sure. My friends call me Woolly."

"Mine call me Dec."

"See you." Woolly left, jabbering away to Gerry as he was carried into the other room.

Declan looked at his body. He knew he was damn lucky. Seeing the struggles of the warriors around him, he knew this place was invaluable. It not only helped soldiers and sailors in some cases literally get back on their feet, but it gave them hope. Every one of them probably had the same dark room they'd hidden in, imagining their dreams fading away. No one should stay in that hell. If they did, then the enemy won. It was up to each of them to keep moving and recapture their lives.

Hauling his body over the side of the tub, Declan found his balance and reached for a towel. As he towel-dried, he vowed to stay strong. He'd get back to active duty and/or active duty ready so that he was in optimal shape to live his life.

Grabbing his crutch, he made his way to the PT room. He could handle whatever the program threw at him. Life was going to be on his terms, instead of the other way around.

———～～———

Later that afternoon, Declan was physically spent but ready for some serious R & R. He'd passed out for two hours after his morning appointment, but there had been no daymares. He was grateful for the radio silence, and now he was prepared to commune with nature.

As he made his way to the balcony door, his cell phone rang. He grabbed it and listened, the pleasant expression fading from his face. When he'd finally put the phone down, his emotions were raw and his face was wet with grief.

He felt even more determined to get outside. Strapping the crutch to his back, he maneuvered his body over the railing. His prosthetic leg was sitting on the coffee table like a work of art. He supposed in many ways it was. It'd taken him a while to get used to it. Still felt strange sometimes, but he liked being able to walk again, with the promise of running in the future. He'd love to feel miles of wet sand passing under him again.

Using his body's agility, his left leg, and his arms, he scaled down the rock wall outside his apartment balcony, reaching the sandy ground quickly. He didn't need the limb for what he wanted to do.

Steadying himself on one leg, he grabbed his crutch off his back and set off, making his way down to the ocean water. The sand was not the most stable terrain, but he was making it work. He didn't care how graceful he looked; stumbling was part of surviving, and he didn't care if he had to do a few face-plants to get to his goal.

Settling in the sand a few feet from the receding waves, he watched them lap at the shore. Closing his eyes, he breathed in and out slowly.

"Thinking about you, kid." He shook his head. He'd wanted to pound something, work out, swim, anything to get the emotion out of him, yet he knew…breathing

in and out…feeling the salty sweet air on his tongue…
this was the best way he knew to honor him.

Lying down on his back in the sand, he looked up at
the sky. Clear blue. No clouds. As if someone took the
color and made it so bright that it needed nothing else
but to be admired.

The sun beat down on his eyes, making them water;
at least he could say it was that, but it wasn't true. He
was sorry to have heard the sad news from Kellogg
Lesterman's father. His son had died of pneumonia,
among several other internal complications. "Kellogg
appreciated your talks. The time you took with him… It
was real special. Thank you." When Kellogg's mother
had gotten on the line, it was all Declan had been able
to do to hold it together. He'd felt the tears flowing and
didn't even try to make them stop.

He couldn't stay inside right now. He needed to be
out in the elements. For Kellogg. For himself.

As he lay on the beach, he couldn't help but wonder
why it hurt so much to know that Kellogg died. Maybe
it was because the kid was so young. He hadn't really
experienced anything mind-blowingly exciting, except
war. That had its own trials.

What about happiness? Making love to a woman
who wants nothing more than you…your touch…your
words…and your presence?

There was just no fucking rhyme or reason to why
death happened. The terrorists and selfish abusers
should have been the first to go, but the crappiest people
stuck around, while the innocents were taken so quickly.
It didn't make a whole lot of sense.

"Tears are just pain leaving the body," Gich would

say. "Let out the rawness and make something new of the energy."

A shadow crossed his face. Was that a giant bird? Declan looked up.

"Is this a private sunbath or can anyone join?" Maura asked. Her toes played with the sand beneath her feet. She looked adorable and the smile on her face was a welcome distraction.

He didn't want to talk. He didn't want to see anyone right now. But there was something special about Maura's presence, as if he could be alone and with her at the same time.

"I'm going for a swim."

"Cool. I'll join you." She took off her sundress, revealing a lovely, bright bikini underneath.

He swallowed down the comment he wanted to make about her frighteningly gorgeous body under a tough-girl exterior. Instead, he made his way to the water. When he was knee-deep, he didn't know what to do.

"Can you dive in from here?"

He nodded.

She held out her hand for the crutch. Then she jogged back to the stone wall beneath their apartments and stashed her dress and the crutch together. It was impossible not to stare at her running back toward him. She radiated strength and beauty.

Splashing past him, she dove into the oncoming waves. Her body made a perfect arc.

He didn't think twice, just dove in after her. His body felt at home in the water, though it took a few starts and stops to get a rhythm that worked. He could do a decent sidestroke and breaststroke, two strokes he used a lot as a SEAL. When he had a handle on things, he looked around to find Maura watching him. Her smile said she appreciated seeing him in his element. When she laughed outright, he said, "What?"

"Nothing." She treaded water as though she were born to it. "Just wondering how it feels."

"How did it feel for you doing gymnastics again, after your accident?"

"Awkward."

"Agreed."

"And good," she added.

"Also agreed."

"I knew it." She splashed him and then spit water in his direction. "When I did parkour movements and gymnastic routines, I found my balance again, like this is how my body is supposed to move. In gymnastics, I forced my body to handle certain positions, and with the parkour, I used the movements my body has to propel forward. It helped me find myself and love the gym again."

He splashed her back. "I love the water. One of the reasons I wanted to be a SEAL. Being here makes me feel alive."

She swam closer to him. "Did you think you lost this?"

He floated onto his back. "Maybe. I believe I felt like I was losing myself. That without my leg I wasn't a whole person, and that I could never be that again. But here I am. I'm me. It's reassuring to know that."

~~~

Ah, blessed sex! Back at the apartment, salt water washed off their skin, she could hardly wait to make love. It was easily the happiest part of the day.

"Oof!" she exclaimed as the air whooshed out of her body. "Shift over."

Declan's body was so large, it pushed her body into the bed and denied her air. He moved slightly to the right to take the pressure off.

They kissed and played for a while, until need took over. He pulled on a condom. In the middle of lovemaking, something changed. She could feel the shift in him, as if a big wall slammed down between them. She sought his gaze.

The look in his eyes was distant.

"Declan," she said softly, but his eyes didn't connect with her.

Instead it felt mechanical as his finger brushed over the tips of her nipples and then swept over her belly.

His face buried into the side of her neck as his fingers probed, making sure she was wet for him. She was. For him, she was always ready. But it didn't change the fact there was a disconnection in the moment.

"Declan," she said more forcefully. Her fingers trailed along his back in an attempt to soothe him and bring him back to her.

There was no response. It was as if he wasn't even there.

He entered her in one movement, and the sheer size of him made her catch her breath.

Her nails dug into his skin and he stilled for several seconds. "Declan," she whispered.

He moaned. "Maura. I need…you."

She hugged him close, whispering in his ear. "I'm here. Stay with me."

As her grip loosened and her body adjusted, he began to move. Slowly. Erotically. And she moaned softly in his ear. "Yes. That's it."

"My Maura. Beautiful, sweet Maura."

"My Declan."

He stilled. His whole body tensed as if he were seeing something else. Someone else.

All at once, his manner changed, and their lovemaking turned hard and aggressive. His head was positioned over hers, but his eyes were looking past her and seeing something else.

She grabbed his shoulders. "Declan, wait."

He kept going and she felt herself fighting him. Pain pushed through her senses.

"Declan!" she yelled, cupping his cheeks with both of her hands.

His eyes moved down to her, and his actions stilled. "Maura?" His eyes focused on her. He seemed confused. "What…"

"Declan, where were you?"

He looked past her, his whole body tense. "I…I don't know."

"No, look at me."

His gaze refocused on her again. He cleared his throat. "I'm here. Sorry. Memories of the Op. Today. The rehab. Kellogg dying. It all slammed into my brain at once in the middle of the peacefulness and pleasure I find with you. I didn't mean to…the frustration and pain…the world just blotted out for a minute."

"It's okay." She moved her hands to his shoulders. Well, sort of okay. Truly it scared her. But she didn't want her fear to be the issue of the conversation. She needed Declan to focus on himself and work through the experience. "What can I do to help?"

He shook his head. "I don't know." He rolled off of

her and onto his back. "Maybe we should stop." He put his arm over his eyes.

She pulled it away. "No. No more hiding and allowing other stuff to take away *our* celebration of life. Tell me what's going on." Looking at him, she saw him as he must have been as a little boy—vulnerable and sweet and so very fragile—and then a shadow fell over his eyes that had nothing to do with innocence.

Climbing on top of him, she forced him to face her. "I'm not moving until you talk to me, so spill it."

He nodded his head. "Fine."

"Don't give me that acronym. I have brothers. I know it means freaked-out, insecure, neurotic, and emotional. Tell me what's happening."

His chest lifted her as he took several deep, long breaths. Finally he spoke. "I've been remembering more about the Op. What happened and the exact moment I lost my leg. So much went wrong so quickly. It's hard to pinpoint the exact moment the events became irreversible, and yet I see the explosion over and over again in my brain, mainly in daymares. The pain... Physically, I knew it was there, but mentally...I had a hard time with it. When I compare that moment to the life Kellogg was leading, I feel like an asshole. I have more of everything...agility, opportunity, health, and you... I'm lucky, Maura. It's just hard to get my brain to understand it."

Tears sped down his cheeks. His eyes held hers. He wiped his face on the side of the pillowcase. "My legs have always been tools, something useful to help me get to where I was going. I've abused the crap out of my body for over twenty years, and my body took it. Now what?"

She waited for him to finish the thought. When he didn't, she prodded him. "Now…you're mourning."

"I'm what?" He looked annoyed and somewhat baffled. "That doesn't make any sense."

"Sure it does." She propped herself up on her elbows. "It's the five stages of grief—check out the Kübler-Ross version—denial, anger, bargaining, depression, and acceptance. Everything is clear, if you consider that you were in the accident and felt the denial at the hospital and now you're angry. I can certainly attest to that emotion."

He looked away and then caught her gaze again. "I'm sorry."

She leaned down and kissed him on the lips. "I know." She kissed him again. This time, she lingered, teasing him, bringing him back to her. "Do you want to keep talking?"

"No," he admitted. "I have a lot of food for thought. Later is better than sooner."

She laughed. "Good to know that I haven't lost my charm."

"Never," he said, placing his hands on his hips. "And since you're lying on top of me, why don't we…"

She moved back, positioning herself over him. "My thoughts exactly." Her hips lowered down until he was deep inside of her. "Keep your eyes on me, SEAL man."

His hands gathered the wealth of her breasts. "Yes, ma'am." His thumb stroked tenderly over her nipple.

She sighed as waves of pleasure rolled over her. Though she was tempted to close her eyes and give in to the electricity building in her body, she kept her eyes locked to his. Those steely, very male eyes, so unfathomable a short time ago, had glints of desire, letting her know his participation was one hundred percent.

Her body grew warmer, slick with sweat, and begged for more as she tried to hold back. His agitation beneath her was a heady drug indeed.

Increasing her pace, she felt an orgasm building inside of her. The electric play inside of her womb was so intense that she felt herself cry out as her body flew over the chasm and climbed once more to new heights.

"Maura." His voice was strained. His body was wet with the same perspiration now as drops merged together where they connected.

"Declan," she moaned.

His breath was coming out in short gasps. His hands ran up and down the sides of her body, urging her, his hard gaze alive with pleasure and holding her own captive.

"One more second…" Holding there, on the precipice of the climax, she felt a wash of power and something so thrilling. She plunged headfirst down the cliff, feeling the waves of climactic release, drinking him clean of all energy and release.

"Maura." He sighed. Relief was written clearly on his face. "I'm sorry I was distant."

Collapsing on top of him, she snuggled her head under his chin and felt his arms encircle her. "I understand. It's just…when we're making love, I need to know you're here."

"Yes." His voice was low and deep as he murmured his agreement. "You have my full permission to call me on my shit. I like that you have the guts to speak up and respect me as you're doing it."

"You're my hero," she said.

His body stiffened. "I'm no one's hero. I'm just a man who's doing the best he can, and who loves this woman."

She lifted her head. "I love you, Declan." She kissed him. It was the first time they'd spoken the words aloud, and she was so overwhelmed by the emotion that tears filled her eyes.

His fingers brushed away her tears. "Hey, no crying. This is supposed to be a happy moment."

"It is." She laughed. She hugged him and then kissed him again. "I'm very happy. I love you."

His hand settled at the nape of her neck. "I love you too, Maura." He drew her head down and kissed her.

She returned the kiss with every ounce of joy in her heart. This had to be the greatest moment of her entire life.

Chapter 16

SIX WEEKS HAD PASSED, AND DECLAN WAS HEALING IN record time. As his body gained strength, though, his damaged leg hurt like the bone was being stabbed with needles every time he put weight on it. He had to do something about it.

Visiting any doctor for an injury was at the top of his least-favorite-items list. He actually loathed it. As he pushed open the door, he was surprised to see the room was filled to capacity. Active-duty guys—their youth giving them away—who had lost limbs were everywhere. A few wives were scattered around, but it was mostly servicemen.

The room's sand interior was meant to be soothing and warm, with its earth-colored chairs and array of brightly colored magazines, but it didn't lower the tension of the patients in the room. The emotions could be cut with a knife and carved into a pretty swan. Everyone was itching to scram, and yet none of them would be here without the docs.

"Swifton," called the nurse at the desk. "Dr. Ekkert is ready for you."

Declan stood. He wobbled momentarily, making him grateful that Maura was home. She tended to make little noises or try to grab him. Truthfully, most men would rather fall on their faces than be fussed over constantly.

Making his way slowly to the open door, he nodded

at the receptionist and followed the nurse to an examination room. She didn't say anything, no chitchat or small talk, just pointed and then closed the door behind her.

Surprisingly, it was only about five minutes before the doc came in, a grin on his face, and asked, "So, how's it going, Master Chief?"

Declan nodded his head. "Fine." He smiled at the memory of Maura knowing that particular piece of Navyspeak. FINE: fucked-up/freaked out, insecure, neurotic, and emotional.

"Any fevers or chills?" The doc listened to his heart and took his temperature and blood pressure. "No? Okay. Let's look at your leg."

Declan pulled up his pants leg, removed the prosthetic limb, and waited while the doctor poked and prodded him. *I'd rather get waterboarded.*

The doctor made a few noises as he looked at his leg. "I'm not thrilled with the look of this. You have an ulcer from an ill-fitting prosthetic, though it's possible there is not enough muscle coverage at the end of the bone." He let go of Declan's stump and looked him in the eye. "Typically, skin breakdown and pain are the symptoms. But my guess is that even if you felt it, you wouldn't say anything."

Declan nodded his head.

"Treatment could be as extensive as revising the whole stump—cutting more bone off so there is more muscle coverage—or getting a better prosthesis." The doctor pulled out a device that helped him measure Declan's stump. "Yeah, I don't like how this is fitting. It's not unusual to have to replace a prosthetic several times…"

Dr. Ekkert grabbed his leg hard and squeezed, making

Declan grimace in pain. "Just as I thought. I knew there was a HO."

Trying to recover from the surprise attack, it took Declan a few moments to get his question out. "Can you explain the, uh, HO?"

The doc was scribbling madly on Declan's chart. He paused and studied Declan. "A heterotopic ossification, or HO, can usually be prevented by taking medication, but sometimes a muscle will be traumatized by an abnormal bone formation. When it sticks out, it's painful and obvious as it rubs against the skin, wearing down the layers. If we let this go, it will be so hard, it'll feel like a bone is growing from your leg."

He tapped his pen against the chart. "Recently, I had a guy who had an incision from chest to pubis and then developed HO under the whole thing. Had to cut it all out because he could not sit up. Felt like a turtle shell."

"Nice, doc," said Declan, not really interested in hearing about anyone else's pain. "So what do we do to fix this? Take a pill?"

"Well, we could try that route, but we'd probably be denying the inevitable, which is that if we take an inch and a half from the bottom and rewrap it with muscle, you'll get a sounder cushion and at the same time, we can remove the HO. It would solve the issue faster."

"Will I be able to run and bike?"

"Like it is now…no. But with the surgery, there is a higher likelihood." He went to the computer and typed in a code, then brought up a calendar. "Our surgical unit has an opening in three weeks. You'll have to recover and do physical therapy again, but that should fix the issue permanently." Dr. Ekkert looked over his shoulder.

"I'd take it, even if you decide to cancel at some future point. There isn't another appointment for eight months, and you really shouldn't wait that long."

"Sold." Declan ran his fingers through his hair, scrubbing his scalp. His stomach gave a roll of discomfort, but he didn't care. Ekkert really knew his business. The thought of recovering again sucked, but if it meant he was no longer in pain and he could possibly be more active in the future, he owed it to himself to do it.

"You'll be hearing from my assistant about necessary blood work for surgery in three weeks. In the meantime, watch those sores." Dr. Ekkert didn't even look up. As Declan pulled on his prosthetic, the doctor typed in the necessary info, gave him a prescription and an appointment-reminder card, and sent him out the door with a nod. Not the most fun he'd ever had at a doctor's office, but not the worst either.

Pulling out his phone, he set a reminder. Then he texted Maura: "One stop done."

The next stop was the base. He slid his ID in front of the scanner, entered the Team FIVE Quarterdeck, and then keyed a code into the dial box to unlock another door. He thought about what he was going to say to the XO and CO of Team FIVE. The talking points were blazed into his brain, and he hoped he'd have a chance to say his piece before they gave him a parting speech.

When he reached the door of the CO's office, it was closed and he could hear voices raised in a heated discussion. That wasn't a good sign as far as he was concerned. Taking a seat, he looked next to him at a Seaman who looked so new to the Teams that he practically had "fresh from the box" stamped on his forehead.

"Master Chief," acknowledged Seaman Albert, his last name stitched on a patch across his chest.

"Seaman," replied Declan, sitting down across from him. "What brings you here?"

"My younger brother rolled from my BUD/S class due to medical. I'm sort of losing my footing without him."

Declan turned his head to the side, studying the Seaman. "Why?"

"Don't know," said Seaman Albert, looking at his feet.

"Helluva cop-out, Albert. What's really going on? You obviously have the strength to have made it through BUD/S on your own and with your class."

"Yes," said the Seaman, looking up. "I just…just can't…"

"Can't what?"

"Having my brother by my side made me feel stronger, as if I could conquer everything, and now I just keep messing up. I didn't store my gear correctly, and another SEAL got hurt tripping over it. I screwed up at the gun range, and I've been shooting since I was ten years old." Seaman Albert's face was splotched with red and freckles.

"How did it make you feel?"

"Like a fool! That's not me, but I can't seem to get over that my brother's not here, and when he calls me, he bitches me out for making it through when he's stuck in the hospital with a broken femur."

A light went on in Declan's head. "I see. So when you don't hear from him…"

"I'm fine." Seaman Albert started to catch on. "When

I talk to him, I fuck up. Pardon me the, uh, swearing, Master Chief."

Nodding his head, Declan said, "No problem. You know that you've got a whole community of brothers now, right?"

"Uh, I guess I never thought of it that way." Seaman Albert looked at the door. "Damn, I don't want to get kicked out."

"Me neither," mumbled Declan.

"What did you say?" asked Seaman Albert, standing on his feet and looking at the closed door like a man on a mission.

"Uh...what are you going to do about it? More importantly, why did you want to become a SEAL? Start with that," Declan advised.

"Yes, Master Chief. Thank you, Master Chief," said Seaman Albert as he walked boldly up to the door and knocked on it.

The XO opened it and nodded at Declan. "Be with you shortly, Swifton. Seaman Albert, come on in. We were just talking about you."

As the door closed, clapping sounded in the hall. The Commanding Officer of BUD/S, Commander Martin Parks, came around the corner.

Declan stood and shook hands. "Parks, it's been a long time."

"Sure has. Nice chat with that Seaman. Let's step into the conference room a minute." The Commander gestured with his hand.

They entered the room and sat down in chairs along the side.

"You were pretty good with him," Parks began.

"Just some psychobabble I learned a while back. I think it's called the velvet steamroller. Comes in handy." Declan was curious why Parks wanted to chat.

"You're two courses short of completing your coursework for your bachelor's degree in counseling. How long would it take you to go on and get your master's?" Park's question was a leading one that could move them back into talking about the Teams or have Declan jumping into civilian life. The choice of direction was a no-brainer.

Declan recognized it and nodded his head. "I plan on finishing it up next spring. I could start the postgrad work the following semester."

"You have a lot of self-motivation." The statement didn't need a response. "I heard about the last Op. You know how news travels." Commander Parks rubbed his chin. "I came here today specially to ask the CO about you. What's going to happen to you medically, etc. You know that Diego is retiring in four months, and there is no one at your level that isn't already slotted in, so I'd like you to fill his shoes. He oversaw Third Phase. A new part of the duty is an additional program. You'd coordinate with a couple of retired frogmen who work in conjunction with a few headshrinkers and career-placement counselors, helping the tadpoles who ring out move back into the regular Navy. In a pinch, you might oversee the changeover of instructors for Conditioning/First Phase and Underwater Combat Skills/Second Phase responsibilities too. Pick up any extra slack. You know how it is."

Declan knew very well how it was. He'd done his stretch at BUD/S before, but only as an instructor. Now he was being asked to be a coordinator of not one, but two programs: Third Phase of Land Warfare Training and the Transition-Out Program. He laughed silently.

"What?" asked Parks, with a curious expression on his face.

Declan couldn't resist saying what was on his mind. "Damn, you want me to be a Gich."

"Christ, there's only one of those. Thank God." He laughed, a bass-sounding chuckle. "But yeah. Pretty much."

"If it means I can stay in the Teams, well, hell yes, I'm game."

Commander Parks stood. "Good to hear. It's damn hard to train people to do what comes naturally. Other branches keep trying to stick their folks in here, and none of them get it. SEALs need SEALs to train them; we're just different. Let's go talk to your CO and get this moving."

Declan stood. As he started for the door, he paused. "My CO put you up to this, didn't he?"

Parks didn't speak for a few seconds. That was as much a confirmation as an actual reply. "He wouldn't have recommended you if you weren't perfect for this position. I, of course, completely agree."

"That's pretty flattering," said Declan, feeling the emotion well inside of him. He thought of all the platoons of men that make up a Team and knew others who were in his boat, having lost arms and legs, eyes and ears, or had all sorts of injuries, and he felt damn lucky for an opportunity like this. Whatever it took from his end, and he had a strong notion of what that would be, he would move heaven and earth to make it happen.

Declan had had a full day. The doctor, the Commander of BUD/S, and then the meeting with his CO. It was full of highs and lows and a lot to take in.

Sitting on a sand dune overlooking Gator Beach was the ideal spot for Declan to contemplate his next step. The surf was good and a few SEALs were taking advantage of the afternoon waves and some extra downtime.

The stressors that had been bouncing around his body since he lost his leg were gone. According to his meeting with the CO, the odds were good that he would be rolling into a new assignment in a couple of months. It depended on his medical fitness and readiness. He knew he could make that happen.

Being in the Teams for over twenty-one years, most of his adult life, had taught him a lot about combat, for sure. But the main thing it had taught was courage and compassion and how to honor himself and his Teammates. He was the man that he wanted to be. It was hard to explain to outsiders what being in the military did for his life and how he was going to take that experience with him everywhere he went.

Looking up at the sky, he knew that Maura would be making her way to the balcony soon, waiting to watch the sunset. He liked that romantic part of her that loved nature.

He stood a little uneasily on the sand and took a step. The next thing he knew, he was sliding down the bank very ungracefully. He laughed, knowing it was easier to laugh at himself than to hear it from anyone else. "Well," he said to the empty sand, "guess I had better get that new prosthetic handled before I fall on my face in front of the tadpoles."

Then he pulled off the leg, dumped the sand out of

the cup, and put it back on. He made it the twenty feet to Maura's car, opened the door, and sat down. His phone beeped again, and he checked it. Maura wondered where he was. She was hungry.

Looking at his own midsection, he knew he needed to watch his intake. Since he was planning on teaching at BUD/S, he wanted to set an example, and that meant taking off the ten or so pounds he had put on while he was contemplating his life, or rather scratching his navel.

His mind flooded with possibilities of how he could put his plan into action, and he knew exactly where he wanted to begin the workout. It all involved a place called Froggy Squats and a certain lady who made him want to push himself to be his very best.

Chapter 17

MAURA WAS AS EXCITED AS A KID WITH A STRAIGHT-A report card. Declan was on his way home, and she had so much to share with him. Her only concern was that he hadn't said anything about his appointment with the doctor or the meeting with his CO when she'd talked to him on the phone.

She wanted to put him at ease and didn't know whether she should greet him at the door wearing a negligee or stay in her blue jeans and T-shirt. Was it appropriate that her shirt said, "Split much? Mine is better than yours."

Rummaging around in her dresser drawer, she found fifty shirts with gymnastics sayings on them. Pulling out a sleeveless camisole with lace around the neckline was definitely the best option.

Dashing to the bathroom, she brushed her hair and added a few dabs of her colored lip balm to give her a little sparkle. The thought of going all girly made her laugh out loud. She liked that her someone special was thinking of her as a woman and not a tomboy in grown-up clothes.

In the kitchen, she surveyed her options. Choosing two wineglasses, two plates, forks, and knives as well as spring water and red wine, she filled a tray and headed out onto the balcony for their dinner outside. She was excited to hear his news.

Thinking about her own, she ran back into the apartment and pulled out a thick envelope. Inside was the signed contract turning Froggy Squats officially over to her. All those years of earning purses for her gymnastic events and it had turned into this…she was the owner of a gym.

Pouring herself a glass of wine, she took several sips of the "two-buck chuck," trying to steel her nerves for some actual relaxation, but those worries sat there like a blazing sun. And though the actual sun would eventually sink and give the watchers a show, she knew her concerns would keep pecking at her happiness.

—⁓—

Maura was startled awake by a hand on her shoulder. "What?"

Her handsome beau was smiling down at her. "Are you ready for dinner? Or would you rather call it a night?"

"Dinner please. And I want to hear about your day."

"Okay." He put the bag of food on the table and sat down on the chair on the other side.

Opening the bag, she withdrew the containers of food and pulled off the tops. They had a standing agreement that they'd each help themselves.

When she was done, he took the containers and added food to his plate. Seagulls danced overhead, begging for food. Neither of them gave in to the ravenous flying garbage gulls. The curry would probably sizzle their insides.

Reaching for the spring water, Declan drank half of the gallon bottle without even using the glass. Wiping his mouth with the napkin, he pushed the plate aside and said, "The good news is that I might have new duty at

BUD/S, and the bad news is that I need surgery sooner rather than later. I'm good with the job, but the surgery has a lot of unknowns still."

"Okay," said Maura, recognizing the "I don't want to talk about it" look in his eyes. "Well, um, congrats on the job."

"Yeah." He looked at her steadily. "Don't be so concerned, Maura. When I know more, we'll discuss it, and if surgery means that I can run and work out and pretty much be me again, then I am all for it being ASAP."

Maura nodded her head. "I'm in your corner."

"I know. Thanks for that and for not pushing me to elaborate until I know more." He picked up the envelope. "What's this?"

She gestured with her hand that he should examine them. She watched as he pulled the papers out and read them.

"Hey!" he said, standing up. "This is great news!" Carefully, he put the papers back inside the envelope and stuck the wine bottle on top so it would have no chance of being blown away. Then he walked around the table and pulled her out of her seat and into his arms.

He kissed her. "Why didn't you tell me your news right away? This is wonderful! You must be so happy."

Snuggling her head against his chest, she smiled. "I am." Looking up at his grinning face, she said, "I'm thrilled. It's a whole new experience for me, not only owning the gym but knowing my past has fueled this triumph."

"Are you going to compete in any of the gym or parkour competitions?"

She didn't know. How did she admit that sometimes her own fears got the best of her, when he was facing greater challenges with a brave gusto that could conquer an army?

"Maura." He touched her chin, tipping her face up to his. "I've been honest with you. It's your turn." He assisted her into her own chair and reached over and lifted his own, so they could sit side by side.

"You're right. I'm...scared." Saying those words was like opening her soul and showing him her flaws. "I have a hard time letting go of fear, even when I want to more than anything."

Declan didn't miss a beat. "Shit! That's natural. What's the fear saying to you? Give it a voice." There was no judgment, just another unique Declanism to remember.

"I don't want to set myself up for a competition and then have another accident." The image was a giant dragon about to devour her sense of confidence, and she hated having to admit it. "See, I'm not that strong. Look at you, you can face problems and it doesn't even give you a second thought."

"Yes, it does," he admitted. "I take plenty of time to think about the issues that come my way. *But* my goal, or rather the desire to reach my goal, is greater than any fear I have. Only one emotion can win: desire or fear. So I chose desire."

She shook her head, feeling tears sting her eyes. "I'm not that brave."

"You're choosing that emotion."

Her anger pricked. "No. I'm not. It's reality."

His voice was calm, almost serene, and that pissed her off even more. "Maura, what do you want? Why did you buy the gym?"

She took a deep breath, bringing her feelings from a ten

to a two on the anxiety scale, and said, "I bought the gym so I could pass on my love of it to kids, teens, and adults and continue to build my proficiency with parkour."

"That's your ultimate desire."

"Yes, and my secondary wish is to compete again. Gym to gym. Maybe even build a few careers for some of the members and their kids. I know that world like I know how to breathe: what it takes to reach the Olympic tryouts and how to balance school, family, and life." Warmth spread through her body as she found herself talking passionately about what she craved. Turning to him, she said, "How…do I control…my fear?"

"I bet you can answer it. How did you do it in competition?"

She closed her eyes and pushed her chin forward. "I know that I'm the best and my performance will be awesome. I can see every move in my head. I run through the routine before I step onto a piece of equipment or the mat, and then when I am sure, I begin."

Opening her eyes, she added, "I repeat it exactly as I rehearsed it in my mind, and if something deviates, I improvise." She could feel the smile blooming on her face and the glint in her eye that was always there when she competed. "Like a song playing in my head, the rhythms play out, and when I'm done, I know I've hit my mark and been successful."

"That's the feeling you hold on to, the knowledge of your capability and belief in yourself. That's the key to achievement. The rest of it…any anxiety…" He rubbed his hands together and then wiped away the imaginary dust. "Let it go. Success only." He grabbed her playfully, tickling her, and then pulled her close.

She loved being enveloped in the protectiveness of his arms. She laid her head on his shoulder, feeling the vibration of his chest with her hand as he talked.

"Control what you have control over. Everything else...deal with it as it comes." He drew in a long breath. "If we try to control forces that aren't ours, our efforts will be met not only with failure, but with enormous frustration."

She nodded against his shoulder. "Control my internal dialogue. Concentrate on what I know, what I love." She wiggled against him. "I love you."

"I love you too. We make excellent teammates." Tapping her on the shoulder, he pointed.

She looked up just in time to see the green flash as the sun sank behind the horizon. *Thank you, God, thank you for the gift of Declan.*

Chapter 18

AN ARM HIT MAURA IN THE STOMACH, SIMULTANEOUSLY taking the wind out of her and waking her instantly. She sat up and pushed Declan's arm off of her, but it took her a few seconds to catch her breath.

Looking at the clock, she frowned. It was four in the morning.

Declan groaned.

She reached over to wake him from whatever nightmare he was having, only to find his body covered in sweat. She threw back the covers and felt around his body.

The stump of his leg was slick. Reaching for the light, she flipped it on and examined the limb. The color was bluish in places and his body was on fire.

"Declan, wake up," she ordered. Panic laced through her when he didn't respond. She punched him in the arm.

"Naghhhh," he said as he pulled the pillow over his head. "Too bright."

"Don't do that. You need to wake up." She used all her strength to pull him over. "Declan!"

His body was eerily still. His face looked flushed and his breathing was shallow.

Stretching her arm to the bedside table, she dialed 911. "Emergency. I need an ambulance." As she explained his condition, she pulled on jeans, a bra, and a shirt.

Slipping her feet into her running shoes, the closest shoes she could find, she went to the front door and opened it, repeating her address to the dispatcher.

They wanted her to stay on the phone until the ambulance arrived, so she left it on and placed it on the bedside table. Digging Declan's phone out of his pants, she dialed the number of Dr. Ekkert.

"Answering service. What message would you like to leave? Please start with your name and phone number," said a firm female voice on the other end.

"This is an emergency. I'm calling for Declan Swifton, one of Dr. Ekkert's patients. He's unconscious and running a temperature. His leg has a bluish tinge." Maura could hear her voice climbing as she recited his stats again. "He's not responding and I've called an ambulance."

"Have the ambulance take him to Balboa emergency. I'll let Dr. Ekkert and his unit know." She paused, and the seconds seemed like forever. "Will you be at this number if there are any questions?"

"Yes. Thank you." Nerves had Maura on edge as she hung up Declan's phone and placed it in her pocket. She ran next door for her purse and keys, pulling her balcony door closed behind her and doing the same with Declan's.

Maura sat down next to him on the bed.

"Hello." The attendants came in the door with their kits. She sprang up again, giving them room to work.

"He's breathing. Good sign." The taller male put a pulse ox on Declan's finger and placed a thermometer in his mouth. Maura watched the numbers climb to 103 degrees. "Fever. Rapid pulse. Shallow breathing."

The short paramedic was writing on a digital pad. "Was he on any drugs? Alcohol? Is he allergic to anything?"

"He's allergic to codeine." Maura cleared her throat. "He's had an amputation. I spoke with his doctor. They want you to take him to Balboa."

"Are you family?"

"Yes." She didn't even hesitate. She wouldn't allow anyone to leave her behind, whatever the cost, especially when it came to Declan. "I'm his wife." *Good Lord, I hope the lie doesn't catch up with me.*

The taller one put an IV in Declan's arm and hooked up clear fluids.

The other left the room and came back with a stretcher. "Going to be a challenge. He's a big one."

Maura slung her purse over her shoulder and lent a hand in lifting Declan. *That's my man*, she thought, *all muscle*.

Please, God. Please let him be okay.

"Maura," moaned Declan as they wheeled them into the emergency room.

"I'm here," she said, scooting past the paramedics and coming up alongside him. "I called Dr. Ekkert. He's going to meet us here." She took his hand and squeezed it. The skin was clammy.

His mouth split into a halfhearted grin. "That's my lady." Then he passed out again.

The phone in her pocket started to buzz. Who on earth was calling at four thirty in the morning?

A nurse passing close to her whispered, "You need to take that outside." She watched Maura to make sure she went out the door.

Maura nodded, still in a stupor, as she walked past the ambulance and into the parking lot. Then she answered the phone. "Hello?"

"Who's this?"

Seriously! Who's calling Declan this early? Must be someone he knows well.

Her voice was a short, clipped sound as she responded, "Maura." She was clenching Declan's cell phone tightly with both hands. The stress of waiting, though it had been less than a half hour, was getting to her. *Should I hang up or should I talk?*

A voice was shouting at her. "Maura, this is Leaper. Can I speak to Declan?"

"No," said Maura. "Sorry… He can't speak. I…I mean he's not available."

"What?! Wait. Talk to me."

The same nurse was running toward her and gesturing for Maura to come back inside.

As Maura caught up to the nurse, walking quickly back to the entrance, she added, "He can't talk right now. I have to go. I'm at the hospital with him." She hung up. She'd call back after she had more details. She hadn't meant to be rude, but Declan came first.

"Ma'am, the doctor would like to speak with you. Your husband needs to go in for immediate surgery. It's urgent." The nurse put her arm around Maura, escorting her back inside. "I didn't realize Dr. Ekkert was already in the building."

Inside, she met a thin, athletic man with a white coat and thick worry lines around his eyes. "I'm Dr. Ekkert. Didn't realize the Master Chief was married. His records must need to be updated." He escorted her into a small room and closed the door. Perching on the edge of a table, he gestured to a chair.

"Thanks, but I'd rather stand." Worry gnawed at her gut, and sitting would only make the stomach cramps worsen.

He nodded. "As you know, I saw Declan earlier today. He has an HO that needs to be removed, and we talked about me shortening his femur slightly so he could use a running prosthetic more easily. But the problem appears to be that the blood supply to his shorter leg is compromised. I don't want him to lose the whole femur region, so my first priority is to make sure the flow is oxygenating his leg. If that's successful, then we can do all of that while we're in there. If for some reason, we feel he's been under too long or any complications arise, we'll need to stop and do this in two operations."

"What do you need from me?" Maura squared her shoulders, ready to take on whatever burden was necessary: money, blood, or support.

"A prayer never hurts." He extended his hand, and they shook. "I just want to keep you in the loop. The waiting room is through those doors. We're going to prep your husband for surgery, and then we'll let you know when it's over."

"I'll be waiting," she replied, feeling like a mechanical robot as she headed out of the room. "Wait. Doctor. Can I see him one more time?"

"Sure. This way."

She followed him to a small curtained area. The scrape of the curtain as it was pulled back made the hairs on the back of her neck stand up.

Declan lay on the gurney. He looked so vulnerable.

A small antibiotic IV bottle was hanging next to a larger IV bag.

She studied the monitor he was hooked up to and then she said, "Can I have a minute?"

The doctor left without hesitation. Outside the room, he was speaking with a nurse, though she couldn't hear what he was saying.

She turned her attention to Declan. He looked so fragile. She pulled over a stool, sat down, and laid her head next to his arm. She listened to his labored breathing and could feel the thump of blood through his veins against her cheek.

Tears welled in her eyes, spilling down onto his skin. "Please be okay. I love you, Declan," she whispered as she wept silently against him.

His massive hand moved to cover her small one. He could hear her.

She looked up. She could see him fighting against the fever.

"Love you," he said. His eyes fluttered and then closed again.

Her heartbeat double-timed as she pushed herself up and laid her lips on his. As she kissed him, she tasted her own tears.

Pulling away was the hardest thing she'd ever done. She wanted to stay right here.

"Excuse me, Mrs. Swifton, we need to prep him for surgery," said a different nurse in green scrubs. Her manner was kind but firm as she urged Maura to wrap up her visit. Standing by the door, she looked very imposing. "The anesthesiologist is waiting."

Not wanting anyone to know the truth, that she

wasn't really married to Declan, Maura nodded. She left
the curtained area without a fuss, only looking over her
shoulder once, then headed for the waiting area. It was
the longest walk of her life. Every instinct in her body
told her to go back.

Entering the large empty room painted a variety of
beige and mustard colors did nothing for her mood. The
television in the corner was muted, and one of those
reality shows where people yell at each other was on.

She dropped her gaze. The lines on the carpet
showed it was freshly vacuumed. What an odd thought
to have, but the OCD part of her personality got it and
appreciated something familiar to latch onto. Cleaning.
Order. Decisive action. All of these actions made her
mind feel calmer.

Her body was another matter. It wanted to keep
moving. She circled the room twice, finally sitting down
in a chair that gave her an optimal vantage point for the
door. She closed her eyes and gave in to the tears that
had been threatening from the get-go. Maura cried until
there was no more emotion inside. Then she dried her
eyes and took several deep breaths. *This is as good as
I'm going to get until I hear Declan is safe*.

Her pocket vibrated. She reached into her pocket and
withdrew Declan's phone. Right! She needed to call his
friend back. Pushing a button, she got his most recent
text messages, including an invitation to participate in
the SuperFROG Triathlon from someone named Moki
Martin. She scanned through the other texts, but they
didn't seem that interesting. So she pushed another
button, hoping to get the keypad.

Instead something went into security mode and the

phone locked her out. Now she couldn't let Declan's friend know what was happening. She wanted to scream her frustration; she shook the phone and tried pushing more buttons to get it to reboot.

At the top right corner of the screen, a little dot moving closer to another dot caught her attention. Pretty soon there was a convergence of dots. The phone gave off a heavy vibration that made her hands shake.

"Here she is," said a male voice from the door.

It sounded like the man she had spoken to on the phone. His build was almost as imposing as Declan's, and the look on his face was not friendly.

Chapter 19

"GO IN, YOU NIMROD," SAID SOMEONE FROM BEHIND.

There was nothing more shocking than having a group of men burst into the room and set their sights on her. Maura knew she must look like hell from all the tears, from getting up in the middle of the night, from being at the hospital and not even looking at a mirror, but she didn't care.

"Hi, I'm Maura." She stood up and held out her hand. She had brothers. Big men or not, she wasn't going to be intimated. Nothing was going to get her out of this room until she had word about Declan's safety.

"Use your indoor manners," said a rather buttoned-up looking guy.

"Right." Leaper cleared his throat. "Uh, I'm Leaper, Declan's swim buddy. I spoke to you on the phone." Leaper shook hands with her. He then took the phone that was lying on the floor and pushed a few buttons. "You turned on the locator beacon. That's how we found you."

"Truth is…we were tracking you even before that. The call with Leaper set off a few alarms for us. I'm Sobbit Dahl." The tallish man nodded at her.

"Right. Sorry about that." She rushed on. "I couldn't talk when you called as Declan was about to go into surgery. I was speaking with the doctor and then the nurse. I had to put him first…"

"She's got the balls to be Swifton's wife. Excuse our manners. I'm Miller Roth, and this is Harvey Wilson, Tyler Kidding, Bunks Fox, and that's Hayes Johnson. We're…"

"Teammates," Maura finished. "Yeah, I know. I figured it out." She cleared her throat. "You've been gone a long time. He talks fondly about you guys."

"He better," smirked Sobbit. "Though he obviously didn't invite us to a wedding or a celebration party. That bastard!"

"Blah, blah, blah! It's always about you!" teased Wilson.

Bunks frowned. "Cool it, guys. The lady isn't used to us yet."

Maura liked the banter. It eased the knot in her gut. "I have brothers. Just be yourselves, okay?"

"Sure," said Leaper, throwing both his Teammates a stern look and then escorting Maura back to a chair and sitting down next to her. "Just tell us, in your own time, what's going on?"

"When I woke up this morning, Declan had a fever. The doctor had told him yesterday that surgery might be imminent, but when I couldn't wake him up, I called the ambulance. Now, here we are." She flexed her fingers, trying not to get stressed while she waited. She just loved him so much, she wished she could take his pain away.

"We just got back in town. We *were* going to give Dec some crap over being MIA, when this news sort of changed our plans," said Hayes. "What can we do to help?"

"Nothing." Maura explained the surgery the same way the doctor had explained it. "I don't know how long it's going to be. It could be two hours. Could be ten."

Miller nodded. "What do you need from us?"

"I'm sure Declan would be happy to know that you're here," said Maura. Picking up the water she'd gotten from the cooler in the corner of the room, she took a sip. It was cold on her throat going down.

"Would you like some tea or coffee? I see vending machines," said Bunks.

"You and your stomach," commented Sobbit.

"I'm hungry."

"It's like you have a tapeworm. You're always hungry."

Maura found herself smiling. Sure enough, they reminded her of Declan. The way they teased each other, the way their strength was their massive energy dominating any space they were in, and this underlining kindness. Tears welled in her eyes. "I'm…I'm glad you're here." Having people to share the experience with lightened the emotion considerably.

Leaper reached over and punched Bunks and Sobbit in the arms. "See what you did? You made her cry."

Miller shook his head. "No way. They made her smile."

———

Being in the air-conditioned room for four hours had lowered Maura's core temperature to near freezing. She couldn't drink another cup of tea or she'd be going to the bathroom every five minutes instead of every twenty.

Miller had mumbled something about his car and slipped out a half hour ago.

She wished she could step outside for ten minutes to warm up, but she didn't dare. Walking to the door, she waited for a nurse to come by and then called her. "Nurse. Is there any word?"

The woman, who had been asked the very same question at least a dozen times, shook her head and continued down the hall.

"The least she could have done was answer me with words," Maura said softly to herself.

"They do that. Don't give out information in case it's taken wrong. Declan is strong. He's the ornery type." Miller was standing behind her, holding a Team FIVE sweatshirt and a large bag of food. He grinned. "Only so many candy bars and snack packs a human being can eat."

"Thanks," she said, grateful for the sweatshirt and the reassuring words. Pulling it over her head, she relished the thick warmth. The hem landed at just above her knees. She didn't care; nothing was going to make her take it off.

Miller handed her a Styrofoam box full of hot eggs, toast, and bacon, and a bottle of fresh-squeezed orange juice. Even though it was almost lunchtime, she'd skipped breakfast, and eggs were welcome 24/7 in her book.

Maura practically inhaled the food. Her body was delighted with the fuel and she felt almost human again. Flexing her fingers, she noted even they were warming up. "I appreciate it. What do I owe you?"

"Nothing," said Miller as he tossed his container in the garbage and reached for hers.

She handed it over and stretched. Spending all this time with these guys had taught her a lot about them. They cared about Declan as if he were not just a brother, but also an extension of them. And they cross-referenced their questions to her, waiting for her to slip up.

Telling them the truth—that she lived next door, that she'd become closer to him after he rescued her from a paddleboard accident, and that he might have an upcoming duty assignment at BUD/S—had loosened some of the tongues about Declan's life before her. She enjoyed the stories; it made her feel like he was right here.

———ᴡᴡ———

The staff shifts rotated, and a new nurse came out to speak to Maura. "I can take you back to see him. He's going in and out of consciousness, but he should be waking up shortly. He was in recovery for over an hour and a half." To the rest of the men waiting, she said, "We'll let you know when he's ready for visitors."

Maura followed the nurse through another corridor and was escorted through double doors into the ICU. Walking down a glass-lined hallway, it was hard not to peer into the rooms where people were lying in their most vulnerable state. It didn't alleviate any of her anxiety to see all of the nurses and doctors hovering around the patients and their families.

"In here," said the nurse, gesturing to an end room. The shades over the window were drawn and the room was dark, except for a block of lights behind his bed. It smelled strongly of bleach in there. Maura's nose wrinkled as the nurse brought her alongside Declan's bed. "The doctor will be coming in shortly, if you'd like to take a seat."

Maura couldn't take her eyes from Declan. Drinking in the sight of him, she willed her racing heart to slow down. Taking long, slow breaths, she kept herself from passing out and finally pulled a chair over to the bed and tentatively wrapped her fingers around his.

His lips were dry and cracked in places, and he looked younger and very vulnerable.

"I miss you," she whispered softly, stroking his hand. The room was so silent, her words felt like they echoed.

Dr. Ekkert came in the door. "Mrs. Swifton? Sorry for the delay in speaking with you. I had a second emergency to handle."

She nodded.

The doctor looked worn-out and at the same time relaxed. Grabbing another chair from the corner, he pulled it alongside hers and sat down. "He did great."

"Thank you," said Maura, letting out the breath she hadn't realized she was holding.

"There was a clot in his upper thigh. We got there in time to remove it, and the other surgeries went well. We did a few scans and didn't see any other problems, but to be on the safe side he'll be on blood thinners for a few months. Other than that, he should be waking up anytime now." Dr. Ekkert squeezed the bridge of his nose. "I'll stick around for another hour, if Declan would like to…"

"Maura…" Declan's voice was rough. He coughed.

The doctor stood and picked up a glass of water with a straw, putting it to Declan's mouth. "How are you feeling, Master Chief?"

Declan drank several sips before spitting out the straw. "Hungry."

Maura smiled. "He's fine." Her stress was officially ratcheted down another level.

"Yeah, that's a good sign." Dr. Ekkert pulled back the covers. Before he exposed Declan, he added, "Can you give us a minute, Mrs. Swifton?"

Maura blushed and rushed into the hall. Pretty nice the way doctors watched out for a patient's dignity, even if a "family member" was in the room.

She chose an out-of-the-way corner in which to wait. She rocked back and forth on the balls of her feet, needing some way to expend her energy. Every time she looked toward Declan's room, the curtain was still pulled. What was going on in there?

Sending her gaze down the hall, she could see Declan's Teammates hovering on the other side of the ICU glass door. Their presence reminded her that she needed to tell Declan about her lie before the entire Team descended on him.

"Mrs. Swifton, your husband wants to see you," said Dr. Ekkert as he left the room and headed down an adjoining hall.

Ah, maybe that meant he knew. Maura lingered for the count of ten before she went into Declan's room. She didn't know how mad he was going to be, but she was prepared to rebut his arguments. They were together… okay, sleeping together. In some kind of logical space, didn't that give her the right to be a part of this?

"Well, well, well, here comes the bride." The smile on Declan's face brought a smile to hers. His color was back to normal. He might not have been ready to bounce out of bed, but the vitality he normally radiated was on high beam.

"Declan, I…" She went back to her place by his bed, not sure how to begin.

He grabbed her hand and brought it to his lips. "It was a good idea. You wouldn't have been able to see me otherwise." His lips caressed her skin and shivers ran up her spine. "I appreciate what you did. You saved my life."

Those words lit her heart up. Leaning down, she

kissed him. The weight of her worry had slipped away with the power of that connection.

"Maybe I should put a ring on it," he murmured against her lips.

She drew back and play-punched his arm. "Don't tease. That's serious stuff."

"Now, now, you wouldn't want to beat up an unarmed man, would you?"

"Ah, your Teammates might. They're here," she said and whispered, "and they believe we're married."

"Good! I don't want them to think you're fair game." Declan laughed out loud and then grabbed his gut and his leg simultaneously. "Ouch! Damn it, that hurts. Don't let me laugh."

"Okay, how about this, then… When you're ready to get moving, let me know, because I've read your texts and there is the SuperFROG Triathlon in a short time. We have three months to train for it, and I already signed you up. It's the perfect workout goal for you, and for me to prep myself for my gym competitions."

"Christ, woman, what are thinking? I just had surgery on my leg. I'm a grown-ass man, you know."

"Yeah, and you might have more healing and growing to do, but I know it is not going to slow you." She tapped her foot impatiently. "Either you make plans and keep going or you might as well stay right where you are."

He cleared his throat, choking on his own frustration. "You're right. I don't want you in my life. Get out."

"Too bad," she said, putting her hands on her hips and leaning her face into his. "I'm too stubborn to leave. You're stuck with me. So learn to love it. Because I love you." With that, she turned on her heel and walked to the door. "I'm going to get your Teammates."

"Hey, lady. I want you to know something."

"What?" she asked, turning her head to the side sweetly.

"My mother…she would have really liked you."

Tears welled up in her eyes. "Thanks," she said, her voice full of emotion. "That means a lot to me. I wish I could have met her." She came back over and wrapped her arms around him.

He held her tight, drinking in the delicious scent of her skin and hair. "My Maura."

She nodded her head against his body as the tears fell from her eyes. Then she abruptly pulled back and walked to the door. "I'll send in the guys."

He grinning as he stared at the empty doorway. "I love you too, Maura." He knew in his heart she was the one for him. She'd go toe-to-toe with him and not back off or back down, and she understood him in ways no one else could.

Maura had lived through a traumatic event that changed her world, and she got it—understood that sometimes life was fine and other times it could hurt like hell. He never wanted anyone to feel sorry for him, and neither did she. Yeah, they both had wounds that would take time to heal, but who didn't? And now they could heal together.

Chapter 20

THE NEXT FEW WEEKS WERE GRUELING. KEEPING A SEAL on the couch—or in slow-motion healing mode— was akin to holding down a lion with a flyswatter, especially when he wanted to be moving. Maura had her hands full and it was testing her patience.

Going to work for a few hours every day was her only sanity time. Maura read over the accounts that Mrs. B. had left for her and signed off on them, lingering over the paperwork as long as she could.

With Maura being gone more, Mrs. B. had logged in more hours acting as gym manager. Quite frankly, the woman had a knack. Perhaps Maura should consider having her take over full-time.

Sue Kolls popped her head into the office. "Hey, Maura, are you going to teach the teen class or can I take it?"

"You want to teach it?" Maura was surprised. This instructor was a former Marine Drill Sergeant and more appreciative of the strength-building and spinning classes for adults than working with the teens.

Stepping into her office, Sue approached the desk with precise steps. "Don't tell anyone, but I really like this program. I've never seen teens so excited to do anything. My sister has problems with her kids, and I was thinking if I'm teaching, maybe they can try a class or two for free. I think it'd help her out."

Maura nodded. "Anyone is welcome to take a class for free. No problem. If they do decide to join, they get fifty percent off for our extended-family discount or if they can't afford it, you know we have a program for that too. But I want to know what else this class gives you and what you want to give it."

Sue sat down across from Maura. "I want to expand the program and offer it not just once a week, but daily, Monday through Saturday. I'd like to see the teens have something to be proud of. They're so hungry for direction and activity, and if we can keep them engaged, I believe it will make a difference in a lot of lives."

"I agree," said Maura, pulling out several pages of notes. "Here's a list of our local gyms and their competitive programs. I'd like the teens to start competing locally and statewide in parkour and gymnastics. Would you like to spearhead the superhero teen program? And coordinate with Deidre and get the gymnastics teens to her?"

"Absolutely! I'll begin immediately…permission forms, rules, program schedules…the whole mission." Sue stood up and headed for the door. She paused in the door frame and looked back. "I adore logistics. I…I just want to say, you've made a difference here. This gym was floundering when you arrived. You've created programs that brought in all ages and encouraged an atmosphere of growth, development, and achievement. I'm…I'm glad you came."

"Thanks, Sue." Maura smiled at her as she pushed back from her chair and walked to the window. She looked out at the busy gym: every square foot was in use and there were lines ready to join in. The compliment from Sue was meaningful. Given the fact the woman originally had wanted to be manager, it meant even more.

Several more instructors gave her a greeting or nod of acknowledgment. Perhaps it was time…to let more birds fly. When she was captain of her gymnastics squad, she had learned to create direction and encourage people to develop on their own. She'd used the same technique here, and each instructor had blossomed or left. As of now, they had quadrupled their income.

Going back over to her desk, she picked up her class listing and pen. She was going to ask for volunteers. Out there were plenty of them. It would give her more time to prepare for competition and allow her to spend more time with Declan.

Smiling to herself, she realized this was the beginning of a whole new phase in her life, one where she chose how and when to let go of control.

⁓

Maura let herself into the tumbling room. They used this space for gymnasts practicing floor routines, with additional padding for the toddler, kinder, and single-digit superhero programs.

Springs mounted under the flooring pads provided additional lift. A stack of safety mats in different spots made the difference on the landing of some of those twists and turns and surviving the experience.

Not seeing Deidre anywhere in sight, Maura put down her clipboard, went over to the music controller, and keyed up a mix of her songs. She did a series of stretches and warm-up exercises to loosen her muscles.

When "Satisfaction" came blaring over the speakers, she adjusted the volume and then walked to the closest corner of the floor mat. With a salute to her pretend judges, she began her routine. After doing three front walkovers in fast succession and ending in a flip, she moved into a dance with high leg raises, arm work, and a bouncy little movement with her head. Using her good arm, she balanced herself in the air while she did the split and then pushed off, twisting her body and landing on the ground in the same position. Her arms waved in rhythm to the music, and then she pulled herself up into a back walkover, doing them over and over until she reached the next corner. Pointing her toes in succession as she caught her breath in the corner, she prepared for her two-and-a-half double twist.

Somewhere in the back of Maura's mind she heard the door open, but she didn't pay heed as she started her run and put her body into motion. She knew this routine like she knew the back of her hand, as she'd done it over and over for years. It was part of her last floor routine before the accident.

Her body flipped and twisted, flying through the air, and she landed with her arms outstretched. Maura stood there, breathing heavily, remembering her last competitive event. Her body was primed, and yet was that who she was right now…today?

Deidre was standing in front of her. "Maura, are you alright?"

With a brief nod, Maura said, "Yes, sorry. Did you need the floor? Is there a class?"

After checking the clock on the wall, Deidre said, "Not for another hour. I liked your routine, but you have one arm that hyperextends and another that locks halfway. Is the scar tissue still catching?"

Maura shook her head. "It's called being too lazy to practice. I think I better get on my game, though. I heard from three more gyms in San Diego, and they want to do an adults-only gymnastics meet."

Deidre grabbed her hand. "That's wonderful! Are you really going to compete? Oh, Maura, you're so talented. How can I help?"

"By putting me through my paces. If I'm going to participate and represent my own gym, I'm going to bring something special to the party."

—◦◦◦—

Maura was wiped out. She'd worked her body extremely hard and she ached in places she didn't remember having muscles. As quickly as she could, she packed up her bag in preparation for the trip home.

She stretched, listening to her joints pop and crack. Granted, there was a long way she needed to go before she competed in parkour or even gymnastics, but the overall exercise felt so good to her mind and body that all she wanted was more…tomorrow. For today, she was definitely done. Maybe there would be a nap in her future. She hoped so.

"Hello," said a familiar voice behind her. That voice made her body melt in places.

She turned to see Declan. "Hi," she replied, moving toward him.

They came together in a hug. He nibbled on her neck and ear, under her hair so no one could see. It was delicious, sending tremors of heat through her body.

"What are you doing here?"

Declan grinned. "I'm meeting my physical therapist here. She said that we could start training in the gym for the triathlon, so I'm here to sign up for my membership."

"You don't need one."

"Yes, I do," he said. "I want to support you and the gym. Besides, I ran into some friends out there and they said they'd help me out."

Maura leaned around Declan to see her seven-to-nine-year-old superhero group dressed and ready to go. She waved at them and they waved back. "So that's your fan club."

"Everyone needs a cheerleader." He waggled one eyebrow.

She felt an embarrassingly hot blast rise onto her cheeks. "Declan! I'm at work."

He winked. "I know. I'm sorry." Digging into his pocket, he pulled out a check. "I looked at your rates online. This should pay for the next year."

"Wow, a whole year. You could do six months." She couldn't keep the unspoken accusation from her voice. There were other options out there.

"This is where I want to be. Hell, if I could sign up for ten years, or twenty, I would." He hugged her tight and kissed the top of her head. "One of these days you're going to trust my statements. I only say what I mean, and I don't make promises I cannot keep."

She leaned upward and looked in his eyes. "And…"

"And I love you. That's not going to change." He kissed the top of her nose. "I better get going before my entourage gets restless. You know how kids are about lovey-dovey stuff at that age."

"Yes," she said, smiling at him. "I'll see you at home. I'll make dinner."

"No way. It's my turn to cater to you. I'm cooking," he said, turning around spryly.

"I'd like that." Under her breath she added, "That's my boyfriend." Picking up her bag, she looked around the office and laughed at herself. *Hard to believe I was once scared of talking to him*, she thought. *And now I'm yours and you're mine.* The idea filled her with head-to-toe warmth, and her heart leaped for joy.

Now if she could just find her keys. She pushed the door open and stepped into the fresh air.

A woman bumped into her.

Maura's automatic response was to say "Sorry," but it sat on her tongue and never came out as she stared at none other than Olivia Fenwick. "Olivia? What are you doing here? Do you need directions?"

The petite blond bombshell looked down at her feet for several seconds and then met Maura's eyes. "I was kicked out of the Coronado Community Center."

Maura frowned. "Isn't that open to all residents?"

"Yes, but I, uh, violated some of their rules," Olivia admitted, obviously embarrassed.

That fact did not surprise Maura. After their first meeting, she'd assumed that Olivia was a walking violation to most souls. Letting internal dialogue out unfettered was not the best game plan to win friends. "So you want to join this gym?"

"You can't keep this body looking the way it does without maintenance." Olivia said snidely. "Think about it."

Maura raised her eyebrows. *Really, that's the road you want to go with me.*

Olivia lifted her hands in surrender. "I'm sorry. I'd be shocked if you took me in, after all the attempts I made to steal Declan from you." She rocked onto her toes. "Okay, okay. They kicked me out for having sex on the premises of the gym and for hitting on the members while they were using the facilities. The director told me to get therapy. She thinks I'm a sex addict."

Maura tried not to smile, to sympathize with the woman. Insecurity got the best of everyone once in a while. She wanted to give Olivia a second chance. "We have rules here, too, that are very similar to the CCC's. Definitely no hitting on the members, and no sex stuff on the grounds—we have kids here. Plus, you're not allowed to chat on your cell phone or play video games while on the premises. Can you abide by those rules?" Maura was doubtful, but she enjoyed the adrenaline rush of keeping herself fit and knew the type of dedication it took. "Olivia?"

"I'm thinking." Her shoulders dropped in defeat. "Yes, I can."

"Then right inside the door is the office. Stop there for an application—for residents outside of Imperial Beach, you have to be approved. Fill it out and the staff on duty can give you a tour."

"I, uh, never heard from Declan about the contents of my envelope. Tell him he doesn't need to thank me for the gift I made to NSW."

"I'll let him know." Maura waited until the woman began walking for the door before she added, "Oh, and Olivia, just so you know, you can make your future contributions directly to the organization. He's mine. We won't need to talk about this again, right?"

Olivia pursed her lips and nodded her head. Her face was mottled with red, but she didn't give a single retort. Perhaps the woman was making personal progress.

Maura walked toward the door with a bounce in her step. She'd stood up to Olivia, was secure in her love for Declan, and was running the most successful gym in San Diego. Life was picking up in Imperial Beach.

~~~

A strong wind was blowing over the ocean. There was a slightly salty tang in the air that made her lick her lips several times. Maura could hardly wait to put on her bikini and dip into the ocean. At least this time, she was going to have the good sense to watch the wind and current, but a dip in the ocean felt like a just reward after the day she'd had.

She'd finished a load of paperwork, worked out, seen her man motivated, and dealt with the past. How could things be better?

As she rounded the street corner, she could see a ruckus in the apartment complex's parking lot. As she got closer, she recognized the culprits. Leaper and Dahl were lifting Declan's motorcycle, nicknamed Joy Juice, and his beloved road bicycle, named Paula after the song, onto blocks when she arrived home. "Maura, wait until you see us jack these bikes up," shouted Leaper as he hauled boxes full of chrome parts out of his Mustang.

"What are you two up to?" Maura hesitated. "Wait, don't tell me. I don't want to know." She held up her hands. "I didn't see anything. Just let me sneak upstairs."

"Maura." Dahl touched her arm as she walked by. "We do this, a lot of us…adapt machines for disabled vets. There are those businesses that do it for a price, but these are our family members…we bleed with them. It doesn't matter if we know 'em directly or not, a lot of us go to the homes of disabled veterans and fix their transportation so there's no problem. No doubt on their part that they, these guys, can be independent, have their joy back, or at least their ability to get a ticket for speeding."

"We know Declan's training for a triathlon, so we're going to fix his road bicycle. Should only take a few hours," Leaper explained. "We'll be mid-construction by the time the big guy gets home."

"The motorcycle is his great joy, and he needs it back," added Dahl. "That's my specialty. Though I need some muscle. I guess I should have asked Miller to join us."

"Screw you! I'm strong!" shouted Leaper.

Maura felt her eyes fill with tears. She nodded her head. These two were some pretty remarkable souls, out helping others, assisting Declan. Not needing to be told how or where or why, but just doing it so that their friend could be happy. Leaning over, she kissed Dahl on the cheek. "Thanks," she managed to say. "He'll enjoy having his motorcycle back, and the road bicycle too."

"Did she kiss you? She didn't kiss me!" Leaper yelled. "I need some sugar, baby." He spread his arms wide, waving his fingers like a madman or an octopus looking for food.

Maura held her hands up. "No, uh, maybe next time, Leaper."

The man actually dropped the box he was holding. It clattered as it hit the ground. Then he leaped over the bike, dodged past Dahl, and pulled Maura into his arms. Leaper tipped her back, looked deeply into her eyes, and kissed her forehead. "That's as close as I'm gonna get. I don't want a giant in my face about kissing his girl." He set Maura on her feet and dashed back to the box.

Mirth bubbled up inside of her. She laughed out loud. She hoped she never got used to these guys, that they would always continue to shock, amuse, and amaze her. "Let me know if you need beer," she said as she headed up the stairs.

"Always," said Leaper. "Let the keg roll down."

As she gained the landing, she looked back at them. SEALs. Teammates. Brothers for life—that's how Declan phrased it. Somehow, it felt as if her world had gotten bigger with them added to it, as if she had twice the number of brothers now. Declan had changed her world tremendously. She wondered if he knew how much.

Chapter 21

EVERY SEAL LIKED TO PUSH HIMSELF, TO SEE HOW hard he could drive his body until it gave out. Today was the SuperFROG Triathlon, and Declan was primed for the test.

It was true that several weeks after surgery, he showed a massive improvement in his state of health. Maura was running every morning, and he was joining her for a swim each afternoon. They pushed each other to lift weights and continued to increase the time of their workouts each day. Declan still didn't feel the recovery from his surgery was going fast enough, but for the most part he had greater strength each day, and that counted for a lot. A short time from now was the beginning of the SuperFROG Triathlon, and he actually felt...jittery.

"Roll the nerves into a ball, paint it a vibrant color like red or violet, and swallow it for energy," Gich used to say.

Declan stopped his pacing, centered himself, swallowed the nervous energy, and went back to his equipment check. Dahl and Leaper had done a terrific job on upgrading his tech. He had his road bicycle with the prosthetic already attached, his running leg, and the crutches to help him out of the water and onto the beach. Getting permission for the two crutches had been worth it, because he could move faster using the strength in his arms than most men could run. In his mind, if he could compete in the triathlon, he would be adding significantly to a job at BUD/S, and if he couldn't, well, then maybe it was time to hang it up professionally too. The SEAL Trainees deserved the best. For him personally, a lot was riding on this race.

Packing his extra crutches into separate duffels with labels L and R, he put on his running gear and number. Having signed in and gotten his registration packet the day before, he knew what to expect. First off was the swimming portion, which was 1.2 miles, followed by the 13.1-mile run—a full three loops of the course—and last was the fifty-six-mile biking part. He had done more exercise than that as part of his regular SEAL regime when he was operational. But with the leg, there were going to be challenges.

A noise outside alerted him to Maura's return. She'd started climbing the wall as part of her exercise routine, and now it was hard to get her to use the stairs. "Are you excited?" she panted.

"More than I thought I'd be," he replied. "Go shower and let's get there early to stage this stuff."

"Sure thing." She whipped off her shirt and walked past him.

His eyes were glued to her frame as she unhooked her bra and walked into his bedroom. "No fair!"

"Think of it as inspiration." The shower turned on and he could hear her singing to herself.

The doorbell rang.

Declan closed the door to the bedroom and let in Leaper, Dahl, and Miller. "What are you clowns up to?"

Leaper was stuffing his face with doughnuts from a giant box of Krispy Kremes. "What?" Leaper asked, opening his mouth wide to show the half-eaten gunk inside.

"Gross," said Miller as he sipped his giant Starbucks coffee, which would undoubtedly have a least three shots of espresso in it. Dahl was quiet. That was his way. Declan knew these souls as thoroughly as he knew himself.

"How can you drink that without having a heart attack every morning?" asked Declan.

Miller shrugged. "Lucky, I guess."

Dahl smiled.

Declan nodded. "Something on the counter for you."

Opening the bag, Miller laughed. "Thanks for being my connection."

Leaper swallowed loudly. "Don't tell me he got you more dark-chocolate espresso beans. So fucking gross." Pulling the door of Declan's refrigerator wide, he found the milk, drained it, and then put the empty carton back inside. Slamming the door, he burped loudly and said, "You're out of milk."

"Thanks," said Declan, shaking his head. Leaper had been his swim buddy for a long time, and he loved the guy like a brother. His whole Team was family, but at times— when they were all in real life—he had to laugh at how dysfunctional they must appear to the rest of the world.

"Do you have any manners?" asked Miller, stashing the beans in the small hydration pack on his back.

"No," said Leaper, turning around like a dog chasing his tail. "Where would I put them?" Going to the mirror, he looked in it and then over his shoulder. "See, I have no ass. Isn't that where I'd put them?"

Miller slapped his head. "Get moving and load the gear into the car."

"Why should I? What are you going to do?" asked Leaper, already picking up two bags.

"I'm going to talk strategy."

"Miller Johnson, I'm just as good as you are at that task." Leaper spoke in the voice of a constipated schoolmarm.

"Yeah, but you're standing around guarding gear and I'm swimming, running, and biking alongside of him." Miller made a shooing gesture with his hand. "Go!"

Leaper sniffed. "I'm not appreciated. I'm not loved. No one wants me around. Oh! Candy! Can I eat this Snickers?"

"Have at it," said Declan. He rarely tired of being around them. Truth was that he missed them. When you spent so much time in an individual's pocket day in and out, they became a part of you and your life. Damn, he missed his Team. They were his best friends.

Maura yelled from bedroom. "I'm almost ready. I promise not to put on underwear as my celebratory incentive. Well, they're really running shorts with an insert, so it's sort of like panties, but it's not…"

"Hi, Maura," yelled Miller.

Dahl said, "Greetings, Maura."

"Oh, crap!" said Maura back. She knew those voices. "Hi, Miller. Dahl. Is Leaper out there too?"

"Loading gear," replied Declan. He could hear her sigh of relief. That was Leaper's thing, getting a whiff of something going on and teasing the crap out of someone until they wanted to deck him. Uh, his buddy was a cad, uh, he meant, a card.

The Team had started spending more time over at the apartment and doing things with them since they all came back. He'd had his "confessional" moment, when Maura and he had explained that they weren't really married, but they were serious about each other. His

Teammates had been pissed for about ten minutes of banter and then they had gotten over it. Thus far, their off-duty time had been a blast.

—⁓—

Maura was screaming her heart out. "Go! Go! Go!"

Even with his short leg, Declan was outswimming the semiprofessional swimmers. This probably wasn't fair, since Declan could be considered a professional due to his job. She didn't give one hoot about that, though. This triathlon was about saying "I can" to Declan and his life and prepping for his next duty assignment.

"You got this!" Maura shouted. *Damn, he's fast!*

Miller was out of the water first. He waited while Declan got his crutches, and then they went up the beach together.

Declan was ahead when they reached the station with gear. Leaper stood guard over Declan's leg and shoes. Declan got both of them on and was ready to go as Miller finished tying his.

The two men moved in unison, talking to each other like this was just a kind of casual run.

"Go for it!" yelled Maura. "Get moving!"

Declan waved.

Maura groaned as she went over to help Leaper haul the bags and crutches over to the bike station. Around her she could hear people swearing as they attempted to shimmy out of wet suits and pull on running clothes and shoes. Why anyone would want to put on that much gear for a triathlon, especially in Southern California, was beyond her. The water was warmer here than it was most places. She swam every day and hadn't shivered once.

"Can't I stay and play with them?" asked Leaper.

"No," stated Maura definitely. "Today is about Declan, and if you screw it up, I'll bean you! Got it?"

"Yes, ma'am," he said with a salute, taking all of the gear away from her and carrying it to the next station.

Someday, he'd find the right mate. Leaper just needed someone who was willing to enjoy all that he was. It would definitely take one strong-minded female with a marvelous sense of humor. She'd put on her thinking cap and see whom she could come up with.

Declan was sweating buckets. He felt completely out of shape. He knew part of it was the fact that he had to change his pace with the new running prosthetic. It was geared for only a certain leg stride, and every time he changed the length, he nearly tripped.

Seeing Maura clapping and smiling made it worthwhile. Leaper was standing next to her, giving him the bird.

Declan had to keep from laughing as he reached the station, pulled off the prosthetic, and climbed onto his bike. Wiping his leg down with a towel, he got the sweat off and put a dry cap on the bottom before he pushed it into the biking leg and strapped in.

Slugging down a few sips of sports drink, he nodded to Miller, and the two of them took off on the last leg of the event. He had seen the pride on Maura's face as she hovered just off the sidelines.

He had to admit, he was pretty pleased with his performance. He'd registered as military and not handi-abled, and he was competing against guys from all branches as well as civilians.

Moki Martin, a retired Navy SEAL who'd started the triathlon, had made it available to all active duty no

matter the designation. He had made his mark support-
ing fitness in the community and the Teams. He was a
credit to the community.

"Get moving," said Miller, studying Declan. "I can see
the wheels turning, old man. This isn't the time to think.
You've got to beat me. Or are you a fucking tadpole?"

Declan gritted his teeth, peddling as fast and hard as
he could. "Screw you, FNG, I'm a frogman." Calling
a fellow SEAL a fucking new guy or a West Coast or
East Coast puke was a compliment of sorts between
the Teammates.

Miller smiled as Declan passed him. "Ah, now I see
the resemblance."

———

The men were in sight. Maura threw her water bottle at
Leaper to get his attention. He'd been trying to score a slice
of pie from one of the vendors. That man seemed to have
only two things perpetually on his mind: food and jokes.

Leaper looked at her.

She pointed.

He nodded and picked up the crutches he'd been
holding. The rest of Declan's gear was in the car. If he
wanted a different limb, she'd run back, but she was
betting he'd want to air his short leg and give it a break.

"Yay! Declan! Yay! Miller!" Maura shouted at them,
jumping up and down as the two men crossed the finish
line together, holding their hands up in the air.

Dahl bellowed. This was the shout of a man with a
baritone voice, which sounded more like the sound of a
bull in need of food.

"In a sign of unity, Miller Johnson and Declan

Swifton tie for first place in the military division and second overall," said the announcer.

Declan squeezed the brakes hard, sending his back tire spinning and turning the bike to the side. He got his foot down before the bike tipped over. "What? Second? Miller, man, I'm sorry. We're slipping." He'd done it, completed the race. He was glad he'd tested his stamina.

"*We* are NOT slipping. It's all on you, buddy, and that broke-down bike of yours. Paula is a crappy name for a bicycle. Pick something new. If you had gotten the bike I told you to get, and named it Speedy, we'd be tied for first. Damn, I hope the CO doesn't hear about it. Two SEALs in second—we'll never live it down." Miller lifted the bottom of his shirt, revealing a lean six-pack of abs, and wiped his face.

"Too late." The CO of Team FIVE was standing next to them. "I have to see my men compete. Decent job." He shook hands with Declan and Miller, waving Leaper away when he tried to get in on the action.

"Sir, good to see you. This is Maura." Declan introduced her to the CO as he unstrapped the leg and got off his bike. The bottom of his leg was bloody, but it didn't look too bad.

Maura promised herself she wouldn't hover in front of Declan's boss, so she shook hands with the CO. "Nice to meet you. I've heard good things."

"About me? I doubt it," he replied.

She laughed, and then the CO did too.

"Have a great day. I have to go find a certain Commander from the Helo Squadron on NAS." Lowering his voice, he said, "He bet me that his Helo

Pilots would beat my guys." He grinned broadly. "The wife is going to love what I buy her."

The CO nodded at them and departed. The man literally had a bounce in his step.

Dahl had the good sense to nod at the CO and slip away. He was targeting the female division winner, whose blond hair was being freed from her braids at this very moment. Her smile was bright and she was a stunner.

"Wow," said Leaper. "Good thing you didn't goatfuck this, Declan! We'd be scrubbing latrines if you lost."

"Correction," said Miller. "Declan has new duty, so you and I would be scrubbing…or actually you." He sniffed loudly. "That kind of work is too drudge-like for my tenderly tapered digits." Glancing over his shoulder, Miller sniffed. "Dahl is too much of an artful dodger to get stuck doing anything he doesn't want to. That man is blessed."

"C'mon, you animals. Let's thank Moki, watch the ceremony, and cook up those steaks Maura bought us." Declan leaned over and kissed Maura soundly on the lips. "Thanks for cheering for me."

"Always," she replied. "Come to think of it, I'm pretty hungry myself."

Leaper made kissing noises at Miller, who put his hand on Leaper's face and pushed him away. The bike and Leaper fell over, landing in the grass.

"Nice," said Declan. "Now I need to get a new bike. It has Leaper cooties on it."

"Uh, you can hose them off. Just use bleach," said Miller, getting back on his bike and riding away from Leaper, who had already lifted the damaged bike over his head and was running after Miller.

Chapter 22

DROPLETS OF WATER CLUNG TO MAURA'S SKIN AS SHE stepped out of the waves. Licking her lips, she relished the taste of the salty ocean and looked up at the balcony to see Declan watching her.

She waved and then shook her whole body like a primal animal freeing itself of the wetness.

His laughter floated on the air down to her. She couldn't imagine ever tiring of hearing it. Never in her life had she ever felt such completeness. When she was in high school competing, she'd gotten close to this feeling, but something had always been missing. Fulfillment was not just on a physical level, but also on an emotional and spiritual plane.

The guys were heading over to Danny's for a burger. She was able to catch scraps of the conversation. Guess they didn't want the steaks. No matter. More for Declan and her.

Sitting down on the sand, she turned to face the ocean, giving herself a few minutes to contemplate her life before she headed to the apartment. Wrapping her arms around her knees, she hugged them to her chest.

Learning to trust her instincts when it came to a relationship with Declan had been fraught with hurdles, yet the minute she got out of her own way and trusted herself, their relationship had bloomed. The same could be said of her taking over the gym: her ability to trust her instincts and reach for her goal had provided countless rewards. Membership was up. They were working on training whole new crops of kids interested in practicing parkour and gymnastics regularly. And she'd let go of her need to control every facet of her life.

She had teachers and employees she trusted working for her. And in her personal life, she had placed her most precious part of herself into Declan's hands—her heart.

"Maura, dinner's almost ready. C'mon." Dec's voice carried to her over the sound of the surf and breeze.

Craning her neck, she saw Declan and gave him another wave. "In a minute!" she yelled back.

Standing up, she brushed the sand from her body and suit. She knew she was ready to tell her family about Declan and introduce him to the whole overprotective bunch. There was no doubt in her mind that it would be memorable.

Turning toward the apartment, she walked to the rocks, intending to climb them.

A noise brought her to a halt. She looked over her shoulder.

Shading her eyes, she searched for the noise and saw several boys, probably around eight or ten years old, horsing around in the water. One of them looked to be in trouble.

"Declan!" she shouted. "Hey, there's a problem."

He was on the balcony in an instant, scaling down the rocks in no time. Spotting the boy being pulled out to sea, he used his crutch to take him to the water and then tossed it aside. Most of the beachgoers in this area knew there were places that pulled swimmers out quickly.

Declan dove into a wave, disappearing into the water.

Maura ran down to the water's edge and picked up his crutch before the sea pulled it out with the waves. Again, she shaded her eyes, trying to catch a glimpse of what was happening.

She followed his progress, running down the length of the beach, her breath coming in short gasps and her heart beating a frantic pattern. The parents of the other boys beat her to her destination, pulling them out of the water before they could get dragged into the current.

Declan had reached the boy in trouble, and he anchored him to his body with one arm. With his other arm, he swam quickly out of the current and into more stable waters.

Waves lifted them, bringing them toward the shore faster.

Maura ran straight into the surf to help Declan. She tried to say something, to point, but Declan was already in motion. He'd been giving rescue breaths, and now on the sand, he did CPR on the kid.

The child awoke, coughing. His parents flanked him and then hugged Declan.

Maura gave Declan his crutch and helped him stand.

A lifeguard from farther up the beach arrived, asking what happened. The parents took over, talking at once.

But Declan had Maura moving at a swift pace away from the havoc. Smoke was billowing down onto the beach. "I think our steaks are on fire."

"Oh, no!" She ran on ahead, climbing up the rocks and onto the balcony. Smoke poured out of Declan's apartment, and the fire alarm was beeping. She threw open the front door to create a cross breeze and turned off the broiler. As she pulled open the oven door, flames leaped at her and then slowly lowered until they went out.

She coughed as she headed to the balcony for fresh air.

Declan was climbing over the railing as she stepped outside. "Are you okay?"

"Yes." She rubbed at her eyes. "That was dramatic."

"Just another day," he said with a smile.

She sat down very ungracefully in a chair, picking up his nonalcoholic stout and taking a sip. "You know, this stuff is growing on me." She pushed her hair off her face and took another drink. "SEALs like living under the radar, don't they?"

"Definitely." He nodded. "Well, any thoughts on a meal? Our dinner is ruined."

"Let's go out."

"Okay, but I get to pick the place this time," he said with a wicked grin. "How do you feel about somewhere fancy?"

"I'd love it," she replied, thrilled at the idea of going out. "I'll get in the shower while your apartment airs out and then you can take a turn at my place."

"What's wrong with mine?" Declan looked offended for approximately two seconds and then he grinned wide. "Fine. I'll make a reservation."

"Good. Your place smells like a grill."

"Honey, that's an aftershave scent for me." He grinned.

Declan drove from Imperial Beach to the far side of Coronado. "They call this the Bay Side. There's a ferry that goes across the bay to Seaport Village, which is near the Hyatt, Marriott Marina, and the convention center." He had been to Poehe's a number of times with his Teammates, and most of the staff knew him, or least his visage.

Pulling into a parking space, he felt the nerves of anticipation nipping at his emotions. Bringing Maura here was raising all sorts of endorphins. He'd never brought a date here, though he had given the maître d' a few specific instructions when he called. This night had to be extra special. He'd had to take his super-sexy apartment angle out of the picture due to burnt steaks, but this restaurant was a great contingency plan. He knew he could make the night memorable.

Walking around the far side of the car, he opened the door for Maura and proffered his hand. Unwilling to relinquish her palm, he tucked it into the crook of his arm and walked her to the front door of Poehe's.

An attendant opened the door and they stepped into the cool, blue-lit interior.

"Swifton," said Declan to the hostess, who checked their name off a list and handed them over to a waiter who escorted them up a ramp to a secluded booth with high-backed seats.

"Here are our menus. The specials are listed on the pullout page. If you have any questions, please let me know." The waiter nodded at them. "I'll be back with spring water, unless you prefer bubbles..."

"Spring water is fine, and wine for me," said Maura, knowing that was Declan's preference and something she had no opinion on. Opening the menu, she looked over the entrees. "What do you recommend?"

"The lobster or the salmon," he said. "Uh, will you excuse me for a moment?" He got up and left.

"Sure," she said. Deciding on the lobster, she closed her menu and looked around the restaurant. It was truly stunning. The chandeliers were made of individual lights that hung at the bottom of long wires and moved with the air. Below their seats were rows and rows of windows looking out over Glorietta Bay, and the view of downtown San Diego was stunning, like a Christmas tree with all the lights blazing.

Motorboats sped by and sailboats took a more leisurely tack toward home port. The entire restaurant was hushed even though it was packed with patrons. Many of them were so engrossed in their meals that they hardly spoke, and the looks of delight were evident in their closed eyes and adoring expressions.

Declan sat back down. "Sorry about that."

She smiled. "Declan, this restaurant is amazing. I had no idea such a gem was hidden here. It's like a five-star oasis." She placed her hand on his. "Did you see that chocolate lava cake? Can we order that? It looks amazing."

He smiled. "Anything you want. This is your night."

The waiter arrived, took their dinner order, then left them to admire the view again.

When Declan put his arm around her, Maura scooted closer to him. This had to be one of the most romantic nights of her life, and she didn't want to miss one minute of it.

She leaned her head against his neck and felt him lay his head on hers. There was so much she wanted to say, and yet sitting in silence together was so easy and blissful that she couldn't bring herself to interrupt it.

As the plates of food were placed in front of her, she could hardly wait to taste each morsel. Time passed quickly as they relished each bite, sharing each other's meal and feeding each other forkfuls.

The dessert arrived all at once, one chocolate lava cake dripping with raspberry sauce and one large mango sorbet. Before she had placed her fork into the cake, Declan pointed to the sky.

She turned her head to look and was astounded by the sight.

Fireworks burst in the night sky. Colorful rockets launched high, exploding in an array of colors as smaller explosions sounded below.

Snuggling close, she watched it with him.

Declan whispered in her ear. "Here comes the finale."

Sure enough, a multitude of rockets and colors snapped and boomed in a crescendo. The ever-quiet restaurant goers burst into applause with murmurs of appreciation, and then the noise died down to a whisper.

Maura lifted her fork and dug into the lava cake. It was so rich that two bites in, she couldn't eat any more. "Do you want some?"

"I've had it before. It's akin to taking chocolate intravenously."

"Yes!" she exclaimed, laughing. "Can I take a bite of your mango sorbet?"

He smiled. "I was waiting for you to start it."

Exchanging her fork for a spoon, she scooped some of the cool orange dessert into her mouth. It was tangy and delicious. Taking one more mouthful, she felt something hard and lifted her napkin to her mouth. Expelling the item, she looked at it.

Her eyes filled with tears and her breathing became ragged. "Declan?"

"Will you marry me, Maura?"

As the tears brimmed over, spilling down her cheeks, she nodded. Words were caught behind the lump in her throat.

Holding out the ring to Declan, she watched him wipe it off and place it on the fourth finger on her left hand. He hugged her close as she wept as silently as she could.

"Is everything okay?" asked the waiter, hurrying over.

Declan replied, "I just proposed."

"Congratulations! I'll bring you a bottle of champagne on the house." The waiter moved quickly down the ramp toward the bar.

Declan held Maura as she wept. His large frame provided her a great deal of privacy. He was lucky that he had found the perfect woman.

When her tears stopped, he tilted her face to his and showed what it meant to him that she'd said yes. His eyes locked to hers, his heart racing, he kissed her on the lips with all the love he had inside of him.

As if she read his mind, she said, "Let's go celebrate, Declan. Take me home."

The waiter arrived with their champagne.

"Don't open it. I'll take it with us. Please bring us the check," said Declan.

~~~

Outside, the weather was too perfect not to take advantage of the night air. They strolled along the walkway together, holding hands. Maura knew that Declan was not a PDA kind of guy, so it was doubly meaningful when his fingers squeezed tight.

"Were you surprised?" he asked.

"Oh my goodness, yes," she said, a little breathless. She kept staring at her hand and her fingers kept touching the ring to make sure it was there, and real. "When did you plan this? How?"

"Well, originally we were going to have this moment in my apartment, but the drowning kid and burning steaks changed all of that…" Declan smiled at her. "I called your father and asked permission, Maura."

Maura tugged him to a halt. "You what?" The waterworks began again. He was so respectful, thoughtful, and kind.

He led her over to a park bench and they sat. Declan handed her his handkerchief. She took it, mopped her face, and blew her nose. "So much for my makeup."

"You look beautiful," he said. "You always look gorgeous. You don't need that stuff."

She nodded, not trusting her voice.

"I called your parents and asked to be put on speakerphone. I told them who I was and where I lived and what you meant to me." Declan put his arm around her and pulled her in close. "They asked me several questions about you: What's your favorite color? What was your biggest hurt and regret in life? What do you want to see happen now in your adult life?"

Rubbing his chin for a few seconds and then continuing, he added, "I'm pretty sure I answered them correctly, because I told them how I was going to propose to you and what I wanted our life together to be like, though I was flexible on how that unfolded too."

She looked up at him. "Thank you. I'm sorry I'm so weepy…"

"Hey, it's your engagement. You can cry to your heart's content. I'm honored that those tears mean heart-felt joy for me and for us." He touched his fingers to the side of her cheek, caressing her skin.

Leaning over, he kissed her simply and tenderly. It was a light brush of lips, but the electricity was always there. Pulling back, he added, "Besides, everyone knows you as Mrs. Swifton. I just want to make an honest woman of you."

Through her tears, Maura laughed. She slapped at his arm playfully. "Declan. I love you."

"Same here, bride-to-be, the future Mrs. Swifton."

She liked the sound of that and could hardly believe this moment was happening. "I'm really going to be Mrs. Swifton."

"Yes, you are. Oh, by the way, your parents and all of your brothers are flying out this weekend from their respective homes. What do I have in store for me?"

"Goodness, Declan, you're in for a challenge." She felt sorry for him in that moment. Her family could be a lot to contend with, though she loved them dearly. "There are a lot of them. Knowing them, they'll prob-ably make a vacation out of it."

"Nice! Besides, it can't be worse than Hell Week."

"We'll see," said Maura, wiping her face with the hankie again as she smiled at the notion of her family putting Declan through the wringer. She knew he was right, though; he was a steadfast man, a SEAL of his word, and he'd handle it.

Two police officers—a male and a female—were walking in their direction. They stopped in front of them.

The female asked, "Is everything okay, ma'am?"

Maura couldn't contain herself. "Yes, he proposed. Look." She stuck out her hand and then laughed outright.

The male police officer chuckled. "Congratulations."

"Thanks," said Declan uncomfortably.

The cops moved slowly away, heading toward the center of activity where the restaurants and stores were located. Mothers walked by with babies sleeping soundly in their strollers. The air held a peaceful quality to it, a certain calm and tranquillity. She relished the quiet as she sat beside the man she loved.

"Do you want to go home and get naked?" he whispered.

"Yes," she answered quickly. "Though I wish we didn't have to wait that long."

His laugh was very male. "I have a solution."

The drive to the Naval Air Station North Island took less than three minutes. Declan drove them to the Navy Lodge on the beach. Pulling into the half circle, he left Maura in the car with the engine running and went inside.

Two ladies were at the front desk. Lessie greeted him. "Hello, sir, how can I help?"

"I need a room for tonight. A cottage if possible."

"For only one night?" She raised her eyebrows.

"Yes," he replied. "I'm active duty and I've just gotten engaged." The last part of the sentence felt strange to say aloud, but he was going to work every angle he could to fulfill his plan.

"One moment, sir." Lessie went into a back room.

He looked around the spacious interior. They'd done a good job redoing the place. Noticing an ad for a garden space, he contemplated suggesting to Maura that they get married here. It'd be convenient to book rooms for her family rather than drag half of the SEAL community to her hometown. But it was her day too, and he needed to ask her about her dream.

Lessie returned with a smile. "Sir, we have one cottage, but you need to be out by 0800. If you agree, then it's yours for the night."

Declan nodded. He pulled out his military ID and credit card, secured the room, and then took the key card and got back into his vehicle.

"How did you do? Did we get a room?" she asked.

"Yes. We did very well," he replied. He drove around the last part of the half circle and then cut through the parking lot and turned onto the main road. He paused at the stop sign.

A plane was taxiing to the runway as he reached the access road and turned left. Going slowly down the road, he turned into the first cottage driveway.

"These are the best spots going." He turned off the ignition and pulled the lever for the trunk. Grabbing a bag and a cooler out of the trunk, he went around to the passenger side and opened Maura's door.

"What's that?"

"Well, I'd been working on a romantic getaway for us—a surprise of course—for this coming weekend, but this stuff should work well now."

"With a cooler?"

"Yeah, just add ice."

His future wife rolled her eyes and laughed. "That's my Boy Scout."

"SEAL, dear. Get it right." He winked at her as they headed to the front door of the cottage. "The card is in my back pocket."

"You just want me to grab your butt."

"Anytime you want, and yes." He grinned. "You know if you keep rolling your eyes, they'll fall out of your head."

"Who told you that?"

"Gich. Along with his lecture on how disrespectful it is. What can I say, I was in my teens—though late teens—when I joined the Navy. I was a bit of a wiseass."

"And that's changed how, precisely?" She keyed them into the cottage. "Wow, this is beautiful."

"Gee, thanks." He made a face at her. "Yeah, it's nice. Two bedrooms and only a few steps to a fairly deserted stretch of beach."

Maura grabbed the cooler from his hand and put it on the table. Picking up the ice bucket, she said, "I'm going to go get ice while you unpack our goodies from your bag."

He put down the bag. "Let's trade duties." He picked up the entire cooler and took it outside. Walking down the access road to the community building, he slid the cooler under the ice machine and kept pushing the button until it was filled. Then he picked it up and headed back.

His eyes scanned the beach and he could see an unattended blaze in one of the square fire rings on the beach. *Maybe we should head out there before it goes out. Enjoy the romance.*

Coming back into the room, he nearly choked on his tongue as Maura stood before him in the sexiest black, see-through, lace nightie. He swallowed several times. Putting the cooler on the table, he didn't even bother diving inside it for a near beer. Instead, he went right to her, picked her up, and carried her into the bed. "I'm glad I packed that lacy thing. I think I almost swallowed my tongue."

She squealed with delight. "Declan!"

He placed her gently on the bed and merely grunted an answer as he stripped off his clothes, pulled off the prosthetic, and lay down beside her.

She didn't seem to need any encouragement as she took control, climbing on top of him and pinning down his arms. She leaned her face close to his. "Thank you for the best night of my life."

The kiss was deliriously intoxicating. *More, more, more…*

"May every day and night together keep getting better," he murmured against her lips.

"Hooyah!" she answered. "Did I say it right?"

"Yes, you did," he said, rolling her onto her back. He looked into her eyes. "You're everything I want and didn't know I needed."

Her hands were holding on to his shoulders. "I knew I wanted you the moment I saw you. It just took you a little time to catch up." She looked down and then away. "When did you know?"

He touched her cheek, bringing her gaze back to him. "You don't have to look away anymore when you get shy or embarrassed. You can always look me in the eye. I won't judge you." Brushing his lips against her cheek, he watched the color rise.

"Okay."

"To answer your question," he said as he kissed his way down her neck and up the other side, "I fell for you the first time as I carried you up the beach during that crazy storm where you lost your paddleboard. The second time was when you went toe-to-toe with me when we spoke on the balcony and you wouldn't let me sit in my man cave. The next time was when you said yes, in the restaurant. I look forward to adding to this list for the rest of my life."

Maura pushed him back and her eyes tracked his. "Really?"

"Yes. Life rewards bold actions."

"I was brave for five seconds and it changed my life. Who would have thought?"

He rolled onto his back, laughing.

"What?"

"Of all the things that could blow your mind tonight, it was me admitting to you how much that kiss meant to me." Declan put his hand over his eyes. "Here I thought it would be the proposal."

She straddled his body with her legs. "Me too."

"You bring laughter and light to my life." He grabbed her arms and lowered her to him. "I love you, Maura."

"I love you."

They rolled around on the bed. Maura's lacy nightgown was stripped away in the process so that they were skin to skin. Every touch fed the fires of intimacy and sensuality until Maura was arching into him, aching for completion.

"I want to remember this moment forever, and if…" She ran her nails lightly down his rib cage on either side.

He drew air through his teeth. He was so hard; he had to concentrate on not coming yet. "If we conceive…"

"Then it will be another beautiful memory to add to all the memories we already have." She lifted her hips and lowered herself slowly onto him.

This was the most exquisite feeling in the world. It was impossible to describe with words, and yet the warmth, the wetness, the tight strength…all of it surrounding him, holding him, was akin to what heaven must be like.

His body pulsed with need as he watched her lift herself up and down, driving his body crazy with need. She had this wicked little smile on her lips that made him want to kiss her into submission on the one hand and drive her batty with desire on the other. There wasn't anything on this planet he wouldn't do to make her happy. This was going to be one of his lifelong goals: bringing her utter joy, complete fulfillment, tremendous passion, and endless entertainment.

Putting his hands on her hips, he guided her so she found her rhythm first. He wanted to see that look on her face when she surrendered to her need and wallowed in the completion. One night soon, he'd see how many times he could bring her before she gave in and could take no more. It was a delightful torture worthy of much experimentation.

"Declan!" He felt her body clench as her sheath spasmed, and she climaxed.

Happiness radiated from her. A low laugh came from her throat along with a panting and breathy sigh.

He gritted his teeth, not willing to come yet. *Hold on*, he repeated over and over. *Hold on*.

Rolling his hips, he changed the rhythm to bring her again.

Maura's back arched as she came a second time, and this time he couldn't wait any longer. He needed to join her.

Rolling her onto her back, he set a swift pace that had her writhing underneath him and clawing his back as she moaned his name over and over. Finally, he could endure the velvet bliss no longer and gave into the pleasure, coming in an explosion of completion.

Coming together was like linking into a universal power, an energy that made him feel like they were one being. And in this oneness, all possibility was real and everything conquerable. If he could have opened his eyes, he was sure they must glow.

Sliding to his side, he pulled her with him.

Her exhaustion was beating at him like a bird's wings, and he gathered her closer, bringing the covers over them.

"Thanks," she whispered, her voice hoarse.

They were still connected. He was deep inside of her.

As he was starting to pull out, she said, "Stay. Please."

He nodded his head. He could deny her nothing. This would be his Achilles' heel. She was his anchor for heart, mind, body, and soul.

Her arms cuddled into his chest as her breath came out in small puffs, displacing tiny hairs on his chest.

"The most perfect night of my life…" she said as she drifted off to sleep.

He listened to her breathing for a long time, feeling her heart beat alongside his, before he allowed his eyes to close and gave in to his own need for rest.

This time as he drifted away, there were no night terrors. There were only dreams of him and her, and their life together.

Chapter 23

THE SATURDAY FOLLOWING THE ENGAGEMENT proposal, in the parking lot in front of their Imperial Beach apartments, three men crowded around a motorcycle. Around them children skateboarded and teased each other, and the road behind was at a standstill as cars filled with people were headed to the beach.

Declan, Leaper, and Miller finished the last of the modifications for Declan's beloved motorcycle, Joy Juice. Grease covered them in odd places on their hands, face, and clothing, but the laughter coming from those three was hysterical.

Maura shaded her eyes as she watched them start the engine. It was followed by slaps on the back and probably words of appreciation, not that she could hear anything with the motor that loud.

A few neighbors poked their heads out and pointed. They seemed pretty adamant about the noise. Maura wasn't sure how they could differentiate it from all the other noises around them, but she made a gesture letting them know that she'd handle it.

Going down the stairs, she interrupted the three stooges and yelled, "Stop revving the engine. You're aggravating the neighbors."

"What?" yelled Declan, putting a hand to his ear.

Maura flipped the key, turning off the engine.

"How did you know how to do that?" asked Leaper.

"No one ever asked me, but I had a Harley when I was fourteen. It was my mom's, and I rode it all over my parents' property, at least until my car accident. After that I shied away from pretty much all moving vehicles for a while."

The men stared at her briefly, seemingly assessing her. Not Declan, of course. He beamed with pride—not that he'd had anything to do with her skill set.

"Told you she was cool!" said Leaper, jabbing Miller in the shoulder.

Miller went after Leaper, and two men mock-scuffled.

Declan came around the bike and grabbed Maura's hand. "Are we pissing off the neighbors?"

"Affirmative." Maura gestured to the neighbors standing on the balcony, looking down on the scene with very unhappy expressions on their faces.

She couldn't resist shouting to the guys who were now wrestling. "Hey, guys, save it for the gym."

"Or the bedroom," added Declan with raised brows.

"Ha, ha," said Miller getting in a last gut punch before he stepped out of Leaper's reach. "Besides, I didn't start it."

Leaper groaned. "My fault. It's always my fault." He hunched over, playing up the fact he was nursing his "wounds."

Maura looked at her watch. "Miller, you better get moving. Isn't your date with Sue Kolls at 1800?"

Miller grabbed her wrist and stared at it. "Damn, I only have thirty minutes. It's going to take me at least that long to get home. Dec, old buddy...can I use your apartment to clean up?"

Declan looked at Maura. The two of them had a silent

conversation. "Sure," he said, "but be quick. I'm going to take Maura for a ride, and I want you gone when I get back."

He took his house key off his key ring and tossed it to Miller. "Leave the key on the table and the balcony door open when you leave."

"Sure thing," said Miller, taking the steps two at a time.

Leaper sat down on the sidewalk. He looked sullen and unhappy. "What am I supposed to do? My swim buddy is getting married. Miller's got a date. Sobbit, Tyler, and Bunks are riding up the coast to attend a screening in La-La Land, and Hayes and Wilson are in Julian at some retired Frogman's party. What the hell?"

Maura put her hand on his shoulder. "I promise, I'll find someone for you."

The man cradled his stomach like a kid with a tummy ache. "A lot of good that does me now. I need something to do."

She held up two fingers, gesturing for him to wait two minutes. Pulling her cell phone out of her pocket, she dialed the gym. "Hey, is the superhero class running today? Uh-huh. Two classes. No, three, because we have an adult version now. Great! I'm sending down the perfect helper. His name is Leaper. He'll be there shortly."

"What have you just committed me to?" Leaper looked doubly unhappy.

"Let's see, a day of playing with ropes, balance beams, kids, teens, and adults—many women in their twenties that like to dress in costumes and work out." Maura waited for the news to sink in.

"Nice," he said, nodding, a smile growing on his face. "I can walk there and pick up my car later?"

Maura held her grin in check. "Sure can. Get going. Just ask for Mrs. B. when you get there."

The man was on his feet in seconds. He stretched his arms over his head and took off at a run. Rounding the corner, he didn't even look back.

"Good one," said Declan.

"Tell me about it. If he doesn't meet someone in that adult superhero class, the man is doomed. They're all Comic-Con fans—you know, comic books, graphic novels, cosplay, superhero TV and films, and animation—and given that Leaper is a real-life hero as well as a crack-up, I'm pretty sure the ladies will go nuts." Maura leaned up and kissed Declan's chin. "Where are we going?"

"You'll see. Hop on."

Declan opened the back hatch and pulled out two helmets. He gave one to her and secured one on his head. Then he climbed on the hog first, sliding his prosthetic into a foot holder and securing a brace along the back side to keep it in place. Turning the key, he held in the clutch and cranked up his Joy Juice.

Maura made sure the strap was secure. Doubts poked at her from the back of her mind that this could be dangerous, but she squashed them into pulp and let her excitement show. Wrapping her arms around his waist, Declan took a dirt path through a field and then wove his way through the streets until he could find a spot to cross the busy road. Soon they were hauling it down the Strand doing seventy, with the wind batting their cheeks and the sun beating down on them.

At the first light, Declan turned off. He gestured to a security guard and took them down a long road. Again they wound through residential roads until they reached a home with a Sold sign on it.

Declan pushed a button and the kickstand went down automatically. He turned off the key, and the silence was quite loud for a few seconds.

Maura got off the bike and put her hands on her hips. She looked at Declan. "You didn't!"

Flowering herbs filled the entryway, along with balloons and vases of roses. A sign on the wall said, "Welcome to the Home of Mr. & Mrs. Swifton."

Covering her mouth with her hands, Maura walked from room to room. "There are two extra bedrooms. Oh, look at all this closet space, and a full bathroom, a double-garage… And this laundry space is great. I can set up a permanent ironing and steaming place here. The kitchen is open-concept, and the dining room is huge, and so is this living room."

"Wait until you see our room." Declan took her elbow and led her into the master suite. "It has a steam shower and a standalone tub, and the view…"

She broke his grasp and ran to the double doors. Throwing them wide, she stepped out onto the patio and walked to the railing. Opening the gate, she went down the gangplank to a dock where a double kayak was tied up. The front seat said "Hers" and the back said "His."

Overwhelmed with joy, she wanted to cry. "I don't know if I can keep back the floodgates."

"Then don't. It's one of the best parts of you that you share your emotions easily. Let the waterworks roll."

Declan's smile was bright and warm, his eyes filled with love. He pulled her into his arms. "Is it your favorite surprise…as of now?"

"Getting there," she said as she rubbed her belly. "Someday, I hope to fill these rooms."

"Yes, the Navy's symbol is Neptune, and that's definitely a god known for blessing fertility."

Maura wiped the tears from her cheeks. "Can we go look at the house again?"

"As much as you like."

As they reached the patio, she stopped him. "What if I hadn't liked it?"

"My Teammates would have had a great place to stay, and hopefully, they wouldn't wreck the staple of my life savings." Declan turned her toward him. "You really do like it, don't you?"

"Yes," she said. "It's the perfect place to begin growing our family."

"Begin?" he asked. "How many kids are we having?"

"I'll let you know when I'm done, but I'm thinking at least five."

"I was thinking two or three."

"Whoops! You should have asked me that question earlier, because multiples run my family. My granddad on Mom's side was a twin, and my grandmother on Dad's side was too."

Declan leaned against the wall. "Why didn't they deliver the hammock chair yet? I need to sit down."

"You bought me the chair—the double seater—that we saw in Seaport Village?"

"Yes, though I guess we're going to need more than one," he sighed.

"As Wordsworth said, 'The external world is fitted to the mind.'" Her hand caressed his butt as she led him inside. "So we'll decide how many kids we want and stick with it. I'm told, after the first child, the others are easier."

"Check, please…" Declan murmured, heading to the bathroom, where he turned on the water in the shower and stuck his head inside. "Just give me a minute to adjust," he shouted through the spray. "Multiples."

—⁓—

Declan had spent the rest of the next two weeks packing and moving boxes. They'd spent the following weeks cleaning and preparing the house, and then throwing a small welcome party. Add in a wedding, a honeymoon, and a lot of very vigorous exercise, and the time had flown by.

Today was the end of a very active four months, which had included surgeries, recoveries, physical therapies, moving, an engagement, and a wedding, not necessarily in that order. It was hard to believe so much had changed in his life.

Turning his Harley, Joy Juice, into the Amphibious Base, he flashed his ID and headed not toward the Team FIVE Quarterdeck, but to BUD/S. He was starting his new duty and he was primed for action. He would be testing the trainees and seeing if these tadpoles had what it took to become SEALs.

He knew from his experience that a lot of men had the physical toughness. It was the mental agility and acuteness, the desire to get the goal despite the odds, that separated many talented athletes from their wish to be a

SEAL and plopped them back into the general population of the Navy. The ones that made it through BUD/S and Hell Week had an indefinable quality that meant they could be leaders *and* followers, that courage and commitment to their Teammate and their oath came before their own needs. Their dedication was unwavering.

Declan knew the wives took on a similar commitment when they married a Team man—not an easy thing, because a SEAL wasn't just a SEAL while he was active duty. That way of life and sense of responsibility and duty was forever. Once a SEAL, always a SEAL. Men were who they are...forever.

Parking his bike, Declan withdrew the key, stashed his helmet, and headed for the door. He showed his ID and was escorted to his office. Stacks of file folders were loaded on his desk, and a man was waiting in his chair.

"Only a half hour early. I thought I taught you better than that," said Gich, sticking out his hand. "Christ, I was two hours early on my first day at BUD/S."

"Yeah, and you probably weren't getting any either. Those of us with wives have other duties, you know." Declan laughed before he swatted away the hand and leaned down to hug the man. "Good to see you, Commander. What brings you here?"

Gich spread his arms wide. "I've had three different offices in this place, and I've got to say, this one is the best." Then he resettled in the chair. "Besides, if I'm going to have you following in my footsteps, I have to make sure you do it right." Gich's bullshitting was a great way to begin this new journey.

He'd play along. "What's your advice, Commander?

Tie the tads up and throw them in the ocean or stick with the pool?"

"That's stage one, my boy, you know that. No, I'm talking about when you're in the mountains. I know this place that has the best pie. Before the stage begins, you need to stock up, and then there is this little pub with darling waitresses—not that you're looking anymore—but you can bring a few of your Teammates who are single…"

Sitting down in his chair, Declan pulled closer to the desk. He'd thought that being behind a desk would mean the end of his time in SEAL Team. Instead it was a phase of his career he was eager to experience. If he could be anything like the man sitting in front of him, he would consider his life well lived, because Gich had saved lives with his actions in combat and at home, and his teaching in the Teams was legendary. He was a role model to everyone, but to himself, he was just an ordinary guy. That was a SEAL, someone who didn't need to be recognized for the glory.

Yeah, he'd be happy to be just like the most outstanding man he knew, Gich. With a wife like Maura at his side too—a woman who was independent, passionate, honest, and the perfect swim buddy—the possibilities really were endless.

"I brought you a present," said Gich, handing him a package wrapped in newspaper. "It was given to me by a brother, before we lost him in battle about a decade back."

Declan unwrapped the package. He looked at the framed print. It was the Navy SEAL Ethos. He read through it, saying the last line aloud: "…the legacy of my teammates steadies my resolve and silently guides my every deed. I will not fail."

Gich stood and the two men shook hands. "I know they're in good hands." And then he walked out of the office.

Picking up the pile of files, Declan opened the first one. He gave the candidate his full attention, making notes on a separate piece of paper on how to push him, teach him, and make him the best SEAL he could be. Because being the best meant pushing oneself every day and living up to the promise of success, courage, commitment, innovation, and achievement.

Epilogue

SITTING IN A C-130, WEARING LEAPER'S COVERALLS because they were the smallest set of winter coveralls that could be located, Maura bit her lip pensively. *What on earth possessed me to agree to this?*

She had bunny boots on her feet, guaranteed to keep her toes from freezing, and giant gloves with warming inserts over her hands. The temperature inside the plane was dropping and her nose was already running. Peeking out from under a neck scarf, there was small gold shiny trident on a thin gold chain around her neck and a glove covered her wedding band. There was no doubt whom she belonged to or who belonged to her.

She pried the handkerchief stuffed into her right glove out of its tight-fitting hidey-hole and wiped her nose and then stuffed it into a pocket in the coverall for easier access.

Declan waited until she was done, then strapped her into the plane and put a set of noise-canceling headphones over her ears. He tapped a switch and a sharp noise sounded briefly. He doted on her.

She shook her head and frowned at him.

He placed a mouthpiece in front of her lips. "You can talk to me."

"Why should I? I look like a polar bear."

"Shhhhhh," he whispered, pointing to the giant cages. "Polar bears eat sea lions."

Maura rolled her eyes and laughed. "Tell me why I

agreed to this again. Why am I traveling on a plane full
of creatures with a below-normal temperature?"

He sat down next to her and strapped in. "This is
prime time. Everyone is off right now and traveling.
Space 'A' flying is optimal when you're active duty
or retired, so most people catch a flight. As you know,
all the domestic flights we tried to Oahu were full.
So I asked a favor of the Marine Mammal guys and
they agreed to allow us to hitch a ride. Keeping these
warrior creatures cool is a priority. We just have to
bundle up."

The C-130 shook as the engines revved. It began
moving as it taxied to the runway. When it reached its
correct position, the engines revved again—this time
longer and higher—until it took off like a flash.

She didn't want to imagine it going out over the
Pacific. She knew she should probably make peace with
it, as they would be out over the ocean for a while.

"I guess I can handle it for a few hours," she acqui-
esced, though the animals secretly intrigued her. Perhaps
while they were in the air, she might get a chance to ask
the Marine Mammal staff some questions. Being around
these creatures all the time had to be interesting.

"Uh." He paused. "It's going to be longer than that."

"What?" she asked, turning her face to his. "How long?"

"Over seven hours, maybe longer."

Her jaw dropped open. "How cold will it be in here?"

"Under fifty degrees." He looked at her sheepishly.
"It will be fun. Really."

Maura laughed. She couldn't stop herself.

The sea lions joined in. *Arrrrrgh. Arrrrgh. Arrrrgh.*
One of them, the largest of the bunch, kept making

moon eyes at her. He nuzzled the bars of his cage and pushed his nose out, sniffing at her.

Three female trainers visited the cages, attempting to distract and calm the creature, but he was obviously smitten. Finally, the short blond trainer walked over to Declan and Maura, who pushed off their headsets to hear her. "Hi, I'm Rocky."

"Maura. Declan. Thanks again for allowing us to join you on the flight." Declan motioned with his gloved hands. "You've got a full crew. Training or Op?"

"Both." She smiled. "Um, I don't mean to intrude, but Gigor has this thing for women when they are, uh, in the family way. Are you by any chance pregnant?"

Maura's eyes went wide. Mentally, she counted the days. It was possible. "I don't know."

"Well, he, uh, acted this way when I had all of mine," said Rocky. "I've been pregnant four times, and the youngest is nine months. Gigor knew before either my husband or me. He's, uh, never been wrong."

Putting her hand over her belly, Maura wondered, *Am I with child?* Closing her eyes, she thought about how her energy had been waning, her stomach had been queasy, and her breasts, specifically her nipples, ached.

Declan put his hand over hers. "Maura, are you okay?"

She opened her eyes and smiled. She nodded her head. "I could be."

He kept his hand over hers and put his other around her shoulders, snuggling in close.

"Sorry to intrude," said Rocky.

"No intrusion," said Maura. "I appreciate the info. I can hardly wait until we land now."

"What's your full name?" asked Declan. "Is it Roxanne?"

"Yeah," said the trainer. "Everyone calls me Rocky. Talk to you later." She went back to her posse to chat with them some more. A tall, muscular man, the guy in charge of the transport and the entire group, joined the women. They opened their packs and drew out food, settling in for the long flight.

They put their headsets back on.

"My mother was named Roxanne. Do you think it's a sign?"

"Do you believe in signs?" she asked.

"I believe in energy, that life rarely unfolds as a coincidence, and that we decide on what makes us happy." He was silent for a long time.

She entwined her fingers with his as they held it on her stomach. "I like the name."

"Me too." Declan cleared his throat. "Are you hungry? I have all of your favorites. Pretty much this whole pack is full of food and drink, and the DVD player is in there with a few our favorite movies."

She couldn't believe it. They'd just agreed upon the name of their first girl. She adored the name, and the look on Declan's face was one she'd remember for the rest of her life. "I'm not hungry per se."

"What?" He looked at her and one of his eyebrows rose. "Here? You want to do it in here?"

"I had visions of the mile-high club, though given the situation, I'm not sure I want to get out of this coverall unless it's really necessary."

"How about I whisper dirty things in your ear?" he suggested, waggling his eyebrows up and down.

"Oh God, you and Leaper didn't exchange personalities before we left, did you?"

He switched off his mic, then hers, and leaning over, he gave her a long, deep, and satisfying kiss. Then he turned everything back on. "Did that feel like Leaper? And don't say yes, because I'll be jealous if you've been kissing him."

She smiled. "No one kisses like you do."

"That wasn't a response," he said, looking disgruntled.

"Ah, a woman rarely kisses and tells," she teased.

He laughed. "Life together is never going to be boring, is it?"

"No," she said. "I just wonder…if we're ready for this."

"A baby. Sure," Declan said nonchalantly.

She opened her mouth and then closed it.

"What?" he asked.

"Remember in my family there are multiples, so it's likely that…"

Declan paled. "I forgot about that." He swallowed and there was an audible sound to it over the mic. "I wonder if they'd hurry up and land."

Maura put her hand on his arm. "We wouldn't find out for a little while now. I can't be that far along."

He took his hand off her stomach and reached into the pack. He popped open the top of the near beer and drank the bottle down in one gulp. When he finished, he stowed the bottle and secured the top of the pack. "Let me tell you the story of a guy from Team THREE. His name is JC, and they thought they were going to have twins, but they ended up having triplets…"

—◦◦◦—

The vacation in Oahu was glorious. This was their honeymoon, for all intents and purposes. Since Declan had started a new duty assignment so quickly after their marriage and all the busyness that happens in life, relaxing in Hawaii was amazing.

They visited the Big Island and sipped Kona coffee, sent back twelve pounds of coffee beans for Miller, and a bought a grass skirt for Leaper. They also found shells and bought gifts for the rest of the Team and a few of the people at the gym.

Lying together in a hammock tied between two palm trees, they watched the waves lap at the sand. Cuddling together, they relished the knowledge of each other and the new life growing in her belly.

"It reminds me of home," she said, falling asleep in his arms.

"Whenever I'm with you, wherever we are, my Maura, I am home." He kissed the top of her head as the hammock swayed gently in the breeze. "My love, this is forever."

Author's Note

"Everyone who is alive has challenges." My grandfather, Dr. H.G.B., wrote this to me in a letter when I was an undergraduate at Boston University. He was a minister, a missionary, a husband, a father, and a grandfather. He was trapped in a concentration camp in Japan during World War II, and when he was released after the war and had regained what he could of his health, he went to Manzanar to help the Japanese-Americans interned there. "Some of us speak of our hurdles and others do not. We make our homes out of what we believe to be the heart of our focused emotions; that can be our families and our love of one another, or it can be the house we build of pain, horrific memory, and torture. It is not our place to judge either way. Rather it is our duty—for those of us that can—to give freely of our joys and to share our personal bounty in a manner that can provide dignity to another. When you think of giving, remember this—it is not for the self we act but for the greater good of man and for the honor of those who have walked before us and sacrificed so that we may have freedom of life, the power of faith, and the willingness to keep living."

I take these words to heart, as does my husband, who is retired from the Teams and a disabled veteran. We both have sought out many opportunities to give. We find the greatest gifts are those that come from generosity of heart or kindness: a smile or a shared laugh, the time spent talking and listening, and/or being a positive presence in someone's life. Making a difference matters.

We want to thank you for joining me—and us—on these journeys. Writing Navy SEAL fiction is a wonderful experience that allows me to incorporate parts of our life and the community's into my stories as well as stretch my own imagination. I am grateful to my husband, friends, and family; to my publishing house, the fine editors at Sourcebooks and the entire staff for believing in me and the value of these books; to *RT Book Reviews* for giving me time away from my Comic Column to craft these stories; to my author friends for their humor and pointers; and to all of the military folks—retired, former, and active duty—who have invited us into their lives. HOOYAH!

May your seas be gentle, your experiences wondrous, and the people you meet have a lasting effect.

—∿∿—

If you would like more information on several organizations that support our veterans, they are listed below. And to those that have served and your families—thank you for your service!

SuperFROG Triathlon
http://superfrogtriathlon.com
Navy SEAL Foundation
http://www.navysealfoundation.org
From their website: "Our mission is to provide immediate and ongoing support and assistance to the Naval Special Warfare community and their families."

Special Operations Warrior Foundation
http://www.specialops.org
From their website: "The Special Operations
Warrior Foundation ensures full scholarship grants as
well as educational and family counseling to the sur-
viving children of Army, Navy, Air Force, and Marine
Corps special operations personnel who lose their lives
in the line of duty and immediate financial assistance
for severely wounded special operations personnel and
their families."
Phone number: (813) 805-9400
Mailing address: PO Box 89367, Tampa FL 33689
Physical location: 1137 Marbella Plaza Drive,
Tampa FL

DAV—Disabled American Veterans
http://www.dav.org/learn-more/about-dav
/mission-statement
From their website: "Providing free, professional
assistance to veterans and their families in obtaining
benefits and services earned through military service and
provided by the Department of Veterans Affairs (VA)
and other agencies of government. Providing outreach
concerning its program services to the American people
generally, and to disabled veterans and their families
specifically. Representing the interests of disabled veterans, their families, their widowed spouses, and their
orphans before Congress, the White House, and the
Judicial Branch, as well as state and local government.
Extending DAV's mission of hope into the communities
where these veterans and their families live through a
network of state-level departments and local chapters.
Providing a structure through which disabled veterans

can express their compassion for their fellow veterans through a variety of volunteer programs."

U.S. Department of Veteran Affairs
http://www.va.gov
From their website: "Federal benefits for veterans, dependents, and survivors."

Acknowledgments

My cherished husband—retired Navy SEAL, EOD, and PRU Advisor—Carl Swepston; the outstanding retired Navy SEAL Thomas Rancich and his remarkable Liz; the incredible Rear Admiral and #1 Bullfrog Dick Lyons and his fabulous wife Cindy; old goat roper John T. Curtis and his marvelous Miranda; inspiring retired Navy SEAL Moki Martin and his family; Greg McPartlin, Navy SEAL Corpsman and the owner of McP's, and his family; retired Navy SEAL Hal Kuykendall and his lovely wife Denise; retired Navy SEAL Jerry Todd and his terrific Pete; Frank Toms (UDT 11/ST1) and his wonderful family; our dear friend Medal of Honor Recipient John Baca; Medal of Honor Recipient Mike Thornton; the Vietnam Era "Old Frogs & SEALs" who contributed comments and stories; and *HOOYAH!* to all of our operational friends.

To—Suzanne Brockmann and Christine Feehan, thank you for being such great inspirations!

To—Marjorie Liu—For brilliant insights!

To—Joanne Fluke and John Fluke—Wonderfully talented souls!

To—DC and Charles DeVane—YOU ROCK! There aren't enough words to express my gratitude.

To—Cathy Maxwell and Kim Adams Lowe—Thanks for being such good friends!

To—Tamara Worlton and Liz LeCoy—Thanks for the friendship and med pointers!

To—Renee, Fiona, and Morgan—Thanks for sharing a precious experience at the ice cream store!

Cheers to my brilliant friends: Laurie DeSalvo a.k.a. Lia DeAngelo; Jan Albertie; Alisa Kwitney; Christina Skye; Angela Knight; Leslie Wainger; Dianna Love; Andrew and Megan Bamford; R. Garland Gray; Mary Beth Bass; Maura Troy; Sheila and Ed English; Domini and Chris Walker; Brian Feehan; Sam, Diego, and Zavier; Maria R. and Joao; Maria M. and Frank; Maria N. and Emanuel; Jessica and Ryan; Kim and Paul K.; Jill and Carl H.; the Lynches; Brenda; Mary H.; Anne M.; Stephanie H.; Rose S.; Mic; Ginger D.; Nonny; Erika; Amy; Katheryn; Kat; Cindy; Lynn; Robyn; Lora; Traci; Trudy; Stacey; Kristy; Simone; Laura L.; the entire BB crew; Sara and Lindsey Stillman, who are marvelous; a shout-out to my cousins, aunts, and uncles; to Kathryn Falk, Kenneth Rubin, and Carol Stacy; and to my agent, Eric Ruben.

Thank you to the Sourcebooks crew—Megan, Susie, Skye, and Danielle; to the marvelous Deb Werksman and Dominique Raccah.

With infinite love and respect to my parents—always!

This book is also dedicated to the memory of our beloved and memorable Madge Swepston, and to the life and legacy of Frank Davidson. Thank you for touching all of our lives. We love you and we miss you!

In case you missed it, read on for an
excerpt from Anne Elizabeth's first West
Coast Navy SEALs book:

A SEAL at Heart

If you're not gonna pull the trigger, don't point the gun.
—James Baker

*Operation Sundial, at an undisclosed location deep
in the jungle*

BLOOD DRIPPED DOWN HIS FOREHEAD AND BLURRED HIS
vision. Wiping it away, Jack forced his eyes to focus. He
squinted, but it was useless.

The helicopter downwash whirled mud and dirt into
the air faster than he could blink, and the clouds of grit
stuck to his face. Nothing shielded him from the suf-
focating pelting of the brownout, making him blind as
hell without his protective glasses.

Gathering the five-foot-ten-inch form of his swim
buddy Don into his arms, he duckwalked as low as
he could, heading toward the belly of the helicopter.
Luckily the rain had stopped momentarily as the rotor
blades cut the air, but it made the moment more surreal.

Whup, whup, whup…

He blew air out of his mouth. His nostrils were caked
with grime, but he could still smell the blood seeping
from the bandages he'd fastened around Don's chest. He

squeezed his swim buddy tightly, trying to keep pressure on the wound.

A stray bullet ricocheted, displacing the air near his face. Where the hell did that shot come from? The helicopter was *so* goddamned loud.

The door of the copter jerked open; the blessed haven was dead ahead. The two door gunners laid down suppressor fire, but it was short-lived aid as enemy bullets took them down. They fell back just within the side door of the helo.

"God help us," Jack muttered under his breath as he finally reached the opening. The men in front of him were practically cut in two by the rounds. There wasn't time to think about them or their families now. With a mighty heave, he lifted his buddy onto the helicopter floor and scrambled in after him.

Coughing the crap out of his lungs, he dragged Don over to the far wall, away from the doorway, and stood up to scan the interior. It took him a minute to take in the carnage. He tried to wipe the image from his eyes as his mind put the gory pieces together. The pilots were shredded. *Damn.*

Making his way to the cockpit, he could see that the glass dome had been compromised and the entire enclosure looked pretty chewed up. "Please let this thing fly." The blades were still turning, so that was a good sign, and neither the cyclic nor collective were hit. But would it be enough to get them out of this hellhole?

He touched his throat to activate the comm mic. It didn't respond. He spoke softly, trying again, "Whiskey. Tango. Foxtrot." *What the fuck!*

Where the hell is everyone?

The rain was starting again, angling into the copter and hitting his face.

Another series of blinding flashes—hard to tell if it was lightning or shots—from outside, but it forced him to move Don, to stash him deeper in the belly of the copter, and momentarily duck for cover.

Pwing! The bullet bounced off metal.

He was pretty sure it was only a small number of insurgents and one sniper firing wildly. Random shots in the dark. Problem was, even a broken clock was right twice a day, and the dead airmen were horrific evidence of the sniper's success.

A volley of shots. A few rebels cross-fired at one another, sending shouts of anger into the air. *Go to it. Maybe you'll hit each other.*

The only good news was that if he couldn't see them, they couldn't target him directly either.

There was no point in sitting tight. He needed to find his Team. After securing Don and rigging a piece of equipment to hold pressure on his swim buddy's wound, Jack went back to the open door. A glimpse of rag-covered muddy boots to the right let him know that an enemy was approaching. Moving quickly into the disrupted cloud of crud, he positioned himself so his vantage point was optimal.

Two Tangos dressed in frayed pants held Russian 9 mms at the ready. Instinctually, Jack withdrew his SIG Sauer, took a breath, and squeezed off several rounds. They dropped instantly.

He checked their pulses. Dead. Now, where were the others? *Here, birdie, birdie, birdie...*

Working his way quickly out of the cloud of dust,

he knew he would be vulnerable, but this was his best option. He had to know what was going on. This mission had gone sideways long ago.

Coming up behind a rebel who was caught up in dislodging a jammed gun, Jack holstered his own weapon and, using bare hands, silently broke the enemy's neck. Slowly, he worked his way around the perimeter of the helo. For now, it was clear.

Lightning split the sky, bathing the area better than a floodlight. It was the vantage point he sought.

A noise caught his attention as a door from the factory flew open, banging against the siding. That was them—his Teammates—sprinting from the interior as flames engulfed the structure. They were coughing and several of them appeared to have minor injuries. Jack held his ground, preparing to lay down cover fire, if required. His eyes were desperately searching for a subversive threat, when an explosion lifted him from his feet and threw him to the ground.

Bam!

Thrown backward from the blast, the back of his head smacked something hard. Black spots danced in front of his eyes and bile scored the back of his throat. Swallowing the harsh rush of acid, he lifted his hand— gun gripped tightly in his fingers—trying to focus on the enemy that should have been coming over the large boulders a few feet in front of him.

Nothing. No one.

The smell of C-4, with its acrid ether odor, filled his nostrils even as thunder shook the sky and rain barreled down.

A sharp burning sensation seared the back of his

skull, going from ten on the pain scale to numb within seconds. Another wave of nausea made his stomach roll and quake as he deliberately forced his way to his knees and then his feet.

The clock is ticking. Fighting the dark spots, he stood wavering for a few seconds before his sight returned to normal and he could search for them… The enemy. His buddies. Or any signs of life.

His eyes widened.

Giant pieces of seared, cloth-covered flesh were scattered over the ground. It didn't compute at first. Those were his buddies, Teammates from SEAL Team ONE, Platoon 1-Alfa, and only a few of them were moving.

Jack was instantly in motion. Grabbing the body closest to him, he felt for a pulse. The steady thump sent a surge of adrenaline through his system. He gathered the man to his chest, trying to keep his hands on his buddy as he dragged him toward the helicopter. The path was wet with blood and mud, and repeating the task several times, he slipped in the sludge as he loaded the bodies closest to him on board.

Only one Teammate, Gerry Knotts, was left and remained exposed. Jack would be a moving target—a perfect bull's-eye—for the enemy's shoot-'em-up game if he attempted it.

Eyes sought his. His Teammate was alive and signaling him. Jack understood and moved to a rock as far from Knotts as possible. Lifting his 9 mm, Jack fired several shots. Bullets peppered around the rock as he quickly belly-crawled back to his original position.

Knotts fired several shots, nailing the Tangos.

Moving up into a dead run, Jack reached Gerry's side

and then helped him stand. Together they rushed into the cloud of dirt and grunge, going for the helo.

They left long streaks of mud along the deck as they rolled inside.

Jack checked…seven men loaded, and he was lucky number eight. His life meant nothing without them.

Finally able to close and secure the door, Jack shoved debris aside until it was easier to move around the cockpit. Quickly moving the pilot's body to properly reach the controls, he straddled the chair and checked the instrument panel.

He held his breath, watching the RPM gauges of the turbine and rotor. The helo hovered. The controls required constant small changes to keep the bird in the air. Sweat dripped off his face. "Come on, baby. That's it! Into the storm.

"Now, let's get the hell out of here." As the helo responded, he sighed with relief. He'd only piloted helicopters a couple of times—all his experience was in fixed-wing aircraft—and he was hoping his brief lessons would be enough to get them back to the rendezvous point.

He had to hand it to her—this bird flew, even all shot up. Just as he was beginning to feel okay about the flight, he noticed black spots at the edge of his vision. With the back of his thumb, he rubbed one eye. Nothing prepared him for his sight going, leaving only one eye functioning.

He squinted at the instruments. The radio was blown and there was no luxury of an autopilot. Keeping a helo in the air was a constant struggle against the torque, the wind, and the pilot's ability. "Come on, Jack. Concentrate!"

Wind buffeted his face courtesy of the bullet-shattered windshield. The smell of ozone was heavy and ripe. He hoped the lightning was over.

Wetness dripped down the back of his neck. He wiped a hand against the warmth, and it came away with fresh blood. His.

Fuck, fuck, fuck!

Looking over his shoulder, he saw the bodies of his Teammates. He didn't know if they were alive or dead. But he could never let them down. He'd get them all to safety—make them secure—even if it was the last thing he ever did.

―⁘―

Coronado, California

No other place on the planet was like McP's Pub in October—the seagulls circling and crying overhead, and the women just as raucous. He took a long pull on his beer.

"Welcome home, Jack," said Betsy. The friendly blond waitress with a wide, pearly white smile and a set of 44Ds grinned knowingly at him as she walked by. Hers was the kind of walk that had her hips swinging, and her tight apron full of change played a musical medley to the movement of her sexy saunter.

Some women can move like their hips are on springs.

For those around him—the suntan worshippers— almost any hot spot on the planet would probably suffice. But for Jack, this tiny island town between Glorietta Bay and the Pacific Ocean was uniquely qualified to be his home. Having been assigned to SEAL

Team ONE and with an apartment only ten blocks away from the Amphib base, Jack thought this was a snapshot of perfection.

He scratched at the gooey tape mark behind his ear. The bandage around his head was gone and he was no longer hooked to IVs or being pumped full of fluids and painkillers, but he wished there were an antibiotic or balm for the one place he hurt the most, his soul.

At Balboa Naval Hospital, the medical staff had told him his number one job was to relax until he was fully healed and had his memory back. There were too many holes, too many memories missing from the last Op. The worst part was… his best friend was dead.

Jack couldn't reconcile it and didn't know how to fix the situation.

The rub was… if he didn't take care of himself, fix the recollection issue, he'd be stuck with the label "acute psychological suppression"—forever. That didn't bode well for him.

Do the familiar. Take it easy. Those were the orders from the medical staff.

With those directions rattling around his brain, it meant finding a place to unwind where he could feel the sun's raw heat on his skin, taste the tang of salt on his lips, and have a cold brew sweating in his hand as he savored each sip. Well, maybe not the alcohol part, but everyone had a vice and his was simple: fresh air, exercise, and a bit of the barley.

Ah, beer! The first sip was always sweetest.

At first, being back in Coronado had been difficult. The layers of emotion had punched him in the gut practically every few minutes. Drink in hand, his mind had started to go numb, turn off, and he went whole hog for the break. McP's was the perfect place to just… be. Where men and women interacted, doing a dance as primal and ancient as time itself to attract each other. As the action unfolded in front of him, he saw a few younger brethren had scored, snapping up the curvy and very willing quarry to set off for more serious play somewhere else. Nature's fundamental dance never ceased to intrigue him, though he wasn't looking.

Listening to the slap of the waitresses' tennis shoes against the slate wasn't quite as sexy as the click of a stiletto, but he couldn't complain. Most of them were paragons, Madonnas—look but don't touch—because they were SEAL wives or friends.

A loaded hamburger with a crisp green salad was placed in front of him. Steam rose from the burger and his nostrils flared. Of course, *this* tasty morsel he would be willing to sink his teeth into anytime.

"Just the way you like it, and on the house," said Jules with a wink, another one of McP's waitressing angels. "'In Xanadu did Kubla Khan, a stately pleasure-dome decree…'"

"'Where Alph, the sacred river, ran through caverns measureless to man down to a sunless sea…'" The reference from "Kubla Khan; or, A Vision in a Dream," by Samuel Taylor Coleridge, was a favorite of his and McP's was a home of sorts, his own pleasure-dome. A framed copy of the eighteenth-century poem sat on his nightstand, a birthday gift from Jules and all of the waitstaff at McP's. Even now he could recite each and every line verbatim. His own life was like that poem, a journey, and very much unfinished. He wanted that chance… to explore.

"Thanks, Jules." Jack grinned, unusually grateful for the human connection. He shifted uncomfortably on the chair. Maybe the incident overseas had shaken him more than he realized. "Hey, how did you know exactly what I wanted?"

Her smile was sweet. "The same way I've known for years that you'd rather drink your calories than eat them. Enjoy lunch, Jack. You're looking skinny." She leaned down and kissed him gently on the cheek.

"Thanks." Part of him wanted to add a sentimental comment about her being a sweetheart or maybe ask about her husband, who was in Team FIVE and probably deployed, but being sappy wasn't his thing. Life was easier with the walls up.

"Don't forget to eat your vegetables." She gave him a big smile before she went back to attending her other customers. Did she know how her aura of bubbling beauty affected men? Probably not.

Releasing the grip on his beer bottle, he placed it on the table and then attacked the salad. It was significantly better than hospital food and MREs. Hooking his fork into the meat, he pulled it out from between the buns. As a SEAL, he was always in training, and he would rather carbo-load with a brew and burn it off running. He wrapped the burger in lettuce and took a bite. The meat was savory and juicy, filling him with welcome satisfaction.

News droned in the background until someone had the good sense to flip on a ball game. There was something peaceful about that… as if it were Saturday and he was a kid again.

Methodically, he ate until the burger and salad were gone. The french fries sat untouched next to the bun halves and a very sad-looking pickle. He lifted his brew, and his lips drew tight, pulling the cold liquid down his throat.

He'd been in the Teams for eight years, and being a SEAL was the basic foundation of his soul. Another enlisted man might state that the military was important, but to Jack it was everything. If he couldn't deploy anymore… well, the concept was too harsh to even contemplate.

His eyes searched, looking for a distraction from his musings. For several seconds his gaze stopped on a large, agile man until his inner gauge dismissed him as a nonthreat. Ever vigilant, there was always a part of him searching for trouble and ready to respond.

At the next table, a dog happily lapped water from his complimentary "pup" bowl. A man in his fifties, probably the owner or an overindulgent dog walker, dropped parts of a hamburger into the water and the dog went crazy—busily fishing pieces out and then chomping, chewing, and swallowing the tasty morsels down as if no one had ever fed him.

Life must be so much easier as a dog. Someone is there to make the meals, walk side-by-side, play, and run. Was that what he wanted? Did he want someone feminine, curvy, and sweet to be there, too?

He'd be better off with a dog. With his schedule he didn't know if either was a realistic wish. His ideal state was being deployed, which didn't leave much time for a home life.

Gripping the cold bottle of beer like a lifeline, he lifted it to his mouth and drank deeply. *God, that tastes good! And it's predictable. Every swallow is the same.*

Off to the side, he could hear the faint buzz of cars and trucks as they sped down Orange Avenue, confirming that everything was in sync here, normal. That was reassuring to a degree, witnessing the commonplace; this is what "everyday" was supposed to resemble. Calm. Steady. Regular.

Why isn't that me? His mind and body couldn't slow down. Closing his eyes, he forced himself to let this familiar place and a beer soothe him. At least he hoped it would. McP's was a special home for his kind. Owned by one of his brethren, there was Navy SEAL memorabilia on the walls, a trident on the T-shirts, and oftentimes the bar would fill with sightseers and froghogs—women who hopped from frog to frog. In the Underwater Demolition Team, or UDT—the precursor to the SEAL Team—these Navy sailors were called frogmen. Later on, the name was changed to better show their areas of operation: SEAL—SEa Air Land—but the age-old name for the women who pursued them never got updated.

Half his Teammates were in committed relationships, and the rest dicked around almost constantly. Lately, his celibacy walk had turned into a preference. It had begun as a way to concentrate on work, and now…

Maybe he just didn't have what it took—a crap tolerance—to be in a relationship.

The back of his head exploded with a sudden and sharp pain. His hand lifted automatically, rubbing over the healing wound and stubbly blond hair.

"Red Jack!" His eyes whipped open, and for a second, he could have sworn that he'd heard Don. That was impossible. His swim buddy was dead, and there was nothing that could bring him back.

Pain squeezed his neck. His vision blurred and for a moment an image of his friend flashed before his eyes.

The rush of emotions for his swim buddy was the kind of tidal wave that could take out a city, and equally as devastating as it crashed over him again and again. He'd have done anything to have Petty Officer Second Class Donald Dennis Kanoa Donnelly alive and well. Sorrow punched his heart, but he'd never show it, especially not in public.

His phone vibrated. Jack had the cell in his hand before he remembered he was supposed to be on vacation— no one would be calling him for sudden deployment.

Punching a button, he accessed the email. Appointments had been scheduled for him: group therapy and individual sessions. *Can't this Frankenstein wannabe leave me alone? I don't need a doctor.*

He just needed to keep it together long enough to go operational again. Being on medical leave was like swallowing two-inch nails whole: it hurt the entire way down and out. He had way too much time on his hands to think. He needed action.

"Petty Officer First Class John Matthew Roaker."

His name was a command that had Jack sitting up straight in his chair. Any other service would have a guy standing at attention before the rank and name had been completely spoken. Spec Ops was different, more laid-back.

"Taking a trip down memory lane?" commented a

gruff man with salt-and-pepper hair and a long bushy mustache. His sideburns were like hairy caterpillars perched on the side of his face. The man took a step closer to Jack and grinned. A fat cigar was clamped between his lips and his voice had lost the hard edge and was warming progressively. "Shit, you look like a newbie jarhead, Jack! We're going to have to mess you up a bit! So you look like a fucking SEAL."

"Good to see you, Commander," replied Jack, already proffering his hand to greet his former BUD/S Instructor, now mentor. With a grin on his lips that spoke volumes of the man's capacity for jocularity, Commander Gich didn't appear to be the kind of guy who could teach you fifty different ways to kill with a knife.

His gaze connected with the Commander's. Jack took comfort in the stare. Emotion hung like a bad painting just behind his own eyeballs, but he pushed past the weight of it. "Sir, it's great to see you."

Jack stood and the men embraced, slapping hands on each other's backs in heavy smacks and then briskly separating. There was a tremendous sense of the familial. Jack needed that right now.

"You too!" said the Commander. "How's the brain? Is it still swelling? I can think of better things to make swell."

"Christ! They're not sure. You know docs. Though, I'm pretty sure the fracture's better." Jack reseated himself, eager to change the subject. "I was thinking about my first drink here, and then there was the Hell Week celebration, when you and I drank until the kitchen opened for the early birds' lunch the next morning." He could practically taste the stale alcohol. Bile threatened to rise, but he shoved it down. Yep, that memory was definitely intact! Why couldn't he have lost that day, instead of the events from the last Op? He needed those memories.

"No shit! You were so hungover from those shots that you puked your guts out in the back of my car." Gich signaled the waitress for a beer. "Still doesn't smell right. But it's easy to find Blue Betty in the dark." His grin could have lit up the darkest depths. "So, how's it going, Jack? What's with the shrink-wrap therapy? I may be retired, but I'm still in the loop."

Shaking his head, Jack said, "I don't know. It's been…" He searched his mind for the word, but he couldn't even find that. Who really wanted to know the inner workings of a SEAL? They might not like what they find in there, and then what? SEALs had more layers than an artichoke.

"Hard, complicated, and disillusioning to come back from a mission that's seriously goat-fucked. You're not the first, Roaker, and unfortunately, you won't be the last. Just don't become a poster boy, it's not your gig."

"Yeah, me a poster boy! Could you see me in Ronald McDonald hair?" cracked Jack without missing a beat. It felt good to have someone giving him shit. Everyone had been so "nice" to him lately that it creeped him out. "Sure I can pull off the look, but all those hands to shake, personal appearances, and then there goes your private life."

"Wiseass!" A shapely blond waitress who could easily be a modern-day Marilyn Monroe placed an icy beer in front of Gich. "Thanks, Betsy. I knew you'd remember how I liked it."

"Anything for you, Gich." She winked at him and headed back inside. The bar was pretty empty for a Tuesday afternoon, but it'd pick up tonight and be packed with military personnel on the hunt for hook-ups and single ladies on the quest for the golden ring. That was old hat for him, and he'd rather work out, clean his guns, anything…

"I can make a few recommendations. There are a couple of medical professionals who use unconventional methods. Alternative healing… it might help." Gich looked at him over the top of his beer as he drank. "The person I'm thinking of does acupressure. Did wonders for my knees and lower back."

"Doctors aren't my preference." Jack contemplated getting a pain pill out of his pocket, but he knew it'd be a dicey mix with the alcohol. He preferred to drink, so he left it in his pocket and took another sip.

"Roaker, you can talk to me," said Gich, drawing on his cigar and puffing out a long thin stream of smoke.

Jack sat silently, briefly weighing his thoughts before he shared them. "Six weeks ago when I left here, I was ready for the mission. Even though there were a couple strikes against it. First, Tucker kept getting changing Intel on the location and how it was laid out. Second, the resources seemed underkill for a plan of this magnitude, and whenever I brought it up, they told me to add as much as we needed. So I did, but it never felt like enough. Third, when we got there, nothing was as discussed; the place was a ghost town outside with only a few people inside. Either the information was terrible, or—"

"You were being set up. Seems unlikely, in the

Teams," said Gich, softly leaning forward. "What happened next?"

Jack shook his head. "I don't know. I don't remember. I can see my feet hitting the dirt and watching everyone take position, and then... nothing."

Gich took the cigar from his mouth. "Did you see Don die?"

"I must have..." Pain ripped through his heart as he pushed hard to make it go away. "But I don't remember any of it. What the hell am I supposed to do? I'm beached like a whale until I can remember, and it's ripping me apart to be this still. I need help."

"You need to get out, have some fun. Don't think. Just react and let go of everything." Gich surveyed him with a critical eye before turning his gaze back to watch the shapely blond go through her routine of serving drinks and taking orders. "The watched pot never boils, or in our case, the undrunk beer only gets warm and flat."

Jack gave a half smile. "I'm not really in the mood for socializing."

"Come on, you'd have to be dead not to appreciate that," Gich said, motioning toward the waitress.

He had to admit the bending and reaching of the busty waitress was rather compelling, but he had more important stuff on his mind and couldn't even consider flirting right now. Shifting in his chair, he found a more comfortable position and said, "What I want to know is how do I... get my warrior mentality back?"

Those words captured Gich's attention as his eyes locked on Jack's. The lesson of finding his equilibrium and balance had been the hardest trick for Jack to learn.

Gich had worked doubly hard with him on that one. They'd developed all sorts of techniques to help him out, but right now, Jack felt like his skin was crawling off his body and he had to nail himself to a chair to keep still. Did other SEALs feel like an alien in a human body?

With a deliberate and slow movement, Gich brought his hand up and rested it gently on Jack's arm. But no matter how slowly he'd moved, Jack still flinched and had an urge to pull away. Forcing himself to be still took some concentration.

"Give it time. PTSD happens. Ride it out." Gich leaned forward and whispered, "And while you're waiting, go get your whiskers wet and your dick licked. You're a fucking hero; you should take advantage of it." He pulled back his hand, grabbed the neck of his beer, and chugged it down. When it was empty, he waved it in the air. "Tonight, Dick's Last Resort. There are all sorts of SEAL fans there. I'm sure the Naval Special Warfare fund-raiser crowd would benefit from laying eyeballs on you, too. Why not go get your pick of the, uh, ladies? Tour some sweet spots and give your brain some time off."

The idea of being surrounded by that many people made Jack's stomach clench, but he knew Gich was right. He had to get back out there. Going from the Op to the hospital, and now home, had not afforded him the opportunity to decompress, let alone figure out how to socialize with anyone of the fairer sex.

Maybe getting hot and heavy would help. He could love 'em and leave 'em as easily as the rest of them, though it seriously had been a while. Love just wasn't a priority the majority of the time, though sex was almost always welcome.

When Don had been alive—God, those words stuck in his throat—it had been easier to go out for a night on the town. His buddy, though married, was a perfect wingman. He would wrangle the ladies in Jack's direction and it was a sure thing that his pocket would have a few phone numbers. Sometimes, he'd even take someone for a spin on the town.

Shit! When the fuck would he feel like himself again?

"Promise me you'll go tonight." Gich was studying him again. A man's word was a bond that was never broken in the SEAL community. Might as well have said, "Put your balls on the table, and if you don't do as I say, I'll slice 'em off and pocket 'em."

Gich would badger him until he agreed, and the Commander ten times out of ten knew best. He'd give it a try. What could it hurt? It couldn't be any worse than spending weeks in a hospital bed.

"Yeah," said Jack. "I'll go." Though he knew he'd probably not enjoy it.

The back of Jack's head squeezed tight again, reminding him that the head injury was still an issue. But as the Commander was fond of saying, "Where the body goes, the mind follows." Maybe a little interaction—some puss and hoots—would go a long way toward finding some kind of relief or momentary happiness.

The beat-up yellow Jeep slid into an empty parking spot only a few blocks from the Naval Special Warfare fundraiser. Jack didn't bother securing the torn soft top. There was nothing of value inside, not even a radio. Though he did shove the Bluetooth speaker under the seat.

The last vestiges of light were slipping from the sky as the ripe smell of seasoned meat filled the air. He was tempted to ditch the NSW event and go to the Strip Club for a steak.

A memory flashed through his mind of grilling T-bones to perfection with Don, his wife, and their five-year-old daughter. God, it was barely two months ago! They'd feasted and Sheila had announced she was pregnant at the meal. A game ensued of toasting her all evening long until she drove the lot of them home.

"Shit!" Jack swallowed hard and forced the vivid moment from his mind. Dwelling on the past, especially the loss of his swim buddy, was not helping. He knew he needed to deal with his friend's death, but until he knew what had happened on that mission, he didn't know how. Maybe once he remembered, he'd finally be able to look Sheila in the eye.

Rubbing his hand over his head, he lingered on the scar. If his buddy's death was his fault, he'd own it. If someone else were responsible for Don's death, he would bring justice.

Without that missing bit of knowledge though, he was in limbo.

Let it go. For at least one night, Jack, you need to be someone else. Take a break from yourself. He nodded his head, deciding his gut was providing good advice.

Pointing his feet in the direction of Dick's Last Resort, he set off. The slap of his feet against the pavement felt good. Anything physical seemed to be healing. This morning he'd run six miles and swum for an hour.

His body had felt somewhat spent, but his mind was still spinning on the hamster wheel.

"Hey, Jack, good to see ya!" Hank Franks, a Master Chief in SEAL Team THREE, slapped his back and then enthusiastically shook his hand. His arm felt like a pump trying to pull up water from a rusted pipe. "Are you on your way to Dick's? Have you met Dan McCullum, our new weapons specialist?"

Jack nodded and shook Dan's proffered palm. "Good to see you again, Dan. Been a while."

"Yeah," said Dan warmly. Pointing to his head, he asked, "How's the noggin? I heard there was some action."

"Healing." Jack withdrew his palm and looked forward. He didn't want to say anything about the Op.

Franks wrapped an arm possessively around the woman walking next to him. Her heels clicked a swift staccato on the sidewalk, keeping time with their pace. "Hey, have you met my wife?"

The lady beside the Master Chief smiled shyly. "I'm Rita. Happy to meet you, Jack." The emerald dress hugged her body as if she were a pinup girl, but it was the humor and happiness in her eyes when she looked at her husband and then switched that intense gaze to Jack that held him captive for a few seconds. He caught the residual affects of her joy and the strength was Grade A.

"Nice to meet you, too," he replied, relieved that he hadn't blurted out some silly comment about Hank's wife having a nice rack or the fact they looked good together. His guess was that Hank had already measured those assets for himself. Giving them all a smile and a nod, he slowed his pace and let them surge ahead.

Social graces weren't his thing. He hadn't been to

Dick's Last Resort in years, but his recollection was that the food was tasty and the beer was ample. That had to be enough to work for him tonight.

After making a show of eyeballing his phone, he pocketed it. Then he looked in the windows of several nearby stores. *Stop stalling!*

He forced himself to walk the extra twenty feet, flashed his military ID, and went inside. The din of voices and music was momentarily deafening. A passing waitress pushed a beer into his empty hand. He gripped it gratefully.

His instincts took charge, taking him to an optimal vantage point, one that afforded him an overview of the comings and goings of the bar. Nothing could halt either that habit or the training, except a conscious decision to set his back to the door. When that happened, he'd have to trust the expressions of the people around him to alert him to danger. It was a hard-earned skill to be able to utilize ordinary passersby as mirrors.

As he drank, he watched a couple argue. The wife was seriously pissed. Jack was glad he wasn't in that guy's shoes. At another table, a group of ladies were making plans for later. Then there was the small group of retired military men lined up on bar stools, chatting about the good ole days, wearing jackets that read Old Frogs and SEALs. Across the room near the bar, several wives gathered together, laughing and pointing as they discussed the auction items and sipped delightedly on mixed drinks. Jack smiled as their conversation turned a bit more racy. He was glad he could read lips.

An alarm beeped on his wristwatch. Time to take an antianxiety pill. Anger lanced through him. What was he, some hundred-year-old man who had to take his medication? He would not die without that little pill, and there was no way he'd let himself get in a situation where he was addicted to something... anything or anyone. Unwilling to spend even another minute contemplating it, he stepped toward the closest trash can and dropped the bottle inside. Relief swept through him. He knew he could do better than those "hunt and peck" doctors who were actually using the process of elimination to guess at courses of action. Besides that, he didn't want to pollute his body with crap.

Beer was his only vice. Basically, it was his carbohydrates—liquid bread.

Ah! He swallowed down the rest of the cold brew.

Another body pushed into his, and suddenly the crowd, the noise, and the smell—everything—was too much. It was overwhelming. And that was his cue to go.

He placed the empty bottle on a passing waitress's tray and headed for the door. He'd done his duty. He came, he drank, and now he was leaving.

The door he had selected as his escape hatch opened before him and a gorgeous brunette stepped through, wearing spikes and a black dress with a very short skirt. Her skin glowed as if she'd just come in from the sun, and she was slightly out of breath. A large basket filled with goodies that she balanced on one hand wavered and then tipped.

In one motion, he was by her side, catching the basket before it reached the floor.

"My hero," she said. "Is this a side job or do you do it professionally?"

A grin split across his face; he knew it must look

pretty goofy, but he couldn't stop it. "Which one do I win brownie points for?"

"Depends…" She smiled, and her eyes sparkled like diamonds in a darkened cave. "I'm Laurie Smith." She held out a now-empty hand.

He shifted the basket to one side and reached forward to take it.

An abrupt woman wearing a badge that read "Salia Sedgwick, I am the Queen! Don't make me fetch my 9 mm!" interrupted him before their hands could connect. This rude lady was actually standing between them. "Laurie Smith! You're late. Give me that basket. This was supposed to be here two hours ago. How am I supposed to do my job when other people aren't doing theirs?"

Jack inserted himself into the conversation. "Ah, Ms. Sedgwick, I'm sure she has a good excuse, or does Ms. Smith need a note from her mother?"

The woman frowned at him. "Well, I never!"

"Never what?" he asked innocently.

Laurie did a lousy job hiding her smile behind pursed lips.

As the organizer snatched the basket and hurried away, Laurie's laughter burst out. "Thank goodness, she left. I almost laughed in her face." She touched his arm. "Thank you. Salia Sedgwick is a handful…"

"A handful of what? Pudding? Meanness? Squishy resentment?"

"All of the above," she said, presenting her hand again. There was something light about her, and as he leaned forward, he could smell a hint of lilacs, as if she'd been rubbing the silky petals on her skin and hair.

This time, his hand connected with hers. As his palm

engulfed her tiny fingers, a small bolt of electricity raced up his arm. Perhaps he could stay at this event for a little while longer.

"Hooyah! Hooyah! Hooyah!" The sound of the crowd grew louder, chanting as glasses were raised. The noise grew until his ears rang, yet it didn't stop him from trying to speak over it.

"My name is Jack."

Once a SEAL

Anne Elizabeth

—⁓⁓—

A hero of her own

What woman hasn't dreamed of what it would be like to marry a Navy SEAL? Dan McCullum is everything Aria has ever imagined—sweet, strong, and sexy as hell. She just never expected how tough the SEAL life would be. Dan could be gone at a moment's notice and not allowed to tell her where he's going or when he'll be back.

Dan has never backed down from a challenge in his life. But this one is his hardest yet: How does he balance his duty to his country with a soul-deep love for Aria? It's going to require patience, ingenuity, and some of the hottest homecomings he can dream up. Because of rhim, this isn't a fling; this is forever…

—⁓⁓—

Praise for *A SEAL at Heart*:

"A beautiful story." —*New York Times*
bestselling author Suzanne Brockmann

"An exciting and poignant read."
—*Night Owl Reviews* Top Pick

"You will not find a better storyteller with such feeling for the hearts of our military warriors." —*Coffee Time Romance*

For more Anne Elizabeth, visit:

www.sourcebooks.com

Way of the Warrior

A romance anthology to benefit the
Wounded Warrior Project

Eight passionate love stories about amazing military heroes by bestselling authors:

Suzanne Brockmann	Julie Ann Walker
Catherine Mann	Tina Wainscott
Anne Elizabeth	M.L. Buchman
Kate SeRine	Lea Griffith

—∿∿—

**To honor and empower those who've served,
all author and publisher proceeds go to the
Wounded Warrior Project.**

The Wounded Warrior Project was founded in 2002 and
provides a wide range of programs and services to veterans
and service members who have survived physical or mental
injury during their brave service to our nation. Get involved or
register for programs and benefits for yourself and your family
online at www.woundedwarriorproject.org.

—∿∿—

For more information, visit:

www.sourcebooks.com

Stop at Nothing

A Protect & Serve Novel

by Kate SeRine

———

When a high-profile investigation goes wrong, FBI Agent Kyle Dawson is transferred back home where he is forced to confront his demons…and the only woman he ever loved. Three years ago, Kyle and Abby Morrow shared a wild, passionate summer—then Abby broke his heart.

Now she needs his help

Kyle never stopped loving Abby. So when Abby uncovers evidence of a human-trafficking ring, leading to her sister's kidnapping, he swears he'll stop at nothing to bring her sister home and keep Abby safe. Caught in a lethal game of cat and mouse and blindsided by their own explosive desires, they must set aside the past before it's too late.

———

"Heart-pounding action and steamy sexual tension. This series is a must-read!" —Julie Ann Walker, *New York Times* bestselling author of the Black Knights Inc. series

For more Kate SeRine, visit:

www.sourcebooks.com

Target Engaged

A Delta Force Novel

by M. L. Buchman

———

Sergeant Kyle Reeves

The premier soldier of the new recruits

Sergeant Carla Anderson

The first woman of Delta Force

If the training doesn't kill them, their passion may—but Kyle Reeves and Carla Anderson blast right in. Show no fear. Have no fear. Then they get the call. The most powerful drug-smuggling ring in Venezuela needs a takedown, and Delta's newest team leaps into the deep jungle to deliver. Giving their all? Not a problem. Giving their hearts? That takes a new level of courage.

———

Praise for M. L. Buchman:

"Buchman writes with unusual sensitivity and delicacy for such a hard-edged genre; his characters are full of deep silences and deeper insights, and their lovemaking is profound, tantalizing, and poetic." —*Publishers Weekly*

For more M. L. Buchman, visit:

www.sourcebooks.com

Hold Your Breath

Search and Rescue Book 1

by Katie Ruggle

—•—

In the remote wilderness of the Rocky Mountains, rescue groups—law enforcement, rescue divers, firefighters—are often the only hope for the lost, the sick, and the injured. But in a place this far off the map, trust is hard to come by and secrets can lead to murder.

That's why Jack, the surly and haunted leader of the close-knit Search and Rescue brotherhood, finds it so hard to let newcomer Louise "Lou" Sparks into his life. But when these rescue divers go face-to-face with a killer, Jack may find that more than his heart is on the line...

—•—

Look for the rest of the Search and Rescue series:

On His Watch (available only in ebook)
Fan the Flames
Gone Too Deep
In Safe Hands

For more Katie Ruggle, visit:

www.sourcebooks.com

About the Author

New York Times bestselling author Anne Elizabeth is an award-winning romance author and comic creator. With a BS in business and MS in communications from Boston University, she is a regular presenter at conventions as well as a member of the Authors Guild, Horror Writers Association, and Romance Writers of America. Anne lives with her husband, a retired Navy SEAL, in the mountains above San Diego.

Too Hard to Handle

by Julie Ann Walker

New York Times and *USA Today* Bestseller

~~~

"The Man" is back

Dan "The Man" Currington is back in fighting form with a mission that takes him four thousand miles south of BKI headquarters, high in the Andes Mountains of Peru. He's hot on the trail of a rogue CIA agent selling classified government secrets to the highest bidder when Penni DePaul arrives on the scene. Suddenly the stakes are sky-high, and keeping Penni safe becomes Dan's number one priority.

And this time she's ready

A lot has changed since former Secret Service Agent Penni DePaul last saw Dan. Now a civilian, she's excited about what the future might hold. But before she can grab on to that future with both hands, she has to tie up some loose ends—namely, Dan Currington, the man she just can't forget. And a secret that's going to change both their lives—if they can stay alive, that is.

~~~

Praise for the Black Knights Inc. Series:

"Each one is full of hot alpha men, strong witty females, blazing passionate sex, and tons of humor. Black Knights Inc. is hands down my favorite romantic suspense series." —*Guilty Pleasures Book Reviews*

For more Julie Ann Walker, visit:

www.sourcebooks.com